Faded Love

Faded Love

Jim Sanderson

INK
BRUSH
PRESS

ISBN 978-0-9824405-8-2
Library of Congress Control Number: 2010936420

This is a work of fiction. Any resemblance of characters in these stories to anyone living or dead is purely coincidental.

Ink Brush Press
Temple, Texas
www.inkbrushpress.com

For Summer Sanderson

Other books by Jim Sanderson

Fiction
Nevin's History (novel). Texas Tech University Press, 2004.

La Mordida (novel). University of New Mexico Press, 2002.

Safe Delivery (novel). University of New Mexico Press, 2000.

El Camino del Rio (novel). University of New Mexico Press, 1998.

Semi-Private Rooms (short story collection). Pig Iron Press, 1995.

Non-fiction
Some Ways of Writing—A Writer's Way: A Supplemental Guide To Writing For Composition and Sophomore Literature (composition text). Kendall Hunt, Fall 2007.

A West Texas Soapbox (essay collection), Texas A&M University Press, (College Station, TX), 1998.

I miss you darling more and more every day
As Heaven would miss the stars above.
With every heartbeat, I still think of you
And remember our faded love.

Bob Wills, "Faded Love"

Acknowledgments

Several stories in this book have appeared in other publications, some in somewhat different forms.

"Don't Empty Houses Ring?" *Pleiades*, fall 1999.
"Endometriosis." *Descant*, 43, 2004.
"The Golden State." serialized in *Iron Horse Literary Review*, 1.2, Spring 2000
    & 1.3, Fall 2000.
"Hemingway's Lighthouse." *Langdon Review,* 2, 2005-2006.
"Like in the Movies." *North Atlantic Review,* 9, 1997.
"Oasis of Love." *New Texas 93.* ed. Jim Lee. Denton, TX: University of North
    Texas, 1993.
"Potential." *Semi-Private Rooms.* Youngstown, OH: Pig Iron Press, 1994, and
    New Mexico Humanities Review, Fall 1983.
"Praying and Drinking." *New Mexico Humanities Review*, Summer 1986.
"Someone To Watch Over." *The Chariton Review*, 26:1, Spring 2000.
"Stripping." *Semi-Private Rooms.* Youngstown, OH: Pig Iron Press, 1994, and
    Ellipsis, 1.3. (1989-90).

Contents

Author's Note

Once I write a story, I often want to give the supporting characters their due, so I write stories for them or put them in other stories. And sometimes I let characters that I've used before interrupt stories that they aren't supposed to be in. So the stories in Part I and II are best read in order. In Part II, "Hemingway's Lighthouse" and "Oasis of Love" belong together. Part IV crams all the characters into one story.

Then too, to me, *a story*, no matter how long, just always seems slightly static, unable to capture our sense of time passing, of our own passing. But even though I never thought that I would write series, I discovered that, to me, *related stories*, no matter how long, whether written or read, may better approximate our sense of time passing, of our own passing. So I also discovered that all my stories, no matter how long, were related. Below is a list of characters and where else they appear. I doubt that they will all be published, maybe no more of them will, but I'm happy that I wrote them because I got to play with these characters' passings.

Characters

Part I: Pooter and Joan appear in *La Mordida* and in *Dolph's Team* (the latest in the Dolph Martinez/Jerri Johnson series).

Part II: Lee appears in *Behind the Pine Tree Curtain* (unpublished). Don appears in "Ladies Man," in *Semi-Private Rooms* and various collections.

Part III: I've mostly forgotten them. But Velda's character, Jerri Johnson, appears in *Safe Delivery*, *La Mordida*, and *Dolph's Team* (the latest in the Dolph Martinez/Jerri Johnson series).

Part IV: Walter and Sarah appear in *Pumpjack* (an extension of "The Truly Talented Writer") and *Dolph's Team* (the latest in the Dolph Martinez/Jerri Johnson series).

Part I
Bailey, Joan, and Pooter

Potential

From his office, Bailey Waller could see the late August sun cook Bob Compton's used car lot. He saw the heat rise off the asphalt, the glare from the new paint jobs and chrome trim. The asphalt was cracking, just like the mesquite-filled desert that threatened to overgrow I-20, which was just across the undeveloped commercial lot behind Compton's dealership. Bailey Waller sat in his glass-walled, air-conditioned office where he should have felt protected.

He looked out at the lot and saw several figures in the heat and said "damn" to himself. Most people would have the good sense not to look at cars at mid-day —they'd come before noon or after six o'clock—but a family of four wanted to buy a car, and Pooter Elam, Bailey's former teammate, college buddy, and hometown Odessa boy, was showing them a five-year-old Buick. Pooter's hands worked like a TV preacher's as he steered the family against the fender of a Buick. Bailey got up from behind his desk and stepped closer to the glass that walled him in from the heat. He watched Pooter pat at his sweating forehead with his fingertips, then hide his hands behind him and shake his fingers, flicking off his sweat. The belly Pooter had been growing since he and Bailey got out of college curled his belt down; Pooter had been a good guard, Bailey thought.

Bailey slipped his hand into the pocket of his Jaymar slacks and pulled out the crumpled clipping from the employment section of Wednesday's *Odessa American*. He read it slowly. Peacock Military Academy needed an eighth grade football coach and history teacher, quickly. Bailey walked back to his desk, sat down behind it, and put the clipping in front of him, reading it over and over. Bailey believed that certain things in your life turn it around for the better. Bailey knew that he could have the important things if only he could see them coming. After all, he had potential. Every coach he had ever had said Bailey Waller had *Po-tential*, *Potential*, like it was two words. Mr. Bob Compton said he had it. Even his freshman history teacher said he had potential. It wasn't something he could define; he just knew potential was something that made getting what he wanted easy.

Bailey looked up and saw the shaking air conditioner that poked through the cracked wood paneling, the photographs hanging behind his desk. Mr. Compton had told him to put those particular pictures there. "Helps business," he said. There was the color photograph of Bailey in his football uniform, number 11. *Bailey Waller, quarterback*, it said underneath.

"Everybody trusts a football player," Mr. Compton had said. Bailey didn't pose like some hot dogs, like he needed mustard, holding a football, sidestepping, giving a forearm, or growling like Pooter. No. He knelt and looked strong, force-

1

ful, competent. Full of potential. There was the newspaper clipping of Bailey and Bob Compton shaking hands. Mr. Compton was welcoming the All-American, who had ruined his knee trying out as a free safety with the Houston Oilers, to the Compton Buick sales team. Next to it was Bailey again—strong, forceful, competent, and full of potential—in his Salesman-of-the-Month photograph. And then there was a blank space on the wall. It matched the blank space on his desk. Only Bailey and Pooter knew what filled those blank spaces. Bailey hid the gold-framed photographs of Joan in his desk drawer.

Bailey picked up the small, silver, aluminum model car with Compton Buick written across its side. He flipped the switch in the back of the car. The tiny headlights came on. Bailey turned the car around in his hands. Bailey believed that he deserved better, but he had more faith than most people his age because he had potential. Which meant that beyond his deserving was a logical, reasonable expectation, of getting better things. All he needed was to maintain his faith until he got his break. He had the clipping, and he had Bob Compton.

He put the clipping back in his pocket, got up from his desk, walked out into the hall, then opened the door to the heat outside. He let the door go and walked down the steps. The hot aluminum handrail seared his palm. He walked between a '78 Chevy Malibu and an '81 Datsun and stopped to look at Pooter. The asphalt burned through his shoes. Pooter had stopped his movement, his hands down at his sides, his mouth forming a lazy *O*. Bailey remembered Pooter as a freshman guard at the University of Texas: a big, dumb, homesick, West Texas boy. Bailey walked through the used car lot and into the glassed-in palace that displayed the new cars. He glanced over his shoulder at Pooter, who looked at him, then back toward his customers, like he was trying to decide between them or Bailey. Bailey could see that Pooter was still plagued by the same habit that hurt him in football, that habit of analyzing even his physical moves and getting paralyzed, instead of acting on instincts and desires.

Bailey stepped into the showroom and turned to his right. The showroom was cool. It chilled the sweat that ran down his back and stained the collar of his fitted shirt. He looked at the four new Buicks, shiny with chrome and buffed paint, parked on the thick red carpet showroom. Though he had worked there for five years, Bailey still wondered how they kept the cars from leaving tracks in the carpet. He stopped to look at the Assistant Manager, Tully Lee, with his telephone pressed to his ear. Tully Lee was a fill-in announcer for high school football games. Bailey knew that his future with the car company was to become someone like Tully. "Compton in?" Bailey asked. Tully jerked his thumb toward Bob Compton's office down the hall.

Bailey walked down the hall and looked at the paintings that Mr. Compton had bought second hand from Holiday Inn. He walked slowly to give himself every opportunity to do everything properly. The point of no return, he thought.

2

Mr. Compton had been good to him. After he spent a summer trying out for the Houston Oilers, after two years of living in Austin bartending and waiting for Joan to get her law degree, after she got the degree and a job in Odessa as a corporate lawyer for Getty Oil, Mr. Compton hired him because of Pooter's recommendation.

Mr. Compton didn't make him dress up in chicken outfits and sell cars on Sunday morning TV commercials that cut into old movies and church services. "I run an honorable, dignified business. I'm not going to embarrass you," he told Bailey. He kept his word even when the automobile business got bad. Compton had inherited his daddy's prime real estate and become one of the city's biggest car dealers. What was more, he was a loyal UT alumnus, and though he had never been a jock, he took care of athletes, to repay them for their services, he always said. But more important, Compton contributed to Peacock Military Academy. Teaching was a more honorable profession than selling cars, and Joan would be surprised and glad to see Bailey was doing something important and honorable. Living up to his potential. He lifted his knuckles to the door to knock.

"Wait," Bailey heard behind him. He turned. Pooter was breathing heavily and sweating. He put his hand below his chin and caught some beads of sweat before they could stain his shirt or tie. "You gonna do it?"

"Yeah," Bailey said.

Pooter wiped his face with his hand. "What the hell for?"

Bailey didn't feel like explaining again, so he shrugged his shoulders. Pooter's face wrinkled, and Bailey knew he would have to give him some kind of an explanation. "Look at you, overweight, sweating like a pig."

"You think you ain't gonna sweat being a coach?"

"It ain't wasted sweat when you're a coach. Goes toward something important."

"You talking bullshit, son. You remember high school. You gonna make less money."

"Money's not important. You got to live up to what you are capable of doing."

"More bullshit." Bailey turned away from Pooter because he couldn't make him understand. "Shit. You like a one-legged duck swimming in circles." Pooter said, "Hell, I gotta get back to my customer."

Bailey turned around, "You left a customer standing out in the sun?"

"Yeah," Pooter said. "You not gonna let me even try to argue you out of it?"

"No." Pooter hesitated, turned slowly, then raced down the hall back to his customer. Bailey turned back to the door and knocked.

He opened the door and looked across the large carpeted office with a built-in bar and expensive aluminum and leather office furniture. He looked at the mahogany desk, clear of all paper, only the opaque protective vinyl sheet on top of it. He looked at Mr. Compton behind his desk.

Bailey walked up to the desk, reached into his pocket, and pulled out the newspaper clipping. He stopped in front of the chair that sat in front of Mr. Compton's desk. "There's a coaching job in Midland," Bailey said, and gently placed the clipping on Mr. Compton's desk. Mr. Compton picked up both arms of his gold, half-framed glasses that hung by a chain around his neck, put them on, grabbed the clipping, and read it. He looked up.

"Sit down," he told Bailey, and Bailey sat into the leather chair that was in front of the desk. As Mr. Compton took his glasses off, Bailey saw the large diamond ring on his right forefinger sparkle and the garnet ring on his right pinky shine. On Mr. Compton's left hand was a simple gold wedding band. "You tell me how you decided I could help you get this job." From the tone in Bob Compton's voice and the beginning of a smile on his face, Bailey knew things were starting well.

He was ready with his answer; he had practiced. "I thought when I didn't make pro that it was just meant to be that I stick with football by coaching. But I didn't have the degree complete nor the teaching certificate." Mr. Compton leaned back in his chair. "Now this job gives me a chance. And, like you said, and what I appreciated so much when you hired me, was that you said you would always help out." Bailey hesitated to get it right. "And I know with all your interests . . ." Compton held up his hand, palm out. Bailey knew it meant for him to stop. Bob Compton was always quick and to the point.

"This is not exactly some college coaching job where you become the next Darrell Royal."

Bailey was ready for that: "I know it isn't like I'm gonna be a real coach, just like playing flag football with Pooter and a bunch of oil rig trash ain't real football. But it's doing something important." Bailey looked at Mr. Compton, then scooted to the edge of his chair. "When you're in a town don't even have a semi-pro team or even a Lone Star Conference college team in it, all that's big is school-boy football. The only way for me to be important here is to coach high school ball."

Compton chuckled and said, "This is not exactly Permian High School with a state championship trophy ever year or so either."

"It's a start," Bailey said. "You know I got the potential. All I need is the start."

"Potential is one thing, Bailey," Compton said. "Getting by another."

"I do better than get by."

Mr. Compton wrinkled up his forehead, then smiled. "I can get you the job, Bailey, but I'm gonna miss you." He took a breath, then continued. "My son plays for Peacock. I would like for him to play." Bob Compton smiled at Bailey, and Bailey knew he meant nothing dishonorable or questionable. Bailey nodded.

"Why don't you go see these folks tomorrow?"

Bailey walked out of Mr. Compton's office knowing the thing had been done, the momentum started, and he knew his potential would carry him through. He told Pooter and took him to lunch at the Steak and Ale restaurant. After lunch, in the Steak and Ale parking lot, Bailey watched Pooter try to squeeze his stomach behind the steering wheel of his M.G. Pooter showed up at college with that car. He had gotten bigger, but the car hadn't.

"Why don't you get a bigger car? They'd give you a demo."

"You get used to something," Pooter said. Bailey asked him to take him by Joan's office. "That why you took me here, so you could embarrass yourself in front of her again?"

"Come on, it's right down Parkway, right down the street."

"You're nuts, son," Pooter said. "Get her out of your head."

"I'm just gonna tell her about my new job," Bailey said, thinking how glad she would be to hear.

"Some big deal."

"Just drop me by and wait. I'll be right out."

"Just busting for her to piss you off again, ain't you?"

"All right, goddamn it. I'll phone her after work." But Pooter dropped him off at the building and waited in the parking lot.

Joan's maiden name (*Phelan*) was added to the end of the string of attorneys' names. They had several suites, all decorated with finer furniture than Bob Compton had. Bailey had seen her office twice. Seeing it, and having gone with her for the interview in San Antonio, he couldn't believe that she had ever considered being a public defender in a shabby office in the San Antonio court-house. He walked into her suite and asked her secretary to buzz her. She wasn't in. Bailey pulled out one of his cards, flipped it over, and wrote, *call me* on it. He decided against putting *love*, then signed it. He gave it to the secretary, then took the stairs down to the lobby of the building.

In the lobby, Bailey saw the elevator doors close in front of Joan's face. He caught himself just before he yelled to her. He raced back up the stairs. As he went up the steps, he thought he must not look too eager. He stopped Joan as she was grabbing the door knob to her suite. "Joan," he allowed himself to shout, and smiled as he ran to her. He could not tell for sure if she pretended not to hear; she opened the door and started to go in. He was able to grab the door knob from her and slam the door shut. Joan gasped.

"Oh, Bailey! Jesus," she said.

She still said "Jesus," Bailey thought, in her own way, trying to cram both syllables into one, while everybody else in West Texas stretched the word out into three or four. He was breathing too heavily to talk. He paused to catch some air and look at her. With her hair pulled back behind her head, and just enough make-

5

up on to let you know she wore makeup, she looked older, but much prettier. She used to look pretty, Bailey thought, back when Pooter called her an Earth Mother; now she was lovely.

"Oh, Bailey, please stop the visits and the calls. Please."

"I got something to tell you."

"It's over between us."

"I didn't come here for that." Bailey breathed in deeply to deliver the news, "I'm gonna coach football and teach, do something important, like you said." He waited for a hug or a short friendly kiss. Joan kissed the tips of her fingers, then gently pressed them against his forehead.

"Do you think you can do it?" she said.

"Sure."

"Bailey, you're gonna have to learn." She stopped, then turned to the door to go in. Bailey grabbed her elbow, squeezed it, and pulled her away from the door. She gasped at first, pulled her elbow toward her side and dipped her shoulder. "Bailey," she said sternly.

"What do you mean?" Bailey said.

"Nothing, let go."

Bailey let go of her elbow. She opened the door and went in, closing it behind her, not even saying "goodbye" or "congratulations."

She was the one who said that he ought to quit selling cars, first gave him the idea of doing something important. Bailey swung at the wall, hit it hard. Then again. He was sure anybody inside the suite heard him. He wanted to kick in the door of her suite and shout to all the associates, "I used to fuck her!"

* * *

Midland had all the oil executives, the millionaires; Mr. Bob Compton lived in Midland. Odessa had the good football teams. But a year at Peacock might move him on. When Bailey got to the Academy, Mr. Compton had already called. He got the job without any problem. He didn't need transcripts or degrees. He had to leave them with the promise that he would go to school during the summers and get some kind of a degree. He called Mr. Bob Compton to thank him, and Mr. Compton told him to take the week off from selling cars to prepare for school.

When he got home, out of habit, he picked up the telephone to call Joan. He knew he shouldn't have, but he did call her, and he asked for his old playbook. She briefly congratulated him on his job, then said she had no idea where his playbook was. When the conversation reached a lull because Bailey was trying to decide whether or not to accuse her of not caring about his playbook or lying about it to him, she politely said, "Good luck," and hung up. Bailey thought about going over to her house, his former house, and tearing it apart until he came across the playbook, but he found it at the bottom of a cardboard box labeled *football stuff.*

During his week off, he woke late in the mornings, but after he woke, he ran and pumped weights to get into better shape for his job. He borrowed an American history textbook from a co-ed who lived above him. In the afternoon he took the book and a six-pack of beer to the pool to study. He always bought bottled beer. Somehow the glass made the beer taste better. He liked to feel the beer in his throat and his belly as well as taste it. He concentrated on the feel and the taste of the beer as he drank it. And when he got bored with studying, he invented a game. He threw an inner tube one of the renters' kids left poolside into the pool; then he would try to throw his bottles through the hole of the tube as he emptied them. He liked to watch the ripples and the small wake the bottles caused gently lap up under the lip at the pool's edge.

And one morning, because somewhere in his memory of high school, when long hair meant a lack of discipline or maybe because he was thinking of his first meeting Joan, back when she was a hippie barber, he got a haircut.

Back then he was a sophomore in college who made the headlines of the *Daily Texan* because of his performance at spring training. He was full of potential, and Joan was a barber at a time when barbers were just becoming hair stylists. It was popular then for a football player to have hair just long enough to have a tuft stick out from under the back of his helmet. It looked good on TV. Now, getting a haircut from a middle-aged woman with blue hair in Odessa, Texas, he thought about how much he wanted Joan the first time he saw her in that barber shop in Austin, off Guadalupe Street, with hippie vendors selling brocade pillows in front of it.

The floor of the barber shop was bare wood. The ripped and scarred leather-covered chairs, some spitting up their insides, still had razor straps hanging beside them. An overhead fan circulated the stale, uncooled air. A man with a shaved head and a gold earring cut a little boy's hair, and Joan cut the boy's brother's hair. Joan wasn't so much good looking but looked good doing what she did, cutting hair. She looked like a dancer because she didn't wear shoes when she cut hair. Getting a haircut from her was like dancing with her. Only later did Bailey learn that she went barefoot because her feet hurt. Then barefoot hair cutting was the most sensual and decadent thing Bailey had ever seen. Her rounded calves, which curved shapely up to the hemline of her old, ragged, print dress, were not shaven. That dress, with the sleeves cut out, had no shape left to it, so she had a safety pin at her waist and barely over her breast, exposing cleavage. Her breasts, large and pointed, seemed about to burst through the thin cloth of the dress.

"Next," the bald headed man with the earring said, and the boy got up out of his chair as the man snapped the bib and looked at Bailey.

"I'll wait," Bailey said. The haircut was worth the wait. It was a dance, a massage, a celebration. She caressed his ears. She rubbed the hair up along his neck. She leaned over the side of Bailey's head to inspect the other side; near the corner of his eye, her breast sagged against the dress. Bent over, her body pressing against the dress, almost touching Bailey, she quivered a bit from standing on her tiptoes. Bailey could smell her breath, the mint she had in her mouth to hide the smell of the joint she had for lunch. He paid her with a check and, after he wrote it, circled his address: the athletic dorm.

"You're Bailey Waller, aren't you?" she asked.

"Yeah," Bailey said, knowing that everybody in Austin knew the third wishbone-T quarterback who was going to take Texas to its next national championship.

That night he sneaked her into his dorm room in a laundry sack, carried her over his shoulder like a bag of dirty laundry. He threw his roommate Pooter's mattress out in the hall and locked the door. After they drank bourbon mixed with coke and smoked some of her dope, he felt the smooth tops of her feet with the sole of his bare foot, rolled next to her and felt their cool thighs touch, and he stuck his hand into her cleavage.

Then he opened his eyes, and he was in Odessa with a blue-haired lady cutting his hair, and he wondered what had happened since then. But then he thought: he had a new job. His life was about to get better.

* * *

His first day of class, Bailey had a dry mouth and a headache from staying out too late the night before. He and Pooter had had a few drinks. For all his reading of the co-ed's history text, he had no idea of what to do or say in history class, so for his first period class he stared at the uniformed, twelve-year-old boys, and they stared back. No doubt, Bailey thought, because they wanted to see what they aspired to be, a one-time All-American football player for the University of Texas. They all looked the same, hair cut close to their heads, white shirts, what looked like hats from an army surplus store. Some even had gold stitching on the black brims of the hats. After fifteen minutes of staring, he told them to read the first chapter and answer the questions at the back of the book. "I'm gonna take those questions up, fellas," he told them, "and they better, by god, be right."

His second period, he didn't get to make the assignment; he fell asleep during the staring stage. He crossed his arms on his desk and lay his head against them. He closed his eyes and did not open them until a small boy who looked like a girl's doll dressed as a soldier tapped his shoulder and said, "Coach, Coach Waller, are you okay?"

"Yes," Bailey said.

The next two periods were better. They were P. E. Bailey gave the boys several basketballs and locked them in the gym to play half-court basketball while he took naps in the coaches' office. Then he had an hour for lunch; then a free period in which he caught more sleep. Finally, sixth period came, time for football practice.

Bailey waited in his office next to the locker room for his team to come in. The first to arrive was a skinny college kid sucking Coca-Cola from a bottle. He was doing his student teaching. As he explained to Bailey, he was the only help Bailey was to have, and he said he was glad to be working under him. He told Bailey he always wanted to play football but that he just couldn't gain weight. "Junior Williams," he said to Bailey, shifted his coke to his left hand, and stuck out his right for Bailey to shake. "I'm proud to meet you. Gonna be an honor working with you," Junior told him. "Oh yeah," he said, "I already give the boys their gear. All right with you?" Junior said and took a swig of his Coke.

The boys, when they showed up, were tinier than Bailey had imagined. Even the little girl soldier doll who had waked him during the second period showed up to play football. Those who could figure out that their pants had pockets for their thigh pads put them in the wrong way. Many weren't sure how to get into hip pads. Once they were dressed, their helmets spun around their heads and their shoulder pads flapped on their shoulders.

On the practice field, Bailey saw they were as clumsy as they were small. They couldn't figure out isometric stretching exercises, so Bailey dismissed them from calisthenics and started drills to find out where his talent was. He had none. He had them run backwards and swivel their hips so he could look for secondary; most of them fell down or tripped over one another. His quarterbacks tried to throw the football like a baseball. His running backs fumbled. His receivers had stone hands. The boys over a hundred fifteen pounds, his linemen, were slow and fat. Only once did Bailey feel anything good. Since no one could throw a ball, he started to toss it to the receivers. On one throw, he dropped back like he had been taught for ten years. And his arm almost naturally cocked behind his ear, and his finger dug into the stitching on the ball, and he felt his arm arching over his shoulder for the over-handed throw; he saw his wrist flipping in front of his face to give the ball spin. He saw the ball, perfect in its flight. But the good was spoiled when the ball hit a boy in the chest and knocked him down. So Bailey sent Junior long on a post pattern and heaved the ball, feeling the power in his arm and the touch in his fingers and wrist, and he watched Junior drop the ball.

When he turned his attention to the linemen, Bailey realized who Bud Compton was; he was the biggest because he was the fattest. From his waist to his neck, he looked like three giant doughnuts stacked on top of one another. He was also the clumsiest and slowest boy. Several times during practice, Bud cried. "See me after practice," Bailey told him.

After practice Bailey waited for Bud inside the cage where they hung their equipment. Junior picked up wet towels and misplaced jocks while the last stragglers finished drying and dressing, then left. Bud was taking his time. These

9

boys, Bailey thought, were not football players. They were rich boys, not like black kids, not rough-necks, not electricians' or plumbers' kids, nor even the few wealthy white kids who hung around with their poorer neighbors through public school education and so became football players. These boys were like their daddies; they didn't want to play football. They wanted to be engineers and accountants and lawyers. Bailey looked around at their smelly gear hanging from racks. He remembered putting on the T-shirts cut off at nipple level and worn to keep shoulder pads from rubbing against skin. The rancid smelling T-shirts would be so stiff from soaked up sweat that they seemed brittle, like they would shatter into pieces. He remembered the feel and the smell of shoulder pads sliding down his arms and over his head, old public school shoulder pads worn by sweating boys for at least three years or more so the foam padding turned hard, started to crack, no longer much cushioning left. If you made it to high school ball and became a starter, you might get new shoulder pads. And if you made it to college, you always got new shoulder pads, and you even got your T-shirt laundered every other day so that it lost the stink and stiffness. As Bailey sat in the locker room smelling the little boy sweat, he knew that these boys would never know about their equipment. These boys would never know what Bailey remembered.

When Bud came in, Bailey led him into his office. He had Bud sit in a chair across from his desk. Bud's hair, still wet from the shower, was slicked across his scalp. His round head looked almost like an out-of-shape football. Bailey looked at him hard.

"How come you're so fat, Bud?"

"My momma says it's glands," Bud said.

"Glands is an excuse, Bud," Bailey said. He looked at Bud, and Bud dropped his head. "You wanna play football, you gonna have to lose some of you."

"Yes, sir," Bud said.

"You ask your momma or maybe your daddy to help you lose weight."

"I really try, Coach," Bud said.

"Try, hell," Bailey said. "You wanna play football?"

Bud looked up at Bailey and then said, "Yes, sir."

"Okay. Then you run on home and don't drink no soda water nor eat no junky food between here and home."

Bud turned to leave but then turned back to Bailey. He looked straight across the desk at Bailey. And Bailey knew that the boy was hiding some kind of great terror. "Coach, sir, I don't really wanna play no football."

"What're you saying?" Bailey said. "You don't wanna play. Why?"

"I don't like it."

"Well, why are you playing?" Bud hung his head and didn't answer. Bailey had heard some of the terror, but not all of it. He tried again. "Now, come on, you tell me why you don't wanna play no football."

Bud brought his head up and was crying, "It scares me, scares me real bad. I go home and tell my mother and she says to quit, but then my father comes home and he says to play football."

"So you're playing football for your daddy."

"Yes."

Bailey leaned back in his chair and thought about what it must be like to be a fat little boy who cared so little about himself that he bloats up like a three-week dead cow. And he tried to feel the terror that showed in Bud's face.

"I know I'm gonna hurt myself," Bud said, and Bailey remembered his senior year, coming back from an ankle injury, what it was like to play scared, hoping for the season to end, a new direction in life to start, a new chance to use his potential.

"Look," Bailey said, "what you wanna tell your kids? You wanna tell 'em about your football playing days in high school, or you wanna tell 'em you grew hair and got fat?" For a moment Bud lost his battle against crying and let tears come into his eyes, then caught himself and snorted. Bailey didn't believe what he had said and didn't really expect an answer, but he got up and closed the door to his office, then sat back down behind his desk. "You can cry if you want to," he said to Bud, but Bud shook his head and walked out of the office. Bailey watched the little stack of doughnuts go through his door and thought that this boy, that none of them, should be playing football.

He got up from his desk and walked out, intending to go home, not even putting on his street clothes. As he walked by the row of benches, he stopped to look at Junior, sitting on the last bench, sipping a Coca-Cola. "We gonna give hell, huh, Coach?" Junior said. Bailey left.

* * *

The rest of the school week did not improve. Bailey had a meeting with the principal of the school, who had been a captain in the army once. The boys called him "commander." Bailey couldn't judge rank by insignia; he knew the man was a captain only by the references to him at his interview and by the sign on his door. "These are basically good boys, Coach," Captain Mayberry began. "But as I'm sure Mr. Compton told you, they need some discipline. That is why they are here, to get a better education, a more rigorous life, and more demands than in public school. They are rich boys, but they are not pampered. Things here are taut."

Bailey felt like telling the captain that he was here only to move on to somewhere else, where there were real kids who wanted to play football and could win for themselves and for him, where he didn't have to play fat boys shaped like piled doughnuts. "Do you understand?" the captain asked.

"Yes, "Bailey answered.

11

But Bailey didn't really understand. He knew that he was going to lose his first football game. He wasn't sure if he was going to play Bud. He had been playing Bud at center, hoping the boy would just take up so much room and look so big that the defense would try to run around him. His history classes were still reading chapters and answering questions at the back of the book while he thought about the team.

The Thursday night before his Friday afternoon game, Bailey sat by his pool, drank beer, and threw his beer bottles into the pool. His landlady had left notes in his mailbox telling him not to throw beer bottles into the pool. He tore up the notes and threw them in the pool too. Though he wasn't sure and couldn't explain it, he felt a terror that his life, like Bud's, was about to unravel. Maybe, he thought being only a kind of a football coach, one with a lousy team of boys who had no business playing, was nothing to be. He squeezed the bottle of beer with both hands. He took a long, slow sip, careful to taste the glass, to feel the bitter cold taste of the beer against the back of his throat. He wasn't sure of anything but the feeling of the beer.

But he could remember his junior year when the Longhorns fumbled away the Cotton Bowl to Notre Dame. Midway through his senior year, he got hurt and had to sit on the bench, the whole time hoping he wouldn't play, and when he did play, he played only to keep from getting hurt. He sat the bench scared, and he played scared because his ankle was hurt enough to knock him out of most of a season, but not enough to keep him out. He felt like he had been cheated because something was about to change his life, and he felt like hiding from it. Then before the last game, he asked Joan to marry him.

"Jesus, think of that," Joan said, "Me marrying a genuine white, Anglo-Saxon, clean cut, all around jock. Guess weirder things have happened." She married him. And living with her, he found out how serious she was about becoming a lawyer who defended poor people and helped society.

Now, this night, he called her. She said she was busy. She didn't stay on the phone long, and Bailey could hear either the television or a voice in the background. Later, Pooter came by. They sat and drank the beers Pooter brought with him.

"So tomorrow is big-time football," Pooter said.

"I'm maybe not going to go," Bailey said.

"You gotta go. You the coach, son," Pooter said. He pulled a can of beer away from the plastic that held the six-pack together. He chugged the beer, took the can in his palm, his fingertips curled over the rim of the can, his thumb against the bottom, and he slowly squeezed it until collapsed. He held it up for Bailey to see. Bailey had seen the trick many times but laughed anyway.

"I ain't gonna win, Pooter. Ain't no way I'm gonna win," Bailey said.

"Hell, son, you gotta lose—you gotta lose. Ain't no big deal, just like playing for TCU or Rice," Pooter said.

"We get as much rain as anybody else," Pooter often said about Odessa. "Just we get it all at one time." The humidity and clouds came just before Bailey's game. Bailey hoped the rain would wash away the field, cancel the game. In the locker room Bailey looked over the boys. On the back row, one let out a barely audible snore. Two others poked each other, played grab-ass. Bailey gave a pep talk. He didn't really know what he said; things that coaches usually said, things about pride and character, he supposed. Junior sat behind him, Coca-Cola in hand, cheering and yelling when he must have thought he should. Finally the boys ran out to the field, and Bailey was up to his armpits in spinning helmets and flapping shoulder pads. Junior slapped him on the back on the way out and said, "We gonna give 'em hell, Coach."

As the game started, black thunderclouds gathered at one end of the field and gradually moved over it. Bailey watched the clouds, and he looked up into the bleachers to see Mr. Bob Compton and his pretty, well-dressed wife sitting close to the front railing, right behind Peacock's bench. Bailey watched Bob Compton push his wind-blown hair into place with the hand that wore the over-sized diamond ring and the pinkie ring.

The first two plays of the game were kickoffs, the first a returned kick against Peacock Academy, the second a fumbled kickoff near Peacock's own one. Peacock was lucky to recover. The third play was a safety because a middle linebacker blitzed over Bud and knocked him backward into the quarterback. Bud knocked the quarterback down in the end zone and the linebacker jumped on him. Bailey watched as Bud got up crying. Bailey heard players on his bench curse Bud, and he knew the people in the crowd were pointing at Bud, talking about him. They didn't laugh or boo because, as Bailey knew, they respected and admired Bud's daddy.

By the second quarter, the terror that he had felt the night before came back to Bailey, and he yelled at his boys. He threw his clipboard on the ground and kicked at it. He cussed his boys, especially Bud, who would either fumble the snap or let the entire defense in over him. In the third quarter, after a boy on the other team ran through Peacock's defensive line, linebackers, and secondary, Bailey's quarterback ran up to him and asked, "Coach?" Bailey didn't answer. "What you want us to run?"

"What you want out of me?" Bailey asked. "What the hell you expect?" And before he could catch himself, almost happening as if it had to happen, Bailey felt himself reaching for the boy, and before he could stop himself, he grabbed the boy's shoulders and shook the boy so hard his head snapped back and forward on his neck. It was as though no boy was in that helmet and those shoulder pads. That standing uniform was just something for Bailey to shake. Then control of his body came back to him and Bailey stopped. For a moment everyone was silent.

"There," Bailey said, "it has been done," the thing that would throw his life off, twist it around. The boy was crying. The fans started to boo. Mr. Bob Compton was on his feet. Even the other team watched. Bailey turned around and saw Bud, crying still, getting off the bench to go in. "Stay there," he said. "Holstead, go in for Compton." Then Bailey went to the bench and sat beside Bud. "You take over," he yelled to Junior.

"Huh?" Junior said.

"You're the coach now, boy. They'll kill me."

Bailey sat out the game next to Bud while Peacock got beat 62 to 0. He watched the clouds and sniffed the air. He did not leave the field; he let them see him. He knew the thing that would twist his life around and hurt him was started, but was not yet finished, so he waited. When the game ended, Bailey ran to the locker room with his little boys. Just as they got into the locker room, the rain started. After the boys left, Bailey ran out the back door of the locker room to avoid Mr. Bob Compton, Captain Mayberry, and irate parents. When he got home, the telephone was ringing. He knew right away it would be somebody he did not want to talk to. The only thing he could think to do was go see Joan.

He parked across the street and ran through the rain and knocked on the door; either Joan wasn't home or wasn't answering. Bailey sat down on the porch to wait. Hot rain drops hit him in the head from a leak in the porch roof. He sat with one shoulder resting against the side of the house, his collar turned up against his neck to keep rain from running down his back, and he watched as the street turned into a shallow river and washed what used to be his yard farther down the block.

After dark a car he did not recognize, a BMW, pulled into the driveway. A man got out of the left side, holding a silk sport coat over his head. He ran to the right side and opened the door. He held the sport coat stretched out in both his hands over Joan's head as she got out of the car. They walked to the driveway, both holding one end of the sport coat to protect themselves from the rain. At first Bailey could think only of what a terrible shame it was to ruin a good sport coat, but then he saw Joan rest her cheek into the soft spot of the man's shoulder.

They didn't see Bailey when they first stepped onto the porch. The man shook his sport coat, and Joan lifted one leg behind her and slipped off her high-heeled shoe. Then she slipped off the other shoe and held both in one hand while she dug with her other hand into the purse slung over her shoulder. She pulled out her keys and stepped toward the door. Bailey stepped in front of her. She gasped, and the man quickly turned around.

"Joan," the man said.

"Jesus Christ. It's all right, I know him," Joan said.

"I'm her husband," Bailey said.

"What are you doing here?" she asked. "Why are you lurking around my house?"

"I'm not lurking."

Joan opened the door, reached inside the house, and turned the porch lights on. Bailey stepped toward her, wanting to go into his house, wanting to see what she and this man had done to it, but she stood in the doorway in a way that said he could not pass. Bailey looked at her. One out of place strand of hair dangled in front of her face. She did not brush it away. Bailey could see she had that look that meant she was slightly drunk. He turned around to look at the man, to see what about him Joan could possibly like. He wore glasses. He was almost bald. He turned back to Joan to ask her why this guy, but instead, looked down at her bare feet.

"Jesus, Bailey," Joan said, "Please leave me alone."

There was that "Jesus" again, Bailey thought.

The man stepped toward the door, but Bailey stepped and turned in front of him. "Come in Duncan," Joan said.

"Duncan?" Bailey said and stayed planted in front of him. Duncan had a moustache that was dripping rain.

"Bailey!" Joan said. Bailey stayed.

"It's all right, Joan, I'll just wait," Duncan said.

Bailey turned around to Joan and looked at the mascara running down her cheek, her wet hair clinging to her head. "I got to talk to you."

"Can't it wait?"

"I really fucked up."

"I'm not surprised."

"Damn it, Joan," Bailey said and stepped toward her, putting his hand out to grab her wrist, but she stepped into the doorway. He reached again, but before he could put his hand around her arm, he felt Duncan's palm on his shoulder.

"I don't believe she wants to talk," Duncan said.

Bailey knew what would happen, and he knew it would feel good. It would come as a relief. It would be the final result, the culmination of all that would hurt him. He whirled around and grabbed Duncan's shirt and swung him against the house. He jerked Duncan up off his feet, and three buttons on Duncan's shirt popped off to reveal a weak chest. Duncan began slipping down the wall as Bailey held the ripping shirt, so Bailey grabbed him by the throat and lifted him until his feet were again off the ground. Bailey cocked one hand behind his ear, ready to smash Duncan's face into the wall. But then he looked at Duncan's face and watched him choking, coughing up some spittle, and he heard Joan yelling at him, calling him a bastard, and he felt her slam the heel of her fist into his back. Bailey got scared because he knew that smashing Duncan's face would not help, and worse, it would not even make him feel better, and maybe worst of all, he realized it was something that did not have to happen. He let Duncan go.

Joan ran to Duncan and put her arms around him. "Get out of here! Get out of here! Damn you! Damn you!" she said to Bailey.

"I could break you in half," Bailey said to Duncan without anger, as though a question to himself and Duncan.

"I know," Duncan said through the spittle caught in his throat and mouth. "I'm sorry about starting it."

"It's okay," Bailey said. He stepped off the porch and walked to his car, no longer noticing the rain.

* * *

The rain turned into a mist within the hour. By morning it would start to evaporate, but now it made pools in the dips in the roads and made cement slippery. Bailey was lucky he didn't wreck his car; he started drinking when he left Joan's.

He left the bars before they closed and carried a case of beer to his pool. He sat in the slow drizzle, trying to feel it against his skin, trying to taste it on his tongue. He felt the drizzle paste his hair to his forehead. Once he went upstairs, he disconnected his telephone and gathered up all the notes that his landlady had slipped under his door warning him about throwing empties in the pool, then threw them in the pool. Two neighbors stood on a balcony across from the pool, but he yelled at them and they went back into their apartment. The landlady came out to evict him or call the police, but when she saw him, she just left him by the pool with his beer.

When Joan came by the pool, the mist had stopped. Bailey saw her from around the neck of the upturned bottle he was drinking from. He lowered the bottle to look at her. She had on shorts and a contrasting top. Her legs were still in good shape, no bulges or waffle marks. Maybe her legs were even better now, Bailey thought—she shaved. And she was barefooted. She stepped onto the wet cement and almost slipped. She caught herself, held her arms slightly away from her body for balance, and walked carefully toward Bailey. Bailey wondered if maybe she had changed into the shorts after sleeping with Duncan. He watched as she got nearer to him, trying to memorize the way she looked and the way she slid on wet cement.

"Want a beer?" Bailey said. She shook her head, looked down at her feet and smiled.

"Forgot my shoes," she said. She tried a new maneuver and walked with quick steps on her tiptoes to Bailey's lounge chair. Bailey hung his legs over the sides, and she sat down on the lower portion of the lounge. "Thank you," she said. "Look, Bailey," she said, "I just found out what happened to you. A friend with the paper called me. Jesus, you made the paper, Bailey. How could you?"

"Don't give me shit," Bailey said.

"Okay, okay. I came to help." Bailey looked at her, tried to see what her game

16

was, then put his beer down and put his hand on her knee. She looked at his hand, then looked back at him.

"I couldn't possibly represent you, but I can find someone who could. And Duncan has decided not to file charges."

Bailey looked down at his hand on her knee, then back at her. "I don't want you nor nobody else defending me."

"What do you want?"

He removed his hand from her knee because suddenly it seemed useless to him to have his hand on her knee. He thought about her question, trying to think of some way to tell her what it was like to be beyond wanting. "I want to know where I screwed up," he decided to say.

"Jesus, Bailey, you hit a minor," Joan said.

"You sleep with him?" Bailey asked.

Joan pressed her palm flat against her throat and chest, "I owe you nothing, Bailey, let alone an answer to that question." She stood up, and he looked at her. "What I do and with whom is my business." Bailey took a sip of his beer and threw the bottle at the tube; it missed and sank. He watched the tiny wake roll toward the edge of the pool and curl up under the lip. Then he looked back up at her. She was looking at the empties in the pool. She turned to look at him.

"It is too my business," Bailey said.

"If you need legal help, call my office," Joan said and turned away from him. Bailey watched as her hips squirmed inside the shorts as she walked away from him. He saw the white half-moons of the upper backs of her thighs as the hem of her shorts rose when she walked. He knew now that he had truly lost her; she would never come back.

About midnight, the pool filling with beer bottles, Pooter came to see him. Bailey felt like vomiting the beer that had long since turned warm. He squeezed a bottle with both hands, then ran one hand up the neck of the bottle to feel the sweat on it. He took a long slow sip of the beer, being careful, trying to fight against the drunkenness, to still feel the bitter but cold taste of the beer against the back of his throat. He tried to concentrate on the feel of the beer in his stomach, but all he could feel was the tight pressure of too much beer. His head was numb. His vision blurred. But he had drunk himself to a clarity of mind.

"Why you been sitting out in the rain?" Pooter asked. Bailey looked up at him. "Hey, how much you had to drink?" Bailey saw the blur of Pooter sit beside him.

"Well, hell, good time to get drunk," Pooter said. Pooter reached into the sack that he carried and lifted out his own six-pack. Bailey heard the fizz of Pooter pulling the tab on the can, and he felt some of the spray. "Hey, hey come here, watch this. Remember, huh?" Pooter chugged the beer. Bailey didn't have to watch because he knew what would come next. Pooter took the can in his palm,

17

then curled his fingertips over the rim of the can. Bailey wasn't too sure of his sight, but he tried to listen. He could hear nothing but Pooter's laugh.

He felt Pooter shake him and say, "Hey, how many you had?" He felt Pooter punch his shoulder. Then Pooter pulled another of his beers from the plastic. Bailey stared at the water, took another sip of beer and concentrated on tasting it. He couldn't. My god, he thought. Then he felt the spray of Pooter's beer, heard Pooter laughing as he deliberately soaked him.

"Jesus, Bailey, son. You a couple over," Pooter said. "But not to worry, your old buddy is still throwing blocks for you." Pooter started shaking him. "Wake up, son. I got you some good news. Ol' Compton come to the rescue. He ain't near as pissed as you think."

Bailey looked over at Pooter and said, "I ain't gonna win, Pooter. I ain't. No way."

"Well, the losing's over. Ain't no big deal. All you done was lose a piss ant junior high school game, for which ain't nobody gonna give a shit nor remember. So Mr. Bob Compton gonna give you your job down at the lot right back to you, son."

Bailey closed his eyes, felt them bulging inside his head. He thought that one point in your life was its peak, wasn't ever going to be anything quite as good. And he knew that point in his life had gone by, and he had never even noticed it.

Bailey blindly threw his beer at the pool, saw and heard the splash it made inside the inner tube. He blinked to clear his head.

"Good shot," Pooter said.

"Shit, Pooter, you don't understand. I ain't gonna win. I had potential. From the beginning I had it."

"That's over, son, you gotta start work tomorrow," Pooter told him.

Bailey rested his head on his knees and started to shake, and Pooter patted him on the back, then left. Bailey knew that Pooter didn't understand and couldn't excuse his shaking. And he knew Pooter was right.

Someone To Watch Over

Not many people showed up at the funeral of the University of Texas' third wishbone quarterback, Bailey Waller: his parents, a few friends from college, Joan (looking radiant in black), and Pooter Elam (Bailey's guard and later sales colleague at Compton Chevrolet). After the service, Joan came up to Pooter and hugged him. They even held hands as they walked out of the Houston cemetery. His big lineman's hand with the battered and broken knuckles encircled her hand. Pooter's palm tingled from the touch of Joan's slender fingers, from the slight scrape and press of her manicured nails.

Joan had been the last person to see Bailey alive. People back in Odessa and in Austin whispered suicide. His body was full of speed and booze, and it was 3: 00 a.m., so they thought that maybe he purposefully pointed the nose of his car toward the guardrail, missed it, and sailed into a deep arroyo just outside of Sonora in that long dusty stretch of I-10 between Junction and Fort Stockton. Since he had lost his coaching job at the private military academy in Midland, he had been despondent. He took to driving to Austin, hoping that his ex-wife, now involved in state politics, would take him back. Joan was the ex-wife, and her name was once again Phelan, not Waller. She told Pooter that Bailey begged her. She had asked him what he wanted. Bailey said that he didn't know but that he did know that he wanted to be closer to her. She told him that she'd help him if he came to Austin. Pooter suspected that what she meant by *help* and what Bailey thought her help would be were two different things.

Pooter and Joan drove back to the Houston airport together, Joan to a catch flight back to her high-profile life in Austin and Pooter to catch the flight back to what his life had become, what it had always been destined to become. In Odessa, way out in West Texas, he sold used cars, the best a big, dumb, ugly West Texas lineman boy could hope for. When she left him to walk down that tube into the belly of her plane, Joan put her palms flat against Pooter's shoulders and lifted herself on her toes to kiss him, and sweat beaded on Pooter's forehead, and a drop rolled down his nose and splattered on his new tie. Pooter watched as she walked away. He watched the sway of her hips, the way they rolled inside the tight business skirt, the determined lean of her shoulder, and the way she held her head upright, away from the lean.

Pooter believed in Bailey, and he believed that Bailey had taken the speed and the booze because he was anxious to get back to Odessa, to quit Bob Compton's car dealership one more time, and to go to Austin to again triumph. Bailey believed in potential, and Pooter didn't believe that Bailey had lost faith in his own potential to finally make good, to reach his own full potential. For Bailey that dream began to hide in Austin. With his ex-wife's help he could find it. For his part Pooter believed in Bailey's potential but not his own. He believed in his own limits. But as he sat in the plane seat, headed back to what he was in Odessa, he remembered Joan's description of Bailey's last night with her. Pooter began to think that maybe he could claim Bailey's potential. Maybe he could go back to Austin and have Bailey's triumph.

So Pooter told his folks, his boss, his boyhood football buddies (now his drinking buddies), his hometown goodbye; he sold his aging sports car to buy a four-door sedan and watched in the rearview mirror as Odessa, Crane, and McCamey faded into the harsh brown West Texas landscape. And he felt as he did in college when he reached the green, water-filled hill country and then came out of the Balcones Escarpment to Austin.

On his first day back in Austin, he walked around campus as he did when he was a freshman trying out for a spot on UT's line. But the feeling was just not the same. Now he was really going to go to school, not just trying to pass so he could play football. Now the campus had changed. Cranes were growing out of the ground and pulling up buildings. Austin had grown to the edge of the campus. Where the crumbling old hovels behind the drag had stood and housed the hippies and returning vets and derelicts were now condos. The few sweat-dripping kids trudging across campus, from shade to shade, to avoid the August sun, looked richer, better dressed, even with their tattoos and baggy clothes. Pooter stood in the heat, and sweat drenched his T-shirt and made a hoof-shaped wet spot in front of and in back of his shorts. He tried to make sense of this new place, this new time, that was related to an old time and place, just like what happened to Bailey Waller.

Pooter suddenly wanted hill country water—Barton Springs, Hamilton Pool, Pedernales Falls, what West Texas didn't have. He wanted to get off this hot campus in the middle of a city expanding all around it and find water, like the times during August two-a-days, when the coaches would turn on the sprinklers on the practice field and the players would slurp up spraying water or even muddy pools. Water gave Austin and the hill country what Odessa, Pooter's West Texas home, didn't have: people, fun, culture, books. And as he started to run for water, he stopped as he saw a blonde student shimmering in the sun. She didn't sweat, she glowed, she reflected. Pooter smiled; she dropped her head. She was what Pooter didn't have. There were trips to 'cuña for a quick one or two with the whores in boystown. Pooter was a lineman; he was clumsy; he was ugly; he was supposed to be dumb. Women didn't really like him.

He didn't run but scooted toward water. Bailey, the third wishbone quarterback at UT, had his pick of women, and he had picked Joan. Pooter was a lineman, and lucky to be that. He could have water, have some of UT, have some of Austin, but women, probably not.

Pooter stopped running and put lineman hands that couldn't catch a ball, weren't really dexterous, just like the rest of him, just big, in his sweaty shorts pockets. An oriental student passed him; she smiled. She was tiny. Pooter could have twirled her. He turned to watch her walk away from him with a sort of waddle. He tasted his sweat in his mouth, licked his lips. Size 44 pants. No suit really fit. Agile in his shoulders and neck. He was a good lineman, the guy who protected Bailey Waller, but Bailey Waller was suspected of purposely pointing the nose of his Camaro toward the deep arroyo on I-10, out between Sonora and Ozona; "suicide run" some called it because it was so deserted. Who was Pooter to protect now? What was Pooter? Water, he could have. Austin, maybe. Women, no.

Pooter watched as the sweat from head, now bald except for tufts around his ears and under the protuberance at the back of his skull (and these tufts stringy and thin), splattered on the sidewalk beneath him. He got his nickname from Bailey Waller because he could spread his ass cheeks on one of those steel tables and make a fart that sounded like a clap or rolls of thunder. In the midst of a pile up, he could fart on command—like at the Cotton Bowl game against Notre Dame, where Bailey fumbled the game away—and players would jump up cussing and laughing. Big, dumb, funny, grotesque. But Pooter, as he was farting in huddles and pile ups, started taking philosophy classes. He never declared a major because linemen were stupid and funny and ugly. And he would have been embarrassed to see on national TV that he, Pooter Elam, wasn't a business, PE, or communications major, but a philosophy major, so he never declared a major. He didn't so much flunk out or give up, like Bailey, after his football eligibility was over, as he guarded this secret. What Pooter might now have was thought, education Pooter looked at his splatter of sweat on the sidewalk. He looked up to see one of those incredibly young, golden, effervescent, female students walking toward him. He smiled. She dropped her eyes. He was a lineman.

* * *

Pooter got his B.A., and then he got his M.A. in philosophy, so then he started working on his Ph.D. "What are you doing?" people would ask. "What can you do with philosophy?" Even some of his philosophy professors would ask, "What future is there in philosophy?" But Pooter had no ambitions of being other than a lineman. In fact, he liked not having any future. He got a job as a bus boy and then became the bartender at the Beanery, just off Congress, down from the State Capitol. The Beanery had been a warehouse for the army one hundred years earlier, and the present owners, discovering that this part of downtown Austin had

21

not been developed, made a bar with good burgers and chili. Upscale places grew up around it. But, as with so many places like it in Austin, the upscale and low-scale customers came in, and some even became loyal.

Pooter made friends with the regulars. One, Ronnie, kept getting cancer and fighting it at the government's expense. All he had left to his name was his bicycle and a pool cue, so he would come by and ask Pooter's view on the V.A. hospital and H.M.O.s. Freddy, who worked for the local L.U.L.A.C be consistent chapter, came in and discussed Mexican-American contributions to the Austin culture with Pooter. And Bess, the 250-pound hospice worker, sometimes cried to Pooter because of the patients that she saw die. Bess, too, was a lineman.

So Pooter had interesting conversations and a place to use his philosophy. What Pooter *did* with philosophy was to become a bartender, who was, really, kind of like an offensive lineman, never the star, but *there* nevertheless. He had water, pools of water, where he could float and feel light and lithe; he had the time to take other courses (anthropology, a course called "Sports in Film and Litera-ture"), and the money to buy more books. What else did he need?

Joan Phelan walked into the Beanery with an entourage of admirers, friends, supporters, donators, and political allies. Pooter had read about her. *The Austin American-Statesman*'s headlines screamed out about her. A lawyer, an activist, a young Democrat, she had become more conservative and thus put together a solid coalition of votes that would probably send her to the U.S. Congress. Young, dynamic, attractive, progressive but traditional, liberal but conservative, radiant; she was the new Texas, ready to assume its post at the national level, ready to take control. Her older, less dynamic opponent was way behind in the polls.

The one-time barber, who had cut Bailey Waller's hair and so stunned him that he snuck her into his dorm room in a laundry sack, with a gaze, with her long, slender fingers, her laugh, her kisses to the cheeks, the handshakes, the radiant smile, the muscular calves that peeked out from her slightly-shorter-than-normal-for-a-politician/lawyer-skirt controlled the men and women who idolized her and promised her contributions. And there was Pooter, the lineman, seeing it all, contributing, by keeping everybody's glass full.

Wined, dined, the guests drifted out as the sun set, and Joan came to the bar to pay the bill. As Pooter took her credit card, she pulled back her head, smiled, and looked as shimmering as any of the young women students crossing the campus at UT. She had beaten her age. "Pooter" came from her lips as though a gasp. "Pooter," as though a mantra.

"Joan," Pooter said.

"What are you doing?" Joan asked.

"I'm crediting your card."

Joan dipped her eyes, like a young golden girl from the UT campus. She brought her eyes back up to look into his and asked, "And what else?"

"I'm doing my dissertation on Whiteheadean Process Philosophy, but I don't want to finish it because then I can't do it anymore."

As Pooter turned away, slid the card into the slot that read the magnetized strip, and then handed the card back to her, she put her hand on top of his. Her hand, her fingers were on his pudgy ol' lineman fingers. She said, "That sounds almost like love."

"I think it's more like your guts, which often have a whole lot to do with love."

She tightened her grip on Pooter's fingers. "I have a benefit, a dinner, a boring political fund-raiser to go to. Would you like to go with me?" Pooter looked down at her fingers interlaced with his. Joan went on: "We can catch up afterward. Stay up with some wine and fill in the blanks."

Pooter thought for a moment and he said, "I hope that I don't embarrass you."

In the old days, Pooter was the only one in their circle of friends who could argue with her or keep up with her arguments. "When she gets like that," Bailey said, while drunk, during one of her tirades, "she makes my dick hard." She was going to save the world, protect an ideal. But she married Bailey and went to work for moneyed people. Now, Pooter thought, the world was going to save her. He was impressed by her will, and of course, her shimmering could bend him to her will.

* * *

Pooter felt trapped in his rented tuxedo. There was a ripple across the back; there were snags under his arms. With one big heave, the thing might explode, and the movers and shakers and moneyed people from Austin, with pieces of Pooter's tux hanging from them, would be looking at him in his underpants and T-shirt. He felt as though they expected it to explode at any moment. Joan was there pressing her fingers against his, against his forearm.

They were seated at the center of the long table at the front of the hall. They had eaten the overpriced meal. The raffle had taken place. And Joan whispered to a handsome man, then leaned back to Pooter. She kept one hand on his forearm and another on the handsome man. Pooter, at one point, placed his opposite hand over her hand on his forearm. The man on the other side of Joan did not hold his wife's hand.

A speaker went to the podium, told some jokes that didn't register, and introduced the mayor of Austin, the man sitting on the other side of Joan. He rose and walked to the podium, leaving Pooter with her other hand. After some political jokes, he introduced Joan, and the beautiful candidate for the U.S. Congress shrugged from under her mink and walked to the podium. The mayor took her right hand in his two and kissed her on the cheek. Her bare shoulders glowing, she smiled, punched the air, pounded the lectern. Pooter, though he paid no attention to what Joan said, was enthralled.

After the speech Joan was surrounded by reporters, well-wishers—*her people*—and Pooter let himself be pushed farther away from her until he was at the very edge of the great hall. He found himself standing next to a small, middle-aged lady. She smiled at him, turned, then looked at him again, "Are you a football player?"

"I was," Pooter said.

"These are terribly boring for me, as I'm sure they are for you."

"I don't know. It's my first."

"Oh, I thought that your wife or . . .or . . . friend. . . had brought you to all of these."

"She's a friend. A good friend," Pooter said.

"She'll probably get elected, you know."

"I hope so," Pooter said.

"Why?"

Pooter thought about why. He answered himself and the lady, "Because she wants to be elected."

The lady smiled and nodded, "I'm not so sure she's good for the state. I'm not sure I'll vote for her. I'm a yellow dog democrat, but not for her. But my husband likes her."

For Pooter philosophy was a protection from politics. He wasn't so much apathetic as scared of politics. He thought for a moment about Joan, Bailey Waller's ex-wife. What would be best for her? Would she be better off as a congresswoman? But Pooter also had the pleasant lady on his mind, "Who is your husband?"

She smiled as though she were surprised that Pooter didn't know, "The mayor. He's very fond of Joan Phelan. I think that he sees some political connection to her."

"And what do you think?"

"I think that we have a family. Two boys about to start college. I wish we were calmer."

Pooter remembered Darrell Royal. "You gotta dance with what brung ya," Pooter said. When the kind lady beside him wrinkled her brow, he said, "Serendipity. Synchronicity." She wrinkled her brows again. "Things are accidental in a chaotic world. But if you are dedicated to the discovery, the accidents happen to those who can make the most use of them."

The mayor's wife giggled and shook her head, "I'm afraid that that sentiment won't win any elections."

"The world is full of apprehension. We apprehend the present moment based on our past experience. We thus can plan for a future that we can't know. Reality, then, is the cutting edge of our apprehension of our past."

"You don't talk like a football player," the mayor's wife said. In ten or so more years of working at the Beanery and reading and studying, he might know something.

Later, Joan lay naked under Pooter's sheet with his arm under her head. She talked about her campaign strategy, the voters she hoped to get, the demographics and voting habits of her potential district. She had been tempted to switch to the Republican Party, but staying a Democrat had been wise. She was the new Texas Democrat. The new contributors wanted a youngish, attractive woman to sponsor. Long ago, when she was what Pooter himself called an "Earth Mother," back when Bailey Waller was humming them pillars, they had all been innocent, naïve; a new world was at hand. Pooter told Joan that he agreed, but he hadn't really been listening to her.

At first he was embarrassed to take her into his apartment. He had a sofa, a table, two chairs, and a bed. That was all. But she shrugged out of her silk jacket, bent over some of Pooter's CDs and picked out what she wanted to hear. She sipped wine while he drank a beer. Then she took his hand and led him to bed.

What happened in Pooter's apartment bedroom was excitement, pawing, anticipation, joy, all demanding lips, skin, the smooth curves of back, butt, and legs. But when the delirium of sex subsided, all Pooter wanted was silence and feeling. He wanted to feel every spot where his body touched hers, as though there was first just that physical mesh of skin and then the seeping of all that she was through the pores of her skin, through his own skin, and into the very heart of him.

Before she went to sleep, Joan curled in Pooter's arm and kissed him on the cheek. She asked if he wanted to accompany her on her campaign. Pooter stayed awake long after Joan fell asleep. He felt the heave of her body as she fell into deeper sleep. He was a lineman. He couldn't remember a better feeling in his life. Austin had now given him sex and a woman.

So Pooter was there for her, as was the mayor of Austin, all the contributors, the campaign managers, and the volunteers. He began to relax, to listen to the speeches, to shake hands, to tolerate the food. Most nights she left him, but on some she invited herself over to his place. Once, she let him into her downtown condo, and in the morning, they drank mimosas and coffee out in the cool air on her balcony. Pooter stopped writing his dissertation because Whiteheadean philosophy didn't seem so important next to Joan. He stopped less often at the campus to talk to graduate students and professors. He found less good company in the habitual drinkers and patrons at the Beanery.

Then with the election approaching, Pooter stumbled to his front door and opened it to find Joan weaving in the doorway. Pooter had closed down the Beanery at 2:00 and had been asleep for some time, so all was a haze to him, but he did know that it was very late in the night. Joan's hair was loose all around her head. She tried to put one foot into Pooter's door but hesitated before she let her foot fall across his threshold. Pooter reached out to steady her. Joan tilted her to one side and smiled. "Oh, Pooter," she gasped in one breath.

Pooter lifted her into his apartment and saw that she had the single leaf of a newspaper crumpled in her hand. Joan, in jeans and tennis shoes and a ski jacket over a man's T-shirt, stood at a slant. She leaned too far forward and fell toward Pooter's sofa. As if pulling from his guard position, Pooter scooped her up before she hit the floor and lay her down on the couch. She smiled at him and poked her fist with the newspaper at him. Pooter took the shredded, wrinkled leaf of the newspaper, smoothed it out over the floor and looked at the headline: MAYOR AND CANDIDATE CAUGHT IN LOVENEST.

"His wife came in just screaming," Joan moaned from the sofa. "She threatened divorce, suing. She looked at me, and said, 'you bitch.'"

Pooter, like a lot of big men, had weak ankles—years of supporting all that weight. His ankles gave. He crumpled toward the floor but caught himself. He looked back at the newspaper, but he could read no more. He reached up to his old bald head and rubbed at the skin and the beads of sweat forming. And with his other hand, he covered his eyes so Joan wouldn't see his face in case he cried.

"I know. I know. I know," Joan said, now quivering from her own crying. "It was too dangerous. What was I thinking?"

Pooter, the philosopher, couldn't stop thinking. And the truth, now apparent and simple, exploded behind his skull. It was too simple for philosophy, too simple for science, for math; it was simple arithmetic. Joan continued as Pooter hid his face with his big dumb lineman's hand. "And it gets worse. This petite woman found out by finding some canceled checks. He had given them to me for my campaign. And I think it was the city's money."

"Oh, oh, Pooter, Pooter," Joan said. "Come hold me. Hold me. Let me feel some ease. Make me feel like my life isn't over."

Pooter shook but hid his eyes and did as he was told. Guts up, two-a-days, fourth quarter. And once again, Joan lay naked in his bed. This time she cried and reviewed her life and all the mistakes she had made with men: Bailey Waller, some guy named Bo Fralix, the mayor, and several minor characters in between them. She didn't mention Pooter.

* * *

Joan's opponent never thanked her or the mayor's wife for allowing him to take the election. The mayor divorced, lost his next election, and Joan went into hiding. Pooter tried calling. He drove by her condo and beat on her door until his knuckles hurt, but she wouldn't answer the door. He thought about breaking the son of a bitch down but didn't know what he'd do if he did. Then, after some weeks, she walked into the Beanery one slow Wednesday afternoon. It was happy hour. Pooter thought that he would have to guide her because she looked unsteady; her eyes looked as though they had fallen deep into her skull. She was pale. What few wrinkles she had, above her lip, at the corners of her eyes, now seemed more deeply engraved. Her hair seemed dull. She just didn't shine. She wore an evening gown, her hair was made up, and she did have a fresh manicure.

"Pooter, Pooter, Pooter," she mumbled. Pooter escorted her to a window seat that overlooked 7th Street. He helped her ease into a chair and asked if she'd like a meal. "Eat something. No charge. I can make you something good. I can run out and buy you something."

"A vodka martini," she said. "I've been drinking vodka."

Pooter went to the bar, made her a martini, and set it in front of her. She stared at it and then out at the street. "Pooter, Pooter, Pooter, my friend," she said. "My very dear friend." Pooter left her to tend to some more customers at the bar, but that word *friend* kept ringing in his ear. *Philosopher*, *lineman* add up to *friend*, just friend, no more. His big shoulders curled forward. He watched from the bar as he tried to talk to one of the regulars. Joan's head made small circles as she stared into the glass of vodka.

After Joan's third vodka, reporters were in the Beanery. They had a microphone in front of Joan's face. Someone spilled her drink, and it flowed off the table onto her gown. The spotlight for a TV camera lit up that dim section of the Beanery, and Joan blinked against it. Pooter tried to listen to their questions and to Joan's answers, but he had a bar to run.

When the UT student who waited tables showed up, Pooter told her to man the bar. Her mouth made an *O*, but she dutifully found her way behind the bar and stared out at the scene. Pooter dipped a shoulder and shoved his way between the reporters, grabbed Joan's hand, and pulled her from the table. "Remember," Pooter said. "You have to get home." He circled one big arm behind her, almost lifting her off her feet and half-dragged and half-carried her to the front door. The reporters parted in front of Pooter after he shoved one from in front of him. He got Joan to her car, took her keys out of her purse, and drove her home. Before she passed out on her couch, she kissed Pooter.

After some weeks, Joan again showed up at the Beanery, and again reporters showed up—only two, then later only one, then none. Joan became old news. But the regulars, Ronnie, recovering from cancer; Freddy, the L.U.L.A.C.; and Bess, who weighed 250 pounds and worked at a hospice, started to sit with her. Bess once started to cry in front of Joan, and Pooter brought her a napkin. "They know the inevitable. They accept it better than you can. And all you can do is watch while they do. All you can do is watch." Pooter wrapped an arm around Bess. Joan had a tear in her eye. Then Pooter left the two women and went back to the bar.

As the Beanery grew more popular, even college students came in for beers;

they all eventually talked to Joan, who sat at the table by the picture window next to 7th street. She was refined. She had been a big shot. She once could have run the state. But she was kinky. Her sexual urges ruined her political career. She became legend. She became the queen of The Beanery. She began to shimmer again but in a different way. She would hold forth, pound the table as she spoke about local and national issues. People would listen and ask her opinion. The regulars at the Beanery, her new world, saved Joan. She would drink until she could hold no more and got tired of the stuff. But she needn't worry, she had Pooter to take care of her. He would drive her home if she needed.

Pooter took pride in watching her from his spot at the bar. He sometimes leaned on his elbows and watched. He was the court attendant, the friend, the lineman, the philosopher. All that he was made sense. And all that Joan was made sense. And Pooter knew that Bailey Waller did not purposefully point the nose of his Camaro toward the railing over the arroyo out on I-10, for Bailey had hope. He had hope in the shimmer of Joan. He believed that that shimmer around her could save him too. That was his potential. As misguided as he was, Bailey Waller never lost hope. The railing came up out of nowhere, and his quarterback reactions steered his car around it. Pooter finally buried his friend.

* * *

The way Joan heard Socorro tell the story, he had bought a twelve pack of beer and was going to share it with Arnie Patton. But he saw Arnie Patton sprawled out across the floor of his crumbling Winnebago and ran to him. He cradled Arnie's head and saw that his friend's eyes had rolled back into their sockets. Arnie had tried to talk, but all that came out of his mouth was spittle. Socorro knew that he couldn't carry his friend far, knew that he might hurt him more by throwing him over his saddle, so he got back on his horse and rode toward Terlingua. Joan was sure he mounted, like she had seen him do when he wanted to show off, all in one smooth motion, the horse running even before he had his butt in the saddle. He was a beautiful man on a horse.

But out of habit, Socorro didn't leave the beer. The July heat was up around 110 degrees, which was why Socorro wanted the beer in the first place. With the gallop and the heat, the beers blew up, one by one, soaking Socorro and his horse, and the horse, fired at and soaked with warm beer, scooted out from underneath him. Socorro was lucky that he landed in desert gravel and missed the claws of the lechuguilla and the bigger rocks.

With beer and sweat caking his body, his horse running toward his stable, Socorro lifted one heavy boot after the other, risking heat exhaustion, and started across the desert. That's when Sister Quinn found him. She was driving on the old rutted back country roads in the broken-down truck that Gilbert Mendoza had given her. She didn't say why she was there. Socorro didn't ask. She always showed up when someone was in trouble. She got Socorro to a phone, and he made his one call—to Joan and told her his garbled story. Sister Quinn then drove him back to Arnie Patton's Winnebago.

After Joan hung up, she sat down behind the register at the Starlight Curio Shop and felt the air conditioning. If she was going to go out into the Big Bend summer heat, which sucked all life out of you, she wanted to absorb as much cool as possible. She dialed the emergency station at Lajitas and tried as best she could to give directions to Arnie Patton's place. When the girl on the other end of the line realized that Joan was calling about that white-haired old man who stumbled around the desert tourist stops heaving his heavy backpack and whistling some tune nobody knew, she said somebody would get there but didn't know when.

Joan walked out on the veranda and saw Pooter sitting in the shade, sipping a beer, staring at the pinks and oranges that the lowering sun colored the buttes, rocks, and distant mountains. Sweat dripped off Pooter's bald head and splattered his chest and shoulders. He was always an agreeable, calm soul, and Joan was glad that he had decided to spend part of his vacation with her. They went way back. He had nursed her through her most embarrassing moment, caught in a love nest with the mayor of Austin. For this sin, she never became a U.S. representative. For the past three nights Pooter had camped out in her condo over in Lajitas. She thought about inviting him into her bed but kept him on the sofa.

She walked down the veranda, and Pooter, feeling the creak of the wooden slats, turned to her. "An emergency," she said. "You want to go or stay?" Pooter stood and smiled. She had left Austin partially because she had become dependent on him. And partially, because she was still young enough to fall once more, on her own, without anyone to pick her up.

As her truck bounced over the rocks in the rutted road, the air conditioning off to give the truck more power, Joan told Pooter what she knew about what had happened. Through the swirling dust in the cab, she saw that dust pasted and caked and mixed with sweat on Pooter's face. The think bill of his baseball cap was not enough to protect him from the sun. His face and the back of his neck were fire red. She looked at her arms. They were almost as brown as Socorro's. In the two years that she had been here, she had dried out. The lines in her body had deepened, her skin darkened. Pooter looked scalded; she looked overly but evenly roasted.

Pooter hadn't said much for three days. He had come during the time of year when the tourists leave and the regulars burrow in. She wondered what he hoped to find, to gain, what he thought of her. The more he studied philosophy, the more imperturbable he seemed to become.

They pulled up to Arnie Patton's wrecked Winnebago and saw the old truck that Sister Quinn drove. "He lives in that?" Pooter asked. They got out, the pickup's doors clicking shut in unison, and Joan felt the sun burn into her bare shoulders and bare thighs. Had she known that she would have been walking through the desert instead of selling souvenirs and curios, she wouldn't have worn sandals, a tank top, and shorts. She picked her way around the bigger rocks, felt the smaller gravel roll over the thin soles of her sandals and sear the undersides of her toes. Pooter stuck out an arm to help her. He had worn hiking boots. Joan opened the door to the wrecked Winnebago and stepped in. Trash, rotting food, empty plastic milk jugs, and water-filled plastic milk jugs lined the floor. Crumpled newspapers filled the cracks in the walls. An undulating trail of tiny ants made its way up one wall. Dust rose from the floor and sifted down from the ceiling. Worse was the smell of unbathed, sweating men. Pooter held his open palm up to his nose.

At the far end of the Winnebago, stretched out, spreadeagled, was Arnie Patton. A white sheet was spread out underneath him; lit candles were placed at each corner of the sheet—an old folk cure chasing away the evil spirits. A bag of melting ice lay on top of his heaving chest. Towels and sheets, soaked in the melting ice, covered his naked body. Sister Quinn knelt beside him and patted his head. Then Joan heard Socorro walk up behind her from the other end of the Winnebago. "That's all the ice, all the water," he said.

Sister Quinn, a large, aging, fat woman, with red hair in ringlets sticking out from under a tennis hat and pasted by sweat to her head, let her butt plomp on the floor of the Winnebago, making the whole thing shake, and then lifted Arnie's head onto her lap. "He's cooler," she said.

Socorro looked at Joan, then sniffed at Pooter. "It's a fucking stroke," Socorro said. "You know anything to do?" he asked Pooter.

Pooter, stinking from the sweat pouring out of him, sidestepped, as though captured or caged in the Winnebago, to Sister Quinn and Arnie Patton's lifeless form. He knelt beside Sister Quinn. "We can comfort him," she said.

"How?" Pooter asked.

"Touch him. Speak to him. Wipe his sweat away." Pooter gingerly touched Arnie's arm.

"No, there's got to be something," Joan said.

"Like what?" Socorro asked, and Sister Quinn cradled Arnie Patton's head.

"Let's drive him to Terlingua. Get him into some air conditioning," Joan said.

"So he can smell and stink and die there?" Socorro snarled.

"Comfort him and wait," Sister Quinn said.

"Why the candles?" Pooter asked.

"In case he believes in evil spirits. If he does, the candles will scare them away," Sister Quinn answered.

"What if he doesn't believe?" Pooter asked.

"I know he doesn't fucking believe in that shit," Socorro said, and Joan wanted to scold him.

"We don't know what he believes, but we can comfort him, touch him, help him die," Sister Quinn said. Pooter grasped Arnie's forearm. Joan's mind shot backward. She wondered if, in what she had told him just prior to his death, she had comforted Bailey, her ex-husband, or had sent him to his death.

Joan felt the rivulets of sweat rolling down her chest; she felt her tank top dampen. It would be even hotter outside, but a few minutes in the sun would turn the sweat stains to lines of salt. She saw an old fan up on a shelf. "There, there," she said and pointed.

"The generator's out of gas," Socorro said.

"I heard of people just cooking, cook from the inside out," Socorro said.

"You're just making it worse," Sister Quinn said. She and Pooter, both stinking and drenched in sweat, touched Arnie and watched him caught in his pain. He seemed still. He let out a low coo. Sister Quinn gently rocked her body so that Arnie's head likewise gently rocked. Then she started some low chant or mantra. It could have been the last rites, or it could have been voodoo. Pooter seemed determined to decipher it.

Socorro didn't trust Sister Quinn. He thought that she was crazy. She had come to this area as a nun, then she started her own church and got Catholicism and the local *santeria* all mixed up. She was a *curandera*, a witch doctor, the locals thought. They said she would turn into an owl and fly around at night. She always seemed to show up when someone needed her. But she started smuggling illegal aliens across the border, and some of them were mules running drugs, so when they got busted, she got caught. After several warnings, the Catholic Church excommunicated her. But she still ran her *templo*, her chapel, did what she could, and lived off charity.

With her back to the wall, Joan slid along the wall of the Winnebago. She looked at Socorro. A jet-black walrus moustache covered his lips. His shoulders curled forward as though the heat and the weight of his past were pushing him into that position. He had told her about the area, introduced her to his friends, had gotten into the habit of calling her "his old lady," but he only hinted at his past. His sweat-stained chambray shirt was buttoned to the neck and at the wrists— keep out as much of the sun as possible. His straw hat, twisted and pulled out of any real shape, slid far down his forehead. He wasn't a native. None of them were, she and Pooter the least native. All of them were expatriates from something or somewhere. This place was like the French Foreign Legion, a place to hide from that past. She suspected that Socorro hid from a crime. He cussed all police officers. He hid from some disgrace. He hid from the different ways he found to make a buck in Big Bend. He lived in a deserted shack in Terlingua, the former ghost town, like the other "squatters." He patched it as best he could, tolerated the heat. He bought the horse and gave riding tours at Lajitas, down the road from Terlingua. He pointed out landmarks, flora, and fauna. What he didn't know, he

31

made up. What did the tourists know? He took long rides by himself. He watched out after Arnie Patton, who had found this wrecked Winnebago to squat in. He had started talking about his and Joan's future together. Joan didn't know why she had let him into her clean, air-conditioned bed. In their long phone conversations in which Pooter usually asked Joan to come back to Austin, she had never mentioned Socorro.

Arnie Patton stuttered; he garbled something. He tried to reach up, but his hand couldn't make it. It got so far, then dropped. Pooter went white and looked at Joan. Sister Quinn kept stroking his face. "Shh, shhh," she whispered. Pooter resumed stroking the man's arm.

"Well, shit, just shit," Socorro said. "Look at this shit."

* * *

When the sun set, Sister Quinn and Pooter grabbed Arnie's shoulders, and Socorro and Joan grabbed his legs. He was sweaty and heavy, but they steered him out of his Winnebago oven and got him into some shade formed by one of the ledges. They gasped for air. Joan had been fighting nausea for an hour. Pooter looked good, invigorated by the cooling desert air. Socorro was still irritable and disgusted. Sister Quinn looked tired and dabbed at the sweat on her face. Someday, Sister Quinn, like Arnie Patton, would give out, give up, or give in to the desert, die in it, and let the buzzards clean up.

As the shadows lengthened, Joan felt her sweat grow chill; she shook. Once that big, undeniable sun ceased, life was again bearable in the Chihuahuan desert. They saw dust rise and then saw headlights. A Border Patrol truck rumbled up, and Agent Dede Pate got out. She looked at Socorro, and Socorro ducked her gaze. She looked at Sister Quinn, "You being a Catholic or a *curandera*?" Sister Quinn didn't answer. "Hello, Ms. Phelan," she said to Joan, then looked at Pooter.

"He's my friend, Pooter Elam," Joan said.

Agent Dede Pate walked to the prone body of Arnie Patton and knelt. She felt the man's throat. "He's dead," she said to Sister Quinn. She stood, and no one said anything. "How long have ya'll been holding a dead man?"

Sister Quinn grimaced, but Pooter answered, "I don't think he was dead the whole time. He slowly lost life. I think that he felt us." Sister Quinn smiled at Pooter.

Together, they pushed the body into a plastic bag, and then they put the bag in the back of Agent Pate's SUV. Sister Quinn shook Pooter's hand and said "Thank you, Arnie thanks you." She looked at Joan but not Socorro. "We made his last moments tolerable."

"How the hell does she know?" Socorro whispered to Joan. "Poor bastard."

Joan watched as Pooter followed Sister Quinn to her old pickup. He yanked open the misaligned for her. Sister Quinn looked at Pooter, smiled, then looked toward Joan. "Do you need a ride?"

"No, no," Pooter said. "I just wanted to say goodbye. I don't know if I'll see you again. I'm just visiting."

Sister Quinn reached out from her driver's side and touched the side of Pooter's face. "I've got to go now but come see my chapel." As Border Patrol Agent Dede Pate eased her truck down the rutted desert road and bounced Arnie's body around in the back, Sister Quinn twisted the keys in her truck's ignition, and Gilbert Mendoza's gift to her coughed to life. Pooter closed the door and stepped out of the way. Sister Quinn followed Dede Pate back down the rutted, boulder-filled road. She waved as she got farther down the road.

Joan couldn't take her eyes from Pooter. He waved and then walked past her and Socorro and into the desert. Socorro started for Joan's pickup. But she followed Pooter out into the desert. "My horse," Socorro said. "I've got to find my horse."

Pooter sat down and stared out into the desert. It was that time of day when you could actually see the dark shadows stretch across the desert to meet the near-darkness of the sun sinking below the line of buttes, ledges, or mountains. "I'd like to sit here awhile," Joan said to Socorro and sat beside Pooter, and then Socorro sat on the other side of her. "You didn't even know him," Joan said to Pooter. "I hardly knew him."

"I keep thinking of Bailey," Pooter said. He turned to look at her. He tilted his head to one side, and then for the first time since they started toward Arnie's Winnebago, Pooter smiled. "Thank you for bringing me here," he said. He quickly jerked his head back toward the sinking sun. Neither spoke while the sun, in a rim of bright colors, dipped below the line of ledges. There was the bright aura of the sun, then darkness.

Bailey Waller had been a mistake. She and that limited jock just didn't have much in common, but he was so charming, so much fun, so vulnerable that he was endearing. She knew that she had used him and hurt him. When he came to her after she had moved away from him and begged her to take him back, she promised to help him get started in Austin, but she told him that she would not get "back together with him." That was over. Then she told him that he had been a mistake. So when he left her house and sent his car into the deep arroyo between Sonora and Ozona, he must have had what she had said on his mind. Pooter thought it was hope, that Bailey was simply tired. But the thought that her last rebuke sent Bailey through the guard rail entered Joan's mind, and she couldn't get rid of it.

The stars were beginning to come out. In this dark, she could barely see the man on either side of her. They were talking, and she might have been talking to them, but she did not know what she said. She conjured old feelings. What she felt when Bo Fralix, the alumni director at UT, dumped her must have been what

Bailey felt after their divorce. Her mother was dying in a room down the hall from the room where Bo Fralix's wife was dying. The affair started in the midst of death; love grew out of sorrow. And Bo finally said that he couldn't watch this wife die and stay with Joan. He had never been true in his life, but now he would, so he asked Joan to leave him alone with his dying wife. The night he told her, he reached to her, but Joan couldn't touch him, so she went through his dark house, crying and shaking with disappointment, and he turned on the lights as she marched through the house to leave him alone in it.

And then Joan's ambition and love met when she spent those nights with the mayor of Austin. She came close to grasping the success that eludes so many people. She had a chance to experience power. She loved the campaigning; she loved the strategy; she loved the mayor. She would somehow resurrect the ideals, find the goals once she got elected. And for a few moments during this heady period when this big, ugly man, Pooter, who turned out to have a heart and brain, appeared in Austin and sneaked under her sheets, she thought that maybe he could rival the mayor. Then the mayor's wife and the press pulled her life out from under her, and she fell into the Beanery. But Pooter was there to catch her.

Gradually she became a character. Pooter guarded her, sent people over to her table. She had company, conversation, a place by the window. And after about a year, Pooter pointed her out to Bo Fralix. Pooter peered at her as she reached out and put her hand over Bo's, and he took both of her hands into his and led her out of the Beanery, back to his house out on the Southwest edge of Austin. They watched deer come up to his back yard to nibble the corn Bo had thrown there. They drank wine. Bo had redecorated, cleaned out his dead wife from the house they both had owned. He had changed it to accommodate Joan, and then he had gone out and found her. He said that he was now ready. He could now be faithful to Joan, faithful in a way he had never been. He said that he wanted someone to watch over and someone to watch over him. She reached for him this time, and he grasped her hands in his. They stood still. To Joan, he was forgiveness, grace, maybe even salvation, but he was no longer love. She let go of his hands, and once again Joan walked through that house, and this time she turned off the lights and closed the door on him. This time he was crying.

Pooter smiled at her when she got back to the Beanery and watched over her even more closely. But he cried when she told him that she was going to leave. He confessed that he loved her, that she was both all women to him and the only one. She had come to Big Bend in winter, seen Terlingua being refashioned by entrepreneurs and exiles from a ghost town into a curiosity, a nice place to get a steak or enchiladas, some supplies, or souvenirs. She would go into exile, do penance, go into the desert, wander in the wilderness. Favors and loans gave her enough to buy part ownership in the curio shop, and cheap Big Bend labor gave her a few profits and air conditioning in the desert. She had a condo down the road in Lajitas. A literate man who wanted to escape opened a trading post and bookstore next to her curio shop. She joined a writers' group and met a few disillusioned intellectuals. In the winter this area was beautiful. In this expanse of nothingness she was beginning to learn about its people, maybe even becoming like them, even allowing Socorro into her bed. She had been comforted, but she wondered if anybody had comforted Bailey.

The stars were not yet fully bright, so she could dimly see the men around her. She shivered. With both hands, she reached into the darkness, wanting to grab something, to hold somebody, to keep away the fear that she would end up like Arnie Patton, to keep away the knowledge that she had really done nothing to help him—or Bailey, or Bo, or the mayor, or Pooter. She had twisted up love and ambition in Austin and lost them both. Now she was growing old, drying up in the desert. Pooter was spending his vacation on her couch. Socorro spent a couple of nights a week in her bed. But they were both still visitors. So she reached for something like love with both hands. Socorro, that near-criminal, the desert rat, found her hand in the dark. She held on to that hand and felt the rough calluses and scars, and when the stars got full and bright, she turned to see Pooter staring at her like he needed some comfort. She had a free hand.

Part II
Lee, Harry, and Stacy

Stripping

"And now, the legs and the face you've seen in the Big Country Mobile Home commercials," the announcer growled into the microphone. "One fine lady. Captain Hook's gives you. . . Ms. Angelica." Captain Hook's had an announcer, a stage with a runway, a carpeted dressing room, clean restrooms, and a long bar that curved around two walls. It was Oklahoma City's best titty bar. A stripper at Captain Hook's didn't have to rely upon tips and table dances to make a living.

Lee, who allowed Charlie Cox, the owner of Captain Hook's, to call her Angelica, walked out onto the stage, and started tapping her fingers and pointing her feet out, then back in toward each other. She wore a G-string, a tight, low-cut black vest, a bow tie, high heels, a black derby, and white gloves. She danced only with her hands and feet to a selection from *Chicago*. It was her Bob Fosse number. "Meat's on the table," she heard from the audience. Charlie Cox still liked her, no matter what, and he told his manager, Leonard, to allow her three of her own numbers a night.

Lee turned sideways to her audience: guys in T-shirts and jeans, just off work. She dipped her knees, pulled her derby low over her forehead, and shook her other gloved hand as she raised it over her head. Then she dropped her head, let the wrist of her raised hand go limp, and strutted down the runway. "Lick some nips," she heard one man shout. At the end of the runway, she turned, unbuttoned her vest, and shrugged her shoulders to let the vest fall. The men clapped. "Lick some nips," the man shouted again. If she was going to work as a nude dancer, she was going to be nude. Lee saw no sense teasing them during the first dance then shedding her top on the second. She wanted few props. She worked in Oklahoma because, though the state had crazy liquor laws, it didn't require pasties like most other states did. And when an Oklahoma titty bar said "all nude," it meant it.

Lee raised the derby up over her eyes; then she briefly closed her eyes, listened to the rhythm, and started to dance. The whistling and cat calling, which usually didn't stop until later in the night when the men got drunk or horny, halted as the men watched Lee's dance. It was cat-like dance that she had choreographed years before for a Dallas Community Theater production of the *Pajama Game*. Sometimes, if she could find suitable music, she used the staccato dance she had made up when she dyed her hair and played Anita for a touring company of *West Side Story*. She had been Cassie in a *Chorus Line* on a tour of Tulsa, Dallas, St. Louis, and Louisville. Had Cassie's number not lasted so long and thus kept other

39

dancers from taking their turns, she would have done it at Captain Hook's. Lee didn't dance much anymore except when she stripped. Occasionally she auditioned for a part or got a recital at Oklahoma City University or the University of Oklahoma. She might have gotten more parts or teaching jobs at the two schools if fewer people knew what she did for a living. But in a titty bar she could steal the time to strut her stuff.

These men with scarred knuckles and brown teeth remained silent and watched her closely because they were seeing something different. They could sense that it was special. Lee hugged the pole in the middle of the stage and wrapped a leg around it and looked at the men. She appreciated them just as they, she knew, were beginning to appreciate her dance as much as her tits and ass. She unwound herself from the pole with Fosse's smooth, hydraulic moves. Dancing Fosse tired her because of the stretching and meticulousness, but Fosse fit a stripper's routine.

The music stopped. Lee let her head drop and bowed. The men hesitantly applauded; none whistled. They didn't know how to react to what they had just seen. Charlie Cox had told her that men expected themselves to act a certain way in a titty bar; and despite beauty or the dance itself, confused men lessened profits. Lee didn't give a damn about Charlie Cox's profits. Later tonight they wouldn't be able to distinguish her own dance from the dances of the other strippers. Their eyes would glaze over; they would smile as they gazed up at Lee, and they would stuff bills in her G-string. Now, even these men knew they had seen something special. Sometimes, after seeing her dances, a man would return to watch Lee.

Her next dance of this set was what Charlie Cox and all the other titty bar owners wanted. Lee gyrated. She didn't twirl her tits, but she bent over, peeked at the men from between her legs, crossed her arms, stuck them between her legs, and rubbed the backs of her thighs and the cheeks of her butt. Even when she danced for Charlie, she found new moves and body angles that the men would think were sexy. She combined moves that other strippers hadn't even thought of. With this dance, she got a few tips. After the men stuck the folded dollars into her G-string, Lee bent over, smelled the beer, tobacco, and spicy lunches on their breaths, and kissed them.

When Lee finished with her dance, she grabbed her vest and ran to the women's restroom and bent over the sink. She tried to breathe slowly and resist the urge to suck in all she could. From her days tap dancing in elementary school, through ballet in junior high and modern dance in college, she had hyperventilated. She could feel the smoke wafting in her lungs. During her performances, she gulped whatever air she could, but the stale air in topless bars was filled with smoke. Several doctors had told her to stay out of these places, but she resorted to catching what fresh breath she could in the women's restrooms.

She ran water and splashed it on her face. She went to the automatic hand drier and pressed the large knob that sent out the hot air. She squatted to hold her head under the hot air nozzle, then her face, then her chest. This machine created more air, even if hot, and dried the sweat. Strippers always had colds.

"Jesus, you need to take it easier," Lee heard from the row of stalls. She looked toward them and saw the auditioning stripper coming out of a stall. She had a G-String, high-top pink tennis shoes, a punk hair cut that looked like a rooster's comb, and a push-up bra on her young, firm, sagless body. She had a butterfly tattoo on her left shoulder. And a long scar, like a tattoo, probably from a Caesarean, ran down from her belly button to her G-String. "If it's easy, it's no good," Lee said.

The young girl, around twenty Lee guessed, stuck out her hand and said, "I'm Monica."

Lee pulled herself from under the hand drier, nodded her head, but didn't shake the young girl's hand. "Charlie and Leonard like that name," Lee said. "What's your real name?" But, before the youngster could answer, the changing temperatures in Lee's body made her feel sick in her stomach; then a lump, which she knew was a cramp, knotted in her hamstring. She cried out but bit her bottom lip to stop the scream and grabbed at the back of her thigh. She tried to hold the cramp where it was and keep it from working its way up into her hip.

"Can I help? Jesus," the youngster said. Gritting her teeth, knowing what she had to do, Lee limped to the sink and lifted her cramping leg to it. She touched her forehead to her knee and kept the leg muscles taut.

Bent over her straightened leg, the sink groaning with her weight, Lee heard the door to the ladies' room open. She looked over her shoulder to see Carol. Carol had a size 42 bust, and those grapefruit breasts had made her lots of tips until, after three husbands and two kids, her hips and belly also started getting big. She was one of those women destined to turn to flab after she gave birth. She was now "retired" from dancing and waited tables because Charlie Cox had replaced her with a younger, thinner girl. "Are you okay?" she asked Lee.

"Yeah," Lee said and straightened up. Carol's gossamer negligee pressed so tight against her tits and hips that it looked like a mist around her. She looked naked but air brushed, like the *Playboy* centerfolds. Lee knew about centerfolds. Years ago, between tours, she had gotten two pictorials but not *the* centerfold for *Penthouse*. Airbrushed so that she looked twenty.

Lee swung her head to look at the new stripper. The youngster asked, "Do you go through this every night?"

"Yeah," Carol said with a hint of malice before Lee could answer.

"I saw your first dance. It was really good, beautiful, but I don't get it."

Lee brought her leg down from the sink and turned to face the younger girl. "It's real dancing," Carol said.

"It's variations on a theme. Just movements. Like Twyla Thorpe says, 'It's just walking.'"

"But, I mean it doesn't make any money. You can't get tips that way. What's it get you?"

Lee hung her head, then brought it up to look at this girl. She had starting feeling maternal toward the younger ones. "Respect," Lee said.

The youngster smiled and walked past Lee and Carol. When she got to the women's room door, she turned and said, "You can't eat respect. I got two kids to feed since my old man ran out." The young girl walked out the door and left it swaying on its hinges.

"Why are they always so tight-assed their first night?" Carol said. Carol's heart tattoos were on both of her inner thighs. Her mother had been a stripper, and as she worked her way up from the dives to Captain Hook's, Carol had danced several times with her mother, who was working her way down. Lee slipped back into her vest. Then Carol said, "She's your new competition."

* * *

At quitting time Leonard told Lee to come into his office. Before he took over managing Captain Hook's, Leonard was a cop. Charlie Cox liked to have ex-somethings—cops, teachers, businessmen, grocery store clerks—run his titty bars. He figured that, as an ex-cop, Leonard could protect his girls. So Leonard kept his .45 in his office and a small .22 under the bar. The guns made Lee nervous. To her, Leonard seemed like that type who was too anxious to use them.

Leonard's office was behind the stage and next to the girls' dressing room. Rather than a door, he had a red drape. When Lee saw the young, auditioning stripper step out of Leonard's office, then look back in to blow him a kiss, she didn't wait to put on her street clothes. She let the young stripper pass by; then she pulled the red drape open and saw Leonard with his hand resting on top of the screen of his new computer and his nose two inches from the screen. His hand formed a fist, and he said "goddamn it." Charlie Cox had had bought computers for all his titty bars to see how much liquor he sold and how much he needed to order. "Son of a bitch," Leonard said and pulled back his hand like he was going to punch the computer screen. His tattoo, a screaming eagle with *U.S. 8th Army* written underneath it, was on his left forearm.

"Leonard," Lee said and sat in the chair across from Leonard.

"Sons of bitches," Leonard said and jerked his head toward the computer. He swiveled his chair toward her. Leonard couldn't keep his eyes from drifting down, then rising up as he soaked up the sight of Lee's legs.

"It's late, Leonard, and I'm hungry and tired," Lee said. Leonard pushed his office chair toward Lee, then leaned back in it. He drummed his fingers next to the computer keyboard. When he hung his head, Lee said, "Oh shit. Shit. Where's Charlie?"

Leonard rolled his chair toward Lee. "Now don't bother Charlie over this." He looked Lee in the face but couldn't keep his eyes from moving down the V of her vest. Lee knew that she should have gotten dressed to talk to Leonard. Leonard had worked in Charlie Cox's bars for nine years, but those years were not long enough for him to grow lackadaisical about strippers' bodies.

Lee turned away from Leonard, scooted her wheeled chair toward the door, and pulled the red drape open. She could see across the dance floor to the bar. Sitting on a bar stool, his back to the bar, his elbows propped up on it was Charlie Cox. Lee felt a clammy palm on her knee and turned to see Leonard patting her knee. "You know, Lee, I liked being a cop," Leonard said and quit patting Lee's knee but lightly rubbed it. "But I had to quit." Leonard's hand moved farther up Lee's thigh.

Lee pulled her leg out from under Leonard's hand, stood up, and said, "Your stupid analogy is bullshit." Lee pushed the red drape aside and walked around the stage and to the bar. She stood in front of Charlie Cox with her hands on her hips. Charlie was a good looking man with blonde hair and deep set blue eyes. His hand moved slowly and deliberately as he sipped his scotch.

"Now, Lee," Charlie said and raised his glass to his mouth so what little light was in Captain Hook's reflected off his diamond pinkie ring. His Porsche was parked outside. His button-down Oxford cloth shirt was crisply starched and monogrammed on the pocket. He had on pleated wool-blend pants and black cowboy boots that probably cost as much as his Porsche. Charlie brought the glass down from his mouth. "Sit by me, Lee," Charlie said.

Lee sat on the barstool next to Charlie and squirmed from the plastic seat biting at her naked butt. She looked down the opposite end of the bar to see Carol pushing a Bissell. Carol would be trying to hear. Charlie downed his drink, and Lee heard the clinking of his ice. He sat the glass on the bar and turned his head in his slow, calculated fashion, and said, "Look at her." Lee looked to see Carol. "It's all she's got."

"Don't patronize me, Charlie," Lee said.

Charlie swiveled toward Lee and laid an open palm across the top of her hand. "The point is that you have so much more than her. You're obviously talented. But I can't make money running a talent show. I wish I could." Charlie patted Lee's hand and moved closer. "Your looks have stayed with you, and you're smart."

"I'm also a dancer."

Charlie smiled. "See? See how smart you are? You have a fast mind. Hell, you could catch on twice as fast as numb nuts Leonard in there trying to figure out which computer key to push." Lee stared at Charlie's forehead and looked at his blue eyes. They never drifted toward her breasts or thighs as Leonard's did. And, though he touched his strippers, he never put clammy palms on them but a warm cupped palm. Lee saw from his expression that he would listen to her, whether she wanted to beg or threaten him, but that he would not let her dance again. "You need to go on. It's time you gave up this kid's game."

"Okay, give me my pink slip," Lee said and tried to slide off the barstool, but the plastic pulled her skin.

"Please. Not so fast," Charlie said and slowly spun around and pulled her around with him until they were both facing the bar. "I want you to manage a place for me," he said. They stared at each other in the mirror behind the bar. "This is not pity. This is an honest chance. I think that you can make money for me."

When Lee swiveled to look at directly him and said, "I don't want to be a businesswoman," Charlie turned toward her and put his cupped palm on her shoulder.

"We're all businesspeople," Charlie said. He pulled his palm down, reached into his pocket, and brought out his rolled wad of bills. He took off the rubber band and peeled off three hundreds and four fifties and handed them to Lee. Lee heard Carol's voice say, "Holy shit."

"That can either be an advance for your new salary, or it can be your severance pay. And, if you ever need anything else. . ."

Lee gritted her teeth and jumped off the barstool, seemingly ripping the skin off her butt. She folded her money into her palm, smiled at Charlie, and said, "Like most people, you did the least you could." She turned away from Charlie, went to the dressing room, slipped her jeans on over her G-string, pulled a sweatshirt over her head, stuck her arms into the sleeves of her Levi's jacket, and made it to her 280-Z in the parking lot before she started crying.

* * *

Lee sat in an all-night coffee shop and drank ice tea and ate a hamburger before she went home to her townhouse. It was the first home she had ever owned. The road shows and the tours never allowed her enough time or money to live anywhere except small one-bedroom apartments. Stripping, commercials, a poster, the *Penthouse* photos, and her tours had given her enough money to buy this three-bedroom townhome in a secure northwest Oklahoma City subdivision.

Lee would have had no problem telling her white, middle-class neighbors how she made a living. She would have liked the shock she would have given them. But instead she told them half-truths about teaching aerobics at the Body Shop and occasionally teaching a week-long seminar on dance in the public junior highs. With the half-truths, the neighbors wondered where she got her money and why she stayed out late, but they didn't get the curiosity that the truth would give them.

Lee flipped on her living room light, then pulled off her high heels. She ground her feet into the soft carpet to let it massage her toes. She pulled off her jacket, sweatshirt, and jeans, and in her G-String, did her stretching exercises. Without her exercises, cramps, with all the creeping subversiveness of age, would form in her legs and move up into her hips.

While she stretched, she reached to her coffee table and spread out the mail in front of her. Nothing but bills. On the lamp stand was the bill from Mini-Maid, the company that cleaned her apartment. After her stretching, Lee went to her refrigerator and took several swallows from a quart of milk. Her doctor had recommended milk for her calcium deficiency.

After she showered and brushed her teeth, she lay in her king-sized bed and checked her answering machine. She had two calls from Fred Wemple wanting a date for dinner. Fred was forty-four, divorced, and fighting twenty-five extra pounds in Lee's aerobic class. She taught the hour-long class at noon three days a week. Many of her aging businessmen students with Baptist wives and spreading paunches had asked her out. None knew what she did for a living.

She had messages from Doris Rhodes at the Oklahoma Commission on the Arts and from Gerry Obermeyer at Midwest City Community College. Both would see her the next day. Expecting Charlie to fire her, Lee wanted to give herself some options before she started the slide down to the titty bars where she would have to rely on tips and table dances.

* * *

Gerry Obermeyer had National Junior College Athletic Association Basketball championship rings on three of the fingers on his right hand. He wore his simple wedding ring on his left hand. His full head of hair, kept firmly in place with mousse, looked like Styrofoam. He sat in his glassed-in athletic director's office and looked out at Midwest City Community College's gym and recreation center's parking lot and tall electric sign. The sign was a gift from Coca-Cola for Midwest City Community College's president allowing Coke to have the sole concessions rights. It flashed out the time, the temperature, coming sporting events, and cheerful, moral messages. Lee had seen the messages before when she had driven by: "God gave me problems, but he also gave me shoulders;" or, "A discussion is an exchange of ideas; an argument is an exchange of ignorance."

"That is some sign," Lee said, and Gerry Obermeyer swiveled his head and his chair to look at Lee.

Obermeyer's chair creaked as he spoke: "Ms. Tomlinson, I can maybe offer you one class this summer, then maybe two or three for the fall. But next spring, if Mrs. Hodgins retires, we will need a dance instructor."

Lee sat with her hands in her lap. She rubbed her charcoal gray linen skirt and felt the collar of her Sunday School teacher's blouse rub her neck under her chin. She looked out at the sign and read the message for the day as it flashed in back

45

of Coach Obermeyer's head: "An error is an error once; a blunder is when it is repeated." Mrs. Hodgins probably liked that sign. Lee knew Mrs. Hodgins. Back before the college got the new million-dollar gym with facilities that rivaled the work-out shops, back when Mrs. Hodgins was acting athletic director at Midwest City Community College, Lee had applied to teach dance. An ulcer and a slight stroke had left Mrs. Hodgins with a limp, so Mrs. Hodgins, a one-time high school P.E. teacher, taught the dance classes at Midwest City Community College while leaning on a cane or sitting down. Once she retired, the college would probably name the building after Mrs. Hodgins. "What about these part-time classes?"

Gerry Obermeyer put his elbows on his desk and studied Lee's resume. "I can send references," Lee said.

Coach Obermeyer ran one hand along the side of his head and left a dent in his hair. "Oh, no," Gerry Obermeyer said. "I don't know much about dancing, but this looks plenty impressive to me. All the shows you've done. A graduate degree from SMU." Gerry lifted his head from the resume to look at Lee. "What does M.F.A stand for?"

"It's a Master of Fine Arts, Coach Obermeyer," Lee said. Earlier, when Lee had introduced herself and called him *Dr.* Obermeyer, Coach Obermeyer had laughed and said that he had no doctorate. When she called him Mr. Obermeyer, Coach Obermeyer told Lee to call him "Coach."

"Now, Ms. Tomlinson, what we need is somebody to teach these kids and the occasional older ladies, bless their hearts, a little lifetime recreational activities. We have regular day-time classes, night classes, and special classes for senior citizens."

The tickling yet hot semi-voluntary nerve in her heart and head made her want to defend dance from Coach Obermeyer and the students at Midwest City Community College. "Yes, yes, I realize that," Lee said.

"You know, we're just a little community college here and don't have much room for a curriculum with art-style dancing. We're not interested in anything fancy. We're just here to help folks."

Lee smiled wider. "That has always been an aim of mine. We should demystify all our arts. Take the name of art away from them and let them be entertainment or recreation." It was the same speech that she had made for Charlie Cox when she applied to be a stripper at Captain Hook's without previous experience and at the age when most strippers retire. She had told Charlie Cox, as she now told Coach Obermeyer, that dance, no matter in what form or for what reason, was still dance and that she could dance.

Coach Obermeyer propped his head up with his hand and squinted his eyes as he listened to Lee. "Yeah, that's a good point," Coach Obermeyer said. "Can you teach country western dancing?"

The nerve twitching in her heart and head caused Lee to choke slightly as she answered, but she raised her hand to her mouth, cleared her throat, and said, "Yes, I don't see why I couldn't."

"That's a popular course," Coach Obermeyer said. "We could always use a course in that for our continuing education department."

Lee closed her eyes, then quickly opened them, and said as much to herself as to Coach Obermeyer, "I can do that."

"Well, Ms. Tomlinson," Coach Obermeyer said and stood, "I'm really impressed with you, and I'll give you a call or have my *secretary* write you a note."

"Is this all?" Lee said. "Is this all you want to know?"

"Oh, I can size up my people pretty fast. Comes from all the recruiting I've done. I know how to get the right folks on my team." Coach Obermeyer held his right hand in front of Lee and shook his ringed fingers. "You seem like you'd be a good community college educator. And I'm rarely wrong about people."

"Well, one question, though, before I leave," Lee said as she stood along with Coach Obermeyer. "Will I get the chance to dance myself?" Gerry Obermeyer cocked his head as he thought about Lee's question. "Will I be able to do my own dancing?" Lee rephrased her question.

"Well, well, no," Coach Obermeyer said and shook his head as if to make himself understand how to make his point. "You don't have to. You just teach dancing here. You don't have to do any dancing."

Lee slowly nodded her head and smiled wider than she had. As Coach Obermeyer shook her hand, Lee let herself ask another question, "Is there any dancing in the drama department?"

Coach Obermeyer again cocked his head and rubbed at his chin. "I don't know. I really don't know. This is the P.E. department. Takes all I have to run it."

"Well, thank you for your time," Lee said and turned away from Coach Obermeyer. When Coach Obermeyer pulled the door open for her, she asked, "Where do you get the sayings for your sign?"

Coach Obermeyer smiled and said, "The company that donated that sign to us gave us a little book with those sayings in them. As athletic director, I get to choose which one to flash. That sign is really something isn't it?"

"It certainly is," Lee said, then added, "I think I'd enjoy working here." She turned away from Coach Obermeyer and walked through his door. As Lee walked out the front door of the Midwest City gym and recreation center, the sign flashed again: "An error is an error once; a blunder is when it is repeated." Lee got into her 280-Z, looked up at the sign, and thought about the impossibility of teaching dance as she understood it, not as Obermeyer understood it, to any student who would believe the sign's messages.

* * *

Lee sat in a cramped conference room with reams of paper around the table. Doris Rhodes sat in front of the one window in the conference room and blocked Lee's view of the Oklahoma State Capitol. To Lee, the Oklahoma State Capitol was almost as ugly as the sign in front of Midwest City Community College's gym.

Doris Rhodes began to talk: "Look at this place. I can't get extra space. Got a shortage of computers and people. Working for this goddamn Republican, give-a-shit-about-the-arts governor ain't worth a bucket of warm spit. You still want a job?"

Lee had worked with Doris Rhodes before. Mrs. Rhodes, the director of the Oklahoma Commission on the Arts, used to hire Lee regularly to be an artist in the schools. Lee taught dancing in the public schools around Oklahoma City. Working for Doris, she could dance with the kids.

Lee wondered what interest Doris Rhodes could have in dance. A dancer knew that lining up her hands and head in a certain way could produce an aesthetically pleasing image. A dancer knew that she had to work with what she had, so a dancer had to be aware of herself: her age, her physique, her face, her limits, her talent. Doris, who was over six feet tall, stacked her hair on top of her head and made herself look seven feet tall. Around the office, Doris wore golden house slippers with curled toes because they were more comfortable than pumps or heels. She wore black, half-framed glasses. And she held herself erect with her shoulders thrown back so that she looked like a drill sergeant. She was as direct in her manner. "I can't send you out to the schools. The budget's gone to shit," Doris said.

Lee could relax more here than in Coach Obermeyer's office. "I need a job, Doris." Doris didn't know what Lee did as a living but probably suspected something that most typically-employed Oklahomans would find disgusting.

"Why are you begging for a job from me? Look at your talent. Your qualifications. What are hanging around here for?"

Lee knew why she was begging for a job from Obermeyer, or Doris Rhodes, or Charlie Cox. She told Doris Rhodes part of it: "I wasn't quite good enough. I should have taken more acting classes. My voice needed to be better."

"Well, hell," Doris said. "It's a shame." Lee shrugged. "I can't give you a job dancing, but I can recommend you for this," Doris said and pushed a job description in front of Lee. Lee first saw the salary, about the same as a full-time teaching job, then saw that the job was with the Commission on The Arts: awarding state grants, traveling to give advice across the state, appearing before the legislature to solicit funds. "You'd be one of my assistants," Doris said. "You're well educated. You have a variety of experience. You look good. I look like shit. You're a woman. I think you could twist the balls of a lot of the old farts in this state."

Lee read the duties a second time, then looked at Mrs. Rhodes and asked,

"Could I dance?"

"Honey, sometimes working for this office makes you want to dance; other times you feel like your feet are planted in cement." Then Doris turned into Lee's mother, "Lee, you need to give dancing up. But you can still be involved." Rhodes shoved the application under Lee's nose. "It's better than teaching for some son of a bitch like Gerry Obermeyer."

Lee looked down at the experience section of the application. Lee didn't want to leave a seven-year blank with only part-time teaching jobs accounting for the way she made a living. "Doris," Lee said, "I'm a stripper. That's what I do for a living. I could do other things, but I like stripping. What happens when I put that down on this application?"

Doris folded her fingers together and looked over her half-frames at Lee. "God, that is a shame. Pisses me off." The corners of her mouth slowly stretched back, "No shit?" she said. "You really take your clothes off in front of men?"

"Yes, Doris. What happens when I put that down?"

"You put that down, you don't get a job because of the stodgy old bastards who run this state," Doris said. Lee stood up and let the application slide out of her fingers and float down toward Doris' desk.

"Wait," Doris said and caught the application before it landed. "Nothing says that you have to list stripping." Doris laughed. "I like the idea. A stripper working for the old Puritans." Doris stood up and held the application out toward Lee.

Lee took a step toward Doris and grabbed the application. "It must give you kind of thrill to have such power over those men? God, it would be fantastic."

Lee had met many strippers who thought like Doris. "For me, there's no power. I just appreciate the dancing. You should have come to see me." Doris smiled, and Lee knew that Doris wanted a better answer. Lee could not give her the speech that she gave to Coach Obermeyer or the community arts patrons, so she spoke while she thought: "Because I don't *have to beg* for money. . . because the men do appreciate me in their own weird way. . . I like dancing in a titty bar better than dancing for the rich, blue-haired, artless ladies who support and watch community dance troupes."

"You're a pretty smooth talker, honey. You'll make a good politician. You've got my vote," Doris held out her hand. Lee hesitated, then shook it.

* * *

Fred Wemple talked about his faith. Lee could feel the hair on his arm lightly tickling her bare shoulder as he tried to use his left hand to help him talk. She could not see him in her dark bedroom. She was glad. In the dark, lying on her back next to him, looking up at the rotating blades of her ceiling fan, she need not really talk to him. "I'm a Baptist, sure. But I don't agree with all the fundamentalism that's going on. I think any person can have a personal relation with God. If a person sees that it's okay for him to drink or dance, then I think that it's fine with God." Fred hesitated and waited for some comment from Lee about her faith. "What do you believe in?" Fred asked after a pause.

Lee believed that believing was not really different from feeling, but she knew better than to tell that to Fred. "I believe that I need to catch up on my sleep. It has been a really enjoyable date."

"Oh, Oh, I'm sorry. I didn't realize. I've been babbling on and on and here you want me to go. I didn't know."

"Please, just get dressed, Fred," Lee said.

Fred was a squat man with a round chest and belly. Lee watched his dark shape as he sat on the edge of her bed and looked over his shoulder at her. She smiled at him even though he probably could not see the smile. He stood and side-stepped, his back to her, so he wouldn't reveal any of his nasty parts to her. Lee covered her face with her palms to keep from laughing. He was clumsy when he exercised, danced, fucked, or stepped into the legs of his pants. He was not aware of his body or of her body. Lee lifted herself to a sitting position and watched Fred dressing, his back still to her. "Thank you for the dinner," Lee said.

"Oh, it was my pleasure," Fred said. His pants and shirt on, Fred turned to face her. "This has been a terrific evening for me. Since my wife and I split up, I've really been so worried about meeting any really nice women, and . . . ."

"I'll walk you out, Fred," Lee said and folded the sheet off her. Fred's form grew straight as he stared at Lee. She walked to Fred, took his arm, and walked him through her dark house to the front door. She unlocked and slowly opened the door. The porch light lit Fred's face and, as Lee knew, lit up her figure. The night air created a shiver in Lee's shoulders, and it ran down her back and chest, forcing Lee to hunch her shoulders and shake. Fred's eyes followed the shiver down Lee's chest and stopped at her quivering breasts. He leaned toward her to kiss her good night, hesitated when she didn't lean forward, then pulled his face away from hers. He stuck out his hand to shake her hand, but Lee crossed her hands over her breasts and hugged herself. "Goodnight, Fred," she said and closed the door when Fred smiled as though saying goodbye.

Lee turned away from the front door, pulled the afghan off her sofa, wrapped it around her chilled shoulders, walked to the refrigerator, and got her quart of milk. She walked back into her living room, sat in her easy chair, sipped her milk, and pulled her legs up onto the seat of her easy chair.

As she sipped her milk and warmed up, Lee shrugged off the afghan and traced the curve of her breast with her forefinger. She could feel the slight droop along with the goose bumps. She moved her hand down her side until she came to her hips and felt a pocket of fat. From the side of her hip, she moved her hand until she felt her female belly, a bulge below her waist. She was not in bad shape for a woman her age. She was not in bad shape for a P.E. instructor at Midwest

City Community College. If Doris Rhodes were an example, she was in fantastic shape for a state bureaucrat. But she was not in good shape for a dancer. She was in fairly good shape for a stripper.

Lee took a drink of milk. It was low-fat milk and tasted slightly sour. Lee raised her knees until she could hug them. Fred had looked around her apartment when she invited him in, and he had commented that he didn't know that she made so much as an aerobics instructor. He had said that she needed a cat or dog so that she didn't have to live completely alone, as though being alone at nights were some great tragedy. Fred had been the first man in her bed in over a year and half. He had been the first man she had had sex with in over a year. There had been two women in that time: both fellow strippers, experiments really. With two interviews for jobs like most people had, Lee thought that she should try a plain man and a plain date. Fred was available. So she had had a plain dinner and plain sex. Lee bounced her head on her knees. She would rather have danced in front of Fred than have fucked him. She would rather have danced in front of any man.

* * *

Lee let the air from the swamp cooler blow her hair back and cool her off. For the dancers' benefit, the Stampede Club had installed a cooler in a wall next to the dancing platform. As "Aquarius" started, Lee pulled her arms out of the sleeves of her blouse and turned to face the men. They clapped and whistled, and Lee started her dance.

Lee kept her body in angles rather than in curves and jerked when she moved. She wanted her dance to look primitive and slightly unnatural. It was sexy, she thought, but scary. She conjured up visions of sex with a space alien in the minds of the men who sat around the foot-high stage. She had rented the movie version of *Hair* and studied, as best she could with the film's editing, Twyla Tharp's choreography. She had stolen from Twyla as Twyla had stolen from Fosse to come up with a dance that was hers. And now, she revealed her dance in the second dance of her first set at the Stampede Club.

The long-haired, greasy-looking men in leather jackets and motorcycle boots, like the men back at Captain Hook's, not yet drunk or horny, stared quietly up at her trying to figure out what they were supposed to think of this dance. They had just watched the 250 pound bar maid with the hairy hump between her shoulders, like a bull's, step onto the stage, which groaned from her weight, casually pull her halter top to her waist to expose enormous tits, then light two thin torches and swallow fire. They were confused.

Later in the night, Lee would premiere another dance. She had watched *Flashdance*, and though she knew the routine was exhausting, she was determined to show her interpretation, complete with a chair and a bucket of water. At the Stampede, when she wasn't dancing, she had to sit with the men and coax them into buying her drinks that were always diet cokes or tea no matter what she ordered. But the Stampede let her do what she wanted to on stage. In return, she gave The Stampede and its clientele a little of what they wanted. She was their star attraction for two nights a week. Her name was on the rented marquee outside by the frontage road next to I-40.

This dance was all in her knees. Lee let them go limp and dangled her arms in front of her, looking purposefully like an ape; then she let the resilience in her knees spring her back up. Doris Rhodes had gotten her the job with the Oklahoma Commission on the Arts, so she got to tell Gerry Obermeyer that she wasn't going to teach any P.E. classes to teenagers and old ladies. With a job that real people did, Lee could afford to work at the Stampede part-time.

Lee twirled then stopped with her knees bent and spread apart on either side of her. Her hands rested on her nearly horizontal thighs. She slowly straightened herself and brought her hands up her trunk, then pushed them inward to pull her breasts up against her chest. She licked a nipple. The music stopped.

The men didn't applaud. They looked at one another and at her. Then a husky man in a denim vest with no shirt underneath it stood. His tattoo, an angry-looking, cigar-smoking Woody Woodpecker, was on his hairless chest. He started clapping. The other men then started clapping and whistling. Several men rolled up dollar bills and held them out for Lee. "Keep your goddamn money," the man in the vest said. "It ain't what she wants." He pulled off his black baseball cap with Harley written across the crown, stepped to the stage, extended his hand, and helped Lee off the stage. Lee wrapped both her arms around him and kissed him square on the lips, even sucked up some of his stale beer breath.

Lee let go of the man and ran to the cramped women's restroom. A teenager leaned against the wall and smoked a cigarette. The cigarette was not helping the girl's nerves at all. She shook all over. Lee methodically breathed in and out, then raised one leg, then the other to the sink and stretched. "You'll do fine," she told the youngster, who had a tattoo of a flower on the back of one shoulder and a tattoo of a bee on the front of her other shoulder. Tonight was her stripping debut.

The young stripper puffed on her cigarette then exhaled. "I'll never be able to do that. It was beautiful." The new girl threw her cigarette on the floor, stomped on it, pulled her shoulders back, and wiped at her eyes. "My break's over."

"Don't worry," Lee said.

The youngster looked at Lee. Her face was young, innocent, and ignorant—though she probably knew more and had certainly seen more than the students at Midwest City Community College. "Why do you go on? You're not a titty dancer. Why do you keep doing this?"

Lee had come to know the answer, but she thought about how to explain it to the teenager. "I cannot, not do it," she told the young stripper and felt for a moment like a teacher at Midwest City Community College.

Endometriosis

Looking into her full-length mirror, Stacy slanted a purple beret across her forehead and liked the way her hair rose out from under its brim. She checked over her shoulder to see that her black skirt stretched tautly across her butt. Turning, smoothing the skirt, she saw no ugly bulges. Pulling her hands up her sides, cupping her breasts, lifting, then pulling her hands away, she saw a hint of cleavage in her burgundy satin blouse. She could do nothing to shape her uterus, but she hoped to fix it with the help of the rest of her body.

When she walked into the Paradise, the throb of the music nearly knocked her back. From listening to friends at Rice, from her high school pals, she knew that she was supposed to like this music. But she didn't. She didn't like the throb. She liked to dance, but not like this. She liked the forms and movements the human body could make, and she liked to watch those movements slowly unwind from a body in a synchronized way; this dancing was too much like convulsing. To her dancing was to be done privately for yourself, or ritualistically with a group of people, or publically in front of an audience, but not with a partner. But if she was to find a suitable father for her child, then this gathered gene pool was as close as possible to a DNA shopping mall.

She dropped her shoulder to squeeze between a clump of people her own age. Young folks, the new adults, disgusted her. Stacy was not infatuated with her own youth; in fact, she was eager to get beyond it. Young folks had no sense. Here was an entrance, an aisle, a walkway, and the patrons of the Paradise merely mashed together, like mindless algae; they didn't step aside, they didn't sit down, they moved in herds. Their consciousness had no brakes, no reasoning; they did only what they wanted, clump together and shout at each other. But it was not sense or intelligence that Stacy was shopping for. She would supply that. She wanted bone structure and good skin.

Stacy got close to the bar and cocked an elbow on it. Soon a bartender asked what she wanted. She thought for a moment about what would look attractive. She wanted a beer, but a beer showed no bold statement. She didn't want a "ladies" drink, those colorful, icy, creamy things that her friends always threw up. "A martini," she said, thought, then added, "with an onion, not an olive." She looked around to see who might have heard. She watched as the bartender shook the gin. When he set a delicate, curved, stemmed glass in front of her, she heard, "Not many chicks drink those," from a voice behind her.

She turned to see a tall boy with dark hair in dove wings on either side of a part in his hair. He was too dark for late fall; he must go to a tanning booth. A few tufts of hair curled out of his starched, open-necked shirt. He looked Italian, maybe. Destiny, Stacy thought. "Right, chicks drink the colorful stuff, then throw it up in their dates' laps."

"I bet you can hold your liquor."

"I like to hold my *licker* by the ears." The boy suddenly stopped. His eyebrows rose. The saying, which Stacy recalled from the boys back at Port Neches-Groves High School, was too much, too soon. She had thought that the boys here would have liked the quick approach.

"Yeah, well, I bet you do." He turned his back to her and leaned against the bar. She scooted to his side.

"Usually I drink beer. I thought that this drink might be more impressive. It's my first night here." He smiled. He wanted to make the advances, wanted to win her. What's more, he was handsome—in a rough way: a crooked grin, one chipped tooth, that hair that he fussed over.

"You here alone?" he asked.

Stacy dropped her head so that she had to raise her eyes to see him. She nodded. "I'm a little scared to be out by myself."

Her doctor had explained her dilemma, one quite common for those young women who suffer from endometriosis. As she listened, Stacy imagined her medical problem as a boy would: her insides twisting up like a corkscrew. What made her a woman wasn't cooperating with her femininity. Stacy almost preferred the rough old male doctor she first saw about the problem. A friend of her grandmother's, he said things like "female problems" and "the plumbing doesn't work right." Her latest gynecologist tried to be gentle, to explain accurately, to be a woman talking to a younger, more vulnerable woman. But Stacy couldn't imagine her endometriosis as something real, tangible, or solid, something like a broken arm. It was a stupid, mean trick of fate, not biology. It was karma for past bad deeds, for moral faults. It didn't seem like "plumbing gone wrong" or "a slight deviation of a woman's natural cycle."

After several band-aid surgeries and one that had left a tiny but visible scar beneath her bikini line, another operation would likely so scar her uterus that Stacy could never have children. However, in the mysterious, magical, ironic way that science worked, a pregnancy might cure the endometriosis. This problem had symbolic heft to Stacy. The term *endometriosis*, Stacy thought, shouldn't be in medical text but in literary glossaries.

When she told her ex-lover about the problem and the solution, he backed toward his bedroom door and shook his head. "Stacy, Stacy, Stacy, honey. I already have two children. I can't do this," Steve had said.

"All you do is supply the sperm," Stacy countered.

Steve put his face in his hands, then shook his head with his hand. "I can't do that." He was an architect. She had met him at an art exhibit at the Houston Museum of Fine Arts. As they sipped the cheap complimentary wine, he told her about the homes he designed. He yearned for some great public commission, but he mostly designed small to medium-sized office buildings. At that time he was married, and Stacy, he said, was what he thought his wife would grow to be. But when Stacy made her proposal, just give her a child, let her raise him or her, take all responsibility, he went into the bedroom of his apartment. She didn't spend the night. It was three days before he returned her call.

The boy at the Paradise, though jerky and goofy when he danced, had an easy grace for his other moves. He had fine chiseled looks, plenty of sturdy, long-living stock behind him, the kind of people who had arrived in this country as peasants escaping Europe and had worked themselves into some upper middle class affluence. He was in college, Houston Community College at present, majoring in business; thus he was practical, unsentimental. A high school baseball player, now a softball player, a drinker, a partier, a good-time boy, interested in college only for vocation, in fact, uneasy with knowledge. Macho, simple, studly. He was not at all the type of boy Stacy would be interested in, but he was the type of boy who would have no objection to Stacy's proposal. Or so Stacy thought from the conversation that was really an interview conducted against the throb at the Paradise.

* * *

When she got him to her room, Joey looked around Stacy's dorm room just as he had stared at the old buildings at Rice. A community-college student attending school in the pre-fab, functional new buildings on the suburban edge of Houston, Joey wasn't used to buildings built when excess and design were a consideration. He wasn't used to a dorm room--or a radiator in that dorm room. "This place is so old," he said as Stacy closed the door behind them. "Damn, Rice! You'd think it would be newer, slicker."

"Rice is old," Stacy admitted.

"And you gotta be smart to go here," Joey said. "So I guess you gotta be smart, huh?"   Stacy turned off the light. She wanted the mood right, and she didn't want him to see the stack of dirty clothes and the empty cereal boxes. Both Stacy and her roommate, Beth, were as slobby as boys. Beth, thank goodness, had driven home this weekend. In the dark, Stacy spotted the silhouette that was Joey and walked to him, unbuttoning her blouse as she crossed the dorm room. "So what's the deal? I thought we were gonna have some beers?" He slurred the words. Stacy had counted the beers he drank, an amazing number. She was surprised that he hadn't passed out. She couldn't decide whether this possibly genetic tolerance or need for alcohol was good or bad for her baby. When she got close to him, she wrinkled her nose and coughed. They both smelled like stale smoke.

"Hey, hey," Joey said as she wrapped her arms around him and started nibbling on his ear. Stacy figured that for her purpose and with this boy, foreplay was necessary. He stuck his hand against her shoulder, backed away from her, and bumped into a TV tray. "Sorry, sorry, man, you get right to the point, don't you?"

"Sorry, sorry," Stacy said and took a step back too but was surprised when suddenly his lips were pressed diagonally across the tip of her nose and her top lip. It was dark, and his aim was bad. She reached to grab his face, twisted to position his face so their lips could press, then steered him toward the bed. As they backed through the dark, they punctured the vacuum that held them together, and she started unbuttoning his starched shirt. He, excited now, grabbed for her blouse, not realizing that it was already unbuttoned, and got handfuls of her breasts. Reaching behind her, she undid her bra just as he pulled back. He held the bra in front of him and then immediately dropped it and cupped his hands around her naked breasts.

As they curled into each other and then across the bed, he never let go of her breasts; she never pulled her lips from his. They twisted out of their clothes, and she felt his hand work up her inner thigh, and then he shuddered again and pulled away from her. "Wait, wait, wait," he said. He fumbled with his knotted pants. And by the light of a distant campus security light that found a way to send a faint glow into Stacy's dorm room, she saw him pull a square patch out of his wallet. "I've carried this for years," he said, as though he had revealed a dark family secret, then ripped the cellophane package that surrounded the condom. With one quick motion he was on his back, his feet were in the air, and he was pulling at his underwear. "We won't need that," Stacy said.

"You can't be too sure," he said. "I've seen the movies and read the stories." Stacy felt insulted. "It's like you're going to bed with all the people who've had sex with the person you're doing, and then all the people they've had sex with too." He wriggled. "No offense," he said and rolled to her.

Stacy rolled away. "We don't need it."

"You don't know about me either."

"We won't need it. I don't like them."

He reached toward his crotch, and Stacy thought she heard a sharp, sucking snap. "Ouch," he said, and Stacy rolled to him.

In the midst of their embrace, she now guiding her hand across his thigh, he rolled away. "What now?" Stacy said. "You would think that this whole procedure would be easier."

"You can't be too safe. We don't really know each other. You don't know if this is exclusive."

He had certainly paid attention in high school sex ed, Stacy thought. "Don't worry," she said. "I trust you, and I know that I'm okay. I've been tested. I'm perfectly okay."

"Okay," he said. She scooted toward him. "But you don't know about me.

Why aren't you worried about me?"

"Ugh," Stacy stood up. "Look, are we going to do this or what? You're a healthy male with a healthy libido. You look like you come from firm, healthy stock. So what is the problem?"

"Hey, I got no problems. You don't give me a drink, play any music. You're like a guy. You're the one with the libido."

Stacy was impressed. He knew what libido was. Then she suddenly felt her nakedness, and she knew that the glow the security light sent through the window highlighted her body. She crossed her arms over her chest. Joey, too, grew embarrassed, for he patted his hand around the bed until he felt his underwear. His legs went back in the air, and in one smooth motion, he had his legs through the holes and his underwear on.

Stacy sat on the side of the bed. "It's not you. It's not your fault." She lay down next to him and pulled the sheet up over her. She reached for the switch to an overhead lamp. They both blinked against the harsh new glare, and he pulled the sheet over himself too. "I need a baby."

"I'll be your baby."

"No, a real baby."

He thought for a moment. "For what?"

"For mine."

"There's adoption," he said.

Stacy chuckled. "No, I need to be pregnant."

His eyebrows furrowed. "You want to be pregnant or have a baby or both?"

"Any combination looks good."

He rolled away from her and then back to her. "So you were gonna use me. Some kind of sperm donor."

"Why are men so upset about it? What is so precious about a little sperm?"

"That's not the right way to have a kid."

"What is?"

"A kid needs a mom and a dad. And who wants to be pregnant? Do women really get some kind of kick or 'glow' out of the 'life growing inside them?'" He had watched the movies in sex ed.

"I don't want to be pregnant; I need a pregnancy." Stacy said as she saw his face wrinkle in the now harsh light. She felt more tender toward him than she had all night. And as she told him the story, he cupped her chin, not her breast. He stroked her shoulder with his forefinger as she described, as well as she could, the irregular convolutions deep inside her. She in turn patted his face. He put an arm around her and pulled her close so that she could smell the smoke on them. She woke the next morning to feel his breath on her bare back.

* * *

Joey wanted to be a father as much as Stacy wanted to get pregnant. So they started dating, and Stacy came to appreciate him. He was simple, straightforward, with modest ambitions. He was a relief after older, more affluent Steve, who seemed skittish when Stacy compared him to Joey. Joey brought her presents and practiced birth control. He was not about to be left out of the plan for her pregnancy. When he saw her curl up and writhe during an attack, when she told him that she felt as though a serrated knife were burrowing out from deep inside her, they both knew that matters were at a crisis. Their marriage was not only natural but practical. Stacy was obliged to tell Steve and Gran about their decision.

To Stacy, telephones had taken much of the drama out of our lives. They enabled more distance than a face-to-face discussion or argument. Fewer senses were aroused, so less communication took place. Which is what Stacy liked about phoning. So Stacy first called Gran and told her what she had decided to do. Stacy listened to the buzz in the receiver. This silence was not something new; Gran had communicated with silence and gestures to Stacy. But, on the phone, Gran was forced to say something. "I guess he's a nice boy?" Stacy wanted congratulations, not accusations, but she hadn't really hoped for more from Gran. Gran suggested a party at the Port Arthur American Legion Hall, the place where she and her latest husband hung out. Next Gran and Stacy debated about who should call Stacy's mother and father. Since Stacy's mother was Gran's child, Gran volunteered to call her. But she insisted that Stacy call her father. Stacy's father, now living with step-children younger than Stacy, muttered "My girl."

Next she called Steve. Stacy had spoken to Steve only over the phone since she had started dating Joey. After the pleasantries, the "*how are you*"s that we don't listen to, Steve sensed that this was an important call, a conversation that could have much more drama, perhaps tragedy, so he wanted to talk in person, but Stacy remained at her desk and gazed out of her window at the Rice University campus. A mother couldn't stay in a dorm at an expensive and elite school. She would soon be going to the community college with Joey. She imagined Steve, pacing back and forth across his apartment. He kept his voice down. Maybe his kids were with him.

"You haven't thought this out," Steve said.

"I've thought about it for almost a year now. It's the only smart thing to do."

"It's a stupid thing to do. You may have thought about it a year, but you've known him only for a couple of months."

"It's stupid just to you."

"Stacy, think, think about what you are throwing away. You have a national merit scholarship. You have a future."

"I'm doing this for my future."

"You're dooming your future."

"Would you give up your kids for a 'future'?"

Really, even with the deep chasm of age, she was smarter than Steve, quicker with words. In the few fights that they had had (and this wasn't really a fight), she had won. "Stacy, what would your mother say?" Steve coughed, probably to suppress his laugh. What would her mother say about Steve? She probably would have asked Steve out. Gran disapproved of him.

"My mother was so happy when I told her that she cried."

"I bet she did."

Since her future was decided, Stacy cut class. It was in between periods, and outside of her window, a swirl of colors passed under the oak trees. The students at Rice were mostly smart Texans. As smart youngsters, they were the geeks, the sissies, the outcasts, the last picks for teams or dates, so they wore blue hair (some Mohawk style), shopped at thrift stores though their parents were mostly wealthy, wore the clothes that their parents thought were cool twenty years earlier. Some tried to preserve class and heritage or practice for their future prominence by wearing expensive, casual, ivy-league clothes. They were very competitive with each other. Anything less than a *B* was a sign that they didn't belong to this elite group, that they'd have to go back to being just another nerd. Every year had a couple of overdoses, lots of drinking binges, at least one nervous breakdown, and sometimes a suicide. Stacy excelled at Rice, but her future rolled around in her mind.

"Stacy, stay in your room," Steve said. "I'll come by."

"Steve, you had your chance."

"What, to 'stand' you, to 'breed?'"

"Well, not quite like that."

"Isn't that what you're doing with *him*?"

"*Him* is Joey. And I'm marrying him."

"So he'll father your child."

"He won't unless I marry him."

"That's absurd. It's stupid."

"Hey, I asked you and then him to breed, and neither one of you would."

"Yeah, but you know me."

"And I got to know him. Who would have thought that males have this strange moral streak running through their libidos?"

"So you really want a child?"

"No, not necessarily right now."

"Well, good holy goddamn."

"But we're talking forever. This is it. Forever. I'm barely twenty. Eventually, you know. I'm a woman after all."

Stacy listened to that buzz in the phone as Steve tried to think of something to say. They'd been talking for over an hour already—one of their longer arguments. Again she glanced outside and felt a breeze come through her window. It was a fine, late autumn day, the first day of the year that had actually cooled Houston down. On this fall day, the city didn't need the air-conditioned bubble that made it tolerable. The cool clear air coming in through her window made Rice feel and look like an Ivy League college.

"Stacy, Stacy, Stacy, call me before you marry him," Steve said. "I love you, Stacy," he added. More buzz. He had never said that. In a way, he was lying. In a way, she did love him. Then he started into the speech that one spurned lover gives to the other over the phone, the one that drags on and on, the one full of both sanctimony and self-loathing, the one that the other lover eventually grows bored with but doesn't hang up on simply because of the past. "Yes, yes," she said. "I know that." But when he cried, she too started to cry. "Goodbye, Stacy," she heard before she could respond and heard the phone click. The receiver's buzz worked its way into her ear. And she was glad that this conversation had taken place through the mediating buzz and distance of a phone call.

* * *

Joey's parents were the sort of middle class people you'd expect him to have. They lived in North Houston in one of the countless suburbs. They worried about Joey, about his future, hoped he'd find something to settle on, thought that perhaps Stacy was it. Talking about their lawn and trees over beer and wine, they doted on Stacy. Stacy charmed them.

Her parents were another matter. Stacy lived in Groves, Texas, which is really a part of Port Arthur, a world of squat, white holding tanks and blinking, rusting, decrepit refineries. During the day, the refineries looked like old, archaic, living creatures. They belched out smoke as though exhaling. Steam spewed out of the pores and fissures in their tough, rusty skin. They were malingering on, sucking in for breath, and exhaling at first gingerly, then mightily. From a distance, at night, with all their arches of lights, they looked like an amusement park, a fairy land. But when you got up close to them, they looked like the set of one of those post-apocalyptic, dystopian movies. Stacy's father worked with a daytime crew that tended these old beasts.

Along with his third wife and her two kids, he was at the reception for Stacy and Joey. "I'm so proud of you," he told Stacy, the same thing that he had said when she went off to Rice. Weekends and a month in the summer had dwindled to occasional visits by the time Stacy was in high school; now she met her father for occasions. Her mother, between husbands, had flown in and was orbiting around the American Legion bar in Port Arthur. She flitted from group to group, the perfect host, though she was not sponsoring the party. Stacy herself, since she was a smart kid and thus a nerd, was not good at entertaining, so she was glad to have her mother take over that chore.

The hosts for the party were Stacy's grandmother and her latest husband, a late-sixtyish man with a shaved head. Stacy had lived with them for the last two years of high school. She had been fascinated by his slick skin (no hair anywhere on him from what Stacy could tell) and his tattoos, not the cool ones like Rice kids wore—butterflies, Speedy Gonzales's, or dragons—but faded, stretched and wrinkled ones—a smoking Woody Woodpecker, a woman in a hula skirt, an anchor, some woman's name that he tried to erase but left only an ink smear with flowers surrounding it. He was a kind but indifferent man to Stacy.

They sat at a long table at the American Legion Hall and drank beer and mixed drinks, one after the other, as friends of her grandmother, mother, father, and step-grandfather slid by the table, kissed the bride, and left their rancid breaths wafting around Stacy's head. Stacy never knew that her parents and grandmother had so many friends. She didn't realize that she had so few. After all, she went to Rice with the nerds, the outcasts, the last ones chosen for the team. Stacy was pretty enough; she knew that. She could have been a cheerleader, could have been popular, but she was weird. She could never enjoy what the kids of the men who tended the dying refineries were interested in. Once she got to Rice, it was as though she forgot that she had a home.

Late in the evening, they all lined up on one side of a long table. On one side of Stacy was her mother. Her flowing, cascading red hair made her pale face shine. Stacy's mother was much prettier than Stacy. She wore a very expensive, tailored skirt and a silk blouse, a single diamond on her necklace. At this party, Stacy's mom screamed class. She had made it out of town by going to work for a travel agency. Schooling herself in etiquette, dress, demeanor, and Spanish, she made a good living giving tours across the United States and Mexico. It was now her business to look simultaneously exotic and classy. Stacy's mother hugged and kissed and flattered people she didn't even know. When she sat down beside Stacy, she patted Stacy's thigh. "Are you sure?" she whispered to Stacy.

On the other side of Stacy was her step-grandfather. He would put his arm around Stacy when his American Legion buddies and their wives would come to tease him rather than congratulate Stacy. "Goddamn good of you to come," he'd say to them.

Next to step-grandad was Joey, who had to bend forward to see past Stacy's step-grandad, to smile at Stacy. Behind the smile was fear. The dove wings on either side of the part in the middle of head fell into his eyes as he leaned to look at Stacy. He was, because of his limits, secure. He was estimable, nothing like Steve or the boys at Rice.

On the other side of Joey was Stacy's father, who looked as if he would explode out of his jacket and tie. "Goddamn, who'd of thought my little girl would be getting married," he'd say to those who came to congratulate or tease him. Then he'd throw an arm around Joey and say, "But she got the real pick of the litter here. A college man." Once he looked at Joey and said, "I hope it's as good on the wedding night as the first time."

Joey had actually won the approval of her step-grandfather and father. He matched them drink for drink, beat them at pool, and told them all the dirty stories that he knew. In a serious tone, he told them that to him the most important thing was family. You never did anything to hurt family. All of them, drunk enough to grow sentimental and serious, had nodded.

Conspicuously absent was Stacy's grandmother. Stacy searched the room for her grandmother. She caught sight of her alone across the cavernous room next to the bar. She had rented only the back wall of the legion hall; the regular drinkers, her friends and some of the friends she shared with her husband, had drifted to their usual places closer to the bar. Stacy whispered to her mother, "I'm going to go talk to Gran."

"But baby, this is your party. These people are here to see you." Stacy smiled to her mother but walked across the sometime dance floor to the rickety card table where her grandmother sat. Gran sucked in on her cigarette and smiled. She crushed the cigarette out in the ashtray and chased the smoke with a sip from her beer. Stacy sat beside her.

"Gran, you were the woman who raised me. What are you doing over here?"

"Needed a breather from those old farts and braggarts. Now I'm just watching." Gran reached into her purse and pulled out a pack of cigarettes. She shook the pack, a cigarette popped out of the opening in the pack, and she grabbed it with her teeth. Stacy picked up her lighter and lit the cigarette.

"The doctor said that you should quit." Gran coughed. She was in the beginning stages of emphysema—the pollution, the cigarettes, smoky bars.

"I tried," she said as she sucked in on the cigarette. Although Stacy's mother was the pretty, shapely one, the lucky one, Gran was still shapely and quite striking, but thin.

"Why don't you come back and talk to them. I want you to like Joey."

"He's all right. It's the others I have a problem with."

"What?"

"I see them all the time. More and more, I want to get off by myself a bit." Gran didn't smile, but pointed with her finger toward the table, which now looked like a mock drawing of *The Last Supper*. "Look at them," Gran said. "Look at your mother." Her mother glowed. When their eyes met, Stacy's mother lost her smile. Stacy couldn't decipher this stare. So Stacy's mother let her smile take over her face, and she blew a kiss at Stacy, and then motioned for her to join the rest of them.

Stacy smelled some smoke around her face and suppressed a cough. "Her boyfriend couldn't make it. He's in Florida somewhere. He wants to marry her, but she's wary. She ought to be," Gran said.

"Gran, that's my mother," Stacy said.

"Yeah, and as you said, I raised you, and I don't begrudge you or her that." Gran leaned toward Stacy, "Somebody had to do it, and I was the logical one."

"Sounds like a real burden."

Gran smiled. "Your mother just had to go."

"Had to?"

"That's right," Gran sucked in on the cigarette. "And do you know how hard she had to work to get herself to what she is right now? Do you know what it cost her?" Stacy stared at her mother, who had risen, to hug an old friend. "It cost her you."

"Now look at the men." Stacy could only look at Joey. His eyes were cloudy from booze. The dove wings at either side of his forehead were mussed and hanging in his face. His eyes now fastened on Stacy. He smiled. He had won their confidence, but in that smile was not just fright but confusion, as though he were missing some parts to a giant jigsaw puzzle.

"They're all good men. Your father, my husband. My old man, Sam, is wonderful to me. Basically he lets me alone. But are any of them what you want?" Stacy looked at Joey. He was raised in a different area by different people. His concerns were staid, reliable, predictable. Her family was off-center, unsure, unsecure.

"But what about the endometriosis?" Stacy could feel a tear forming.

Gran leaned closer and reached to the back of Stacy's head. Gran exhaled and scooted her chair close to Stacy. "Maybe this genetic pool needs to end."

"Oh, Gran," Stacy said. She wanted to laugh, but she felt like a serrated knife was about to grind its way out from her insides. She pulled slightly away from her grandmother to see her. "No children. This pain," she said.

Her grandmother's lips started to move, her eyebrows wrinkled, but instead of saying anything, she patted Stacy's cheek. "Gran, Gran. Oh, Gran." Stacy said.

"It's a shame," Gran said. "But not a tragedy." Stacy felt her grandmother's palm tilt her head, as though from this angle, the world and her dilemma would look different, "It's the tragedies we should always try to avoid."

Stacy breathed in and straightened her head to look at the world and her dilemma from her grandmother's view. Invitations had been sent, so there would be a lot of notes to write. She would confront what followed like Gran would— but without a cigarette. *Endometriosis* was not at all a medical term. It was like *fate*, *foreshadowing*, *pathos*, *hamartia*, or *peripeteia*.

Don't Empty Houses Ring?

Don't empty houses ring? Are magnesium
and scorn sufficient to support a town,
not just Philipsburg, but towns
of towering blondes, good jazz and booze
the world will never let you have
until the town you came from dies inside?
            Richard Hugo, *"Degrees of Gray in Philipsburg"*

To Stacy, telephones had taken much of the drama out of our lives. Now, she was willing to risk drama but was scared of it. Now, when she called Harry, Stacy's fingers punched the numbers automatically without any hesitation or assistance from memory.

With the receiver to her ear, Stacy listened and remembered the tones and remembered listening to those tones. Every day for two years at six, after they had both watched the national news, she held her slim, cordless phone in her hand and pressed the numbers with her thumb. The phone used to bleep in a faster sequence. Her fingers were better trained then. And if she waited into the local news, as she did maybe once a week just to test him, Harry would call within fifteen minutes. They'd decide if they would spend the night at his place or hers and what they'd do in the meantime.

After the third hollow ring, she pressed the lever with her thumb to hang up and think about what she was doing. She didn't want to talk to his machine and wasn't sure how to start talking to him.

But she reconsidered: if Harry was not calling her out of spite, vengeance, or anger, then she would call him. If their affair was to become muttered sarcastic comments to friends and new lovers, then it was not to be blamed on her. She would make an effort. She would be the one to salvage something. She made her thumb go into the contortions that made the old time bleeps, and inside her mind, she sang the song that followed those bleeps: "Honey, this is Stacy."

His empty "hello" worked its way through the phone lines and into her ear. A second and then a third "hello" worked their way through the lines to reach her ear. "Harry, it's Stacy." All she heard was faint static. "Harry, are you there?"

"Stacy," she heard. "You're calling me?" For somebody who was supposed to be smart, Harry could get stumped by, then dwell on the obvious. Then she once again heard the familiar way he talked: hesitant, trying to choose the right words, thinking all the time. Jesus, he used to piss her off when he tried to explain something to her. But now all he said was, "What's going on?" He said it easily, then added with some restraint, "Why did you call?"

Stacy wanted to ask if she needed a reason to call but didn't. She said, "Harry," squeezed the phone between her cheek and shoulder to free her hand, stepped across Don's living room, and checked the front door. "I miss you, you know. I miss talking to you."

"What else do you miss?" Harry, like he'd always done, faked sleaziness. Harry was sexual, he'd try anything, get turned on by anything, but he was never sleazy. He couldn't be. He was too careful. During the actual act, he'd scream and moan and completely give himself over to his lover, just like a woman, but afterwards, when it was time for talk or for just staring at the ceiling, something was missing.

"I miss sleeping with you," she said.

"You mean snoring or fucking?"

"We had great sex."

"So come see me."

"I can't do that. Don't tempt me. I'm trying to be faithful."

"You were never good at faithful. Come see me."

"And what would we do?"

"Whatever you wanted."

"I want to be faithful."

"Faith untempted is not faith."

"I don't want to make any false promises. I can't sleep with two men anymore."

She heard his short breaths through the static and knew from the changed rate of his snorts that he was thinking, planning two steps ahead. "You never had any trouble being with two men when you were with me."

Being funny and vindictive at the same time was Harry's specialty. "Please, Harry, don't be pissy. If you get pissy, there's no use talking."

"Is there any use talking, pissy or not?"

"Harry, I can't come see you."

"Where are you calling from?"

She hesitated, "From Don's."

"You live with him, don't you?" She didn't answer. Harry's voice grew terse. "Are you going to marry him?" She knew that, if she could have seen him, he would have that irritating smirk. Age had made Harry's smile a part of his face. As he talked and stumbled into the stories and anecdotes that amused him, his smile spread wider and wider and squinted his eyes, making wrinkles appear on his smooth face. But when he got pissy, that smile crept into the left side of his face and created a large dimple in his left cheek. When he smirked, he made her feel even more than eleven years younger than he. After the smirk, he'd make some wise-ass comment that wasn't rude but sarcastic.

"I'm not going to marry anybody, not right now."

"No, live with them."

"I would have lived with you. But we never planned anything. We just stumbled into things. We'd have stumbled into a marriage."

"And that would have been horrible."

"Oh, God. I'm going to hang up."

"I'm sorry." Stacy breathed in and heard him grab for breath too. She knew that he was stretched out on his couch, a book or the TV channel changer beside him, his smile shifting from one side of his face to the other as he tried to decide on whether to bite off all his anger or frustration or whatever it was that was still up his ass and be pleasant or whether to keep on trying to beat her over the head with what she couldn't help doing. "So why did you call?" she heard.

"I miss you. I never stopped."

"But at nights, you sleep with someone else."

"You can be lonely and still sleep with someone."

"You're telling me about loneliness." Stacy closed her eyes and imagined him smiling, not smirking, so she wouldn't slam the receiver down.

"Don't make me hang up." Maybe he wanted this fight, like maybe he wanted the punishment. Her therapist and she had talked about this. For some types, like Harry, when the compulsion goes, even if that compulsion hurts, hurting is better than no compulsion.

"But at nights, you go to bed with somebody, and in the morning you wake up with them. And the woman I used to sleep with is gone, so I sleep with nobody. It's a different kind of loneliness."

"Please, Harry. I've heard it before. My counselor says that your analogies are bullshit."

"Maybe your counselor is bullshit."

"Harry, I just said that I missed you. Can't you take it a little easy on me?"

"Six months ago in Doña Aña at lunch, with your mouth half-full of an enchilada, you kissed me and said you loved me. I thought life was great. Then that night, you spent the night with Don."

"I was so restless. I had to do something."

"You love him too?"

"I love you. I love him. And I love Randy."

"But you left Randy, left me, and now you fuck him. And in between him and me was a whole bunch of other guys you thought you loved."

"Oh, God. God, I swear. Look, Harry, the sex with Don isn't that great. I mean he's older than you. It's just not often enough."

"Older than me, huh? He must be ancient. All the more reason to come see me," Harry said. Her therapist and she had talked about sex at the last session. Harry would roll on to his back and rub his hand behind his head as she pulled her tongue down his chest. He would moan, like a woman. His hands were always on her. With Don, like with most men, sex was bargaining, for this, you got that. He never said "no," but the way his head would roll to one side, the way his mouth gaped open, like he was slow-witted, meant "no." Harry'd risk a heart attack for just one more orgasm, like this one more might be his last. But Stacy suspected that he was like that with every woman.

"Look, Harry, you should know, it's never just sex. I can talk to you. You are interested in my life, my ambitions. Don and I don't like the same movies or the same books." Don's hands went right for the vital parts, and after squeezing or wrapping his lips around a breast or a fold of flesh, he'd let Stacy know what to do. Harry let Stacy do the leading.

"So let's go to the movies."

"Harry, I can't."

"So why the hell do you stay with him?"

She stopped, pulled her breath in. "He complements me. I look at him and I see Randy, or everything that I loved about Randy, grown up, settled, established. And it's not so bad."

"So what the fuck about me?"

"It's not the same. We just don't have the same relation."

"Yeah, I'm the one you don't fuck."

"It's not just fucking."

"No, it's not. It's holding someone after you're through fucking and then rolling away from them to go to sleep and maybe once in a while in the night brushing up against them and taking comfort in the fact that they are there and that you want to be there with them."

"Oh, honey." She had let the word slip, the word that he would take the wrong way, the word that would do him some harm. And while she heard him gather his breath, she said quickly, "Can't I miss you and tell you that?"

"And I'm supposed to be the super human or the schmuck who takes it."

"I'm so sorry. I miss you. You want me to hang up?"

"No. It feels good to talk to you."

"Oh, honey, I'm sorry. There's nothing else I could have done."

"I'm angry at you," Harry said, then snorted, then his voice broke. "Finally I'm goddamn mad as hell at you. That's progress, right? And you were wrong. I'm the good guy here. I've got the moral high ground."

She chuckled, didn't smirk: "You're talking about morality?" But he was not about to laugh. He would not let her change the conversation. He had to say what had been building up in him. He had to keep hurting both of them. His smirk was gone. She could see him clenching his teeth and pulling his lips apart to expose his teeth as he talked. "But at nights, I have these dreams about women, about sex with them, about touching them. They're kinda women in general, and when the morning comes, between sleep and consciousness, all of them become specifically you."

"Harry, I want to see you. But Don doesn't understand. You scare him."

"Fuck him."

"Harry!"

"Why?"

"I like lying in bed with him, waking up with him. He teaches me to play golf. We go sailing. We travel. We have this life."

"So he's got money, and I don't. But when the bourgeois lifestyle gets old, when the excitement wears off, then all you got is yourself. And that's what you need to work on." The static on the phone bounced between them.

Stacy wanted to tell him not to forget her completely. She heard his breath tighten. Women are not the ones who use crying. They cry, and then, because they are the ones who are supposed to cry, the man pats their shoulders, says, "there, there," and that's it, all wrapped up. Fixed. But when a man cries, he's ashamed, so his crying won't go away; his crying stays with the woman and with him. But now, a few tears were not going to change Stacy's mind or push her into anything, but then too, she wanted to tell him she would meet him, but she heard the door open, and she yelled into the receiver, "Don's here, I have to hang up." She slammed the receiver, knowing that she left Harry crying, with his receiver still up to his ear and buzzing.

She turned to smile at Don. He looked tired, but with his lazy eyelids, he always looked tired. But Stacy loved that look. He dropped his sport coat from his shoulder and on to the couch. He smiled at her rather faintly. "Who's on the phone?" he casually asked.

"My mother," she said.

"I'm going to get a drink," he said to her, smiled, and went into the kitchen.

After dinner, some drinks, a shared joint, and two scotches for Don, they were both ready for bed. Don stripped off his pants and slid under the sheets. Stacy went to the bathroom, brushed her teeth, tried as best as she could to comb some life into her hair, and stepped into a negligee cut low in front and high around the legs. She turned her back to the mirror, saw her butt, grown a bit larger since leaving Randy.

She came into the bedroom, turned out the light, walked across the bedroom —that had once been strange but that she had now memorized, that she now thought of as her bedroom—and turned on the night light by her side of the bed. Don rolled over and smiled at her. "You're beautiful," he said.

She squeezed in beside him, and he put his arm around her shoulders. "I hate teaching," she said. "I need to do something else."

"You're beautiful, young, and smart," Don said and kissed her ear. "You can do anything that you want." Harry had said the same thing. Randy always told her that she wasn't as smart as she thought she was.

She felt Don's arm start to pull out from behind her shoulders, so she rolled into him and put her head on his chest, felt the slick feel of his chest with the few downy-like hairs, so unlike the stiff, coarse hair on Harry's chest. She licked his slick chest and pulled her eyes up to look into his eyes, and she started to lower her hand from his chest, down his belly, and over the top of his thigh. Don's lids grew heavier still, he blinked, didn't resist. She slid her hand to his inner thigh then stretched her fingers up. He looked down at her with squinted eyes; his mouth made an *O*. When she pulled her hand away, he kissed her, and she smelled the scotch on his breath.

* * *

Stacy repeated, not from memory but nearly from the mere charging of neurons in her brain, the four aspects of character. By the third period, she didn't need her brain. The students jabbed each other with their elbows, didn't dare show interest, and marched to the vice principal's office when she sent them down. During her next two periods, she taught *The Pearl* to seniors who couldn't read. They were a much better-behaved class because they sensed the inevitable and their gruesome fate three months away. Harry drifted in and out of her mind as the neurons charged and converged.

During her resource period, Fred, the football coach, winked at her, and Donna saw him. "A hunk," Donna said and rolled her eyes, "kind of a nice butt." Stacy didn't tell Donna that, while she was still with Harry, she had seen that nice butt, and that was all she saw in Fred, so back to Harry, who at least was interesting in his shortcomings. "But men my age," she told Donna, "pretty as they are, are so dumb." At times Stacy felt that, during her last operation for endometriosis, the doctor must have punctured some part of her that made her a woman. It must have fizzled out of the inch-long incision they made for the surgery. She'd never have kids with all the cutting and slicing of her uterus, so sex, for her, was for free. No bothersome, clumsy birth-control devices, no little plastic circle of pills demanding her attention every morning, rerouting the natural chemical delivery system, making her butt spread, no boogey man, no left-over prudish thoughts about procreation. Sex was for men and now for her. Randy was four years older and couldn't get rid of the idea of his kids playing in their front yard. So Stacy went for older men than Randy, ones with kids behind them, and ended up with Harry, then Don. Neither one had kids, and both had given up on or never had images of children running through the house or playing in the back yard. They cared for and nurtured their own childishness.

The only woman Stacy knew who was roughly in her shape in regard to kids was Lee, a dance instructor at the St. Elizabeth's Health and Wellness Center. Once, in another life, a teenager's life, like every woman, Stacy fancied herself a dancer. And when married to Randy, she thought that dancing would keep her in shape. So she took a class with this Lee. Lee Tomlinson had been a professional dancer, then a stripper, then a bureaucrat for a state arts commission, then a health teacher and dance instructor. None of these professions allowed Lee time for a kid, so in a way, as Lee once told Stacy, Lee had performed a hysterectomy on herself.

After school Stacy met Lee for beers in the patio of the Ginger Man Bar, under the cool shade of an oak. Used to, Stacy and Harry would go to the Ginger Man, and one night, because Harry was tired and because she couldn't sleep, Stacy kissed Harry good night, stayed, and met Don. The sun went down; the dinner crowd came and left; the regulars came in and listened to a really bad singer; and Stacy admitted all to Lee.

"I need something to happen," she told her. "And it will tell me what to do."

"Something with men, or something with a job, or going back to school?"

"One of those things, just one of those."

Lee reached into her purse and pulled out her vice and her treasure, a pack of cigarettes. She looked at Stacy and smiled, then shook the pack so that a butt popped out. Stacy shook her head, and Lee raised the pack and pulled the butt end out with her lips. "Oh hell," Stacy said and reached for a cigarette. Lee smiled and shook her pack so that a butt popped out for Stacy.

Lee's muscles had stiffened but still made the hard bulges in her tights, the kind that the young women in her dance classes wanted. Stacy hoped that her genes, eating and work-out habits, and discipline destined her to look like Lee. Of course, as with Lee, no child would ever stretch out her stomach muscles and leave them in little ripples. Stacy spent her life looking healthy and was afraid of cigarettes, but smoked exactly one—four days a week.

"You won't find what you want or need in a man. Just get away for a while," Lee said and smoke came out of her mouth. She quickly stuck the cigarette back in her mouth.

"That's what Harry always said." Stacy shrugged her shoulders.

Lee pulled her cigarette out of her mouth and looked at the lit end. "Maybe those years dancing in bars addicted me to nicotine. I didn't start smoking until I quit dancing."

The singer screeched some Bob Dylan song, and some man looked at Stacy and then at Lee as he made his way to the restroom. "See, you smiled at him," Lee said and inhaled on her cigarette.

"So?" Stacy asked.

"So nothing."

"How did you get so smart?"

"I'm getting to that age where a woman becomes invisible." Lee glanced at Stacy. "A man gets some character when he get wrinkles, and a woman just gets worn. People don't 'see' a woman past forty."

Stacy twirled the pint glass in front of her face, "You 'see' somebody, don't you?"

Lee smiled. "No."

Stacy looked around, saw the man go into the restroom, and rested her eyes on Lee's gaze. "What about sex? Hell, don't you ever just want a man around?"

"When I was a dancer, I actually got a thrill from it. The dance, I mean. When I became a stripper so that I could dance once in a while, some men would actually appreciate the dance. Nakedness was a part of it. The sex was the dance. Then as I got older and slid down from gentlemen's clubs to titty bars, I didn't even care if the men saw me. I didn't even notice. It was just the dance. And I realized that no man could match it." She puffed again, cocked her head to look at Stacy, and smoke came out of her mouth as she said, "Then I stopped dancing."

"Well, see there," Stacy said.

In the light coming from the kerosene torches, Stacy looked closely at Lee's wrinkles. Whatever it was that pushed up her cheekbones had fallen into pockets around her mouth and bulged on either side of her jawline.

"But you've been with men?"

Lee narrowed her eyes, but as she began to speak, her eyes lifted up above Stacy's head. Stacy turned around to see the guy who had just gone to the bathroom standing behind her. He shifted his body away from her when he saw Stacy look. Stacy swung her head back toward Lee, and Lee planted her elbows on the table and leaned toward Stacy: "Men have this long stretch of clitoris between their legs, and whatever they bump that thing into, it gets aroused." She sipped her beer and leaned back in her chair. She spoke louder, probably so the man behind them could hear. "Breasts are marvelous things. For all their fascination with them, men don't know how to treat breasts." Lee shifted her eyes up to the man behind Stacy. And Stacy turned to see him pull himself back from them, like they smelled.

"I don't dance much anymore. As for sex. . ." Lee inhaled the last bit of cigarette before it burned the filter. "Afterwards, don't you find yourself thinking that it just wasn't worth the before or the after?"

Stacy squirmed for a moment in her chair while conversations with her counselor floated like bubbles in her head, then one popped. She told her: "Do you think that sexual desire is gender specific. Or do you think that there is just the one desire? The 'procreant urge'?"

They cut off the serious conversation that Stacy had wanted because Lee had work to do and because Stacy had Don wondering where she was.

In the parking lot, Stacy hugged Lee and told her thank you. Stacy had tilted the glasses that Lee seldom wore, and as Lee raised her hand to adjust her glasses, the flat of her hand brushed against Stacy's breast. As Stacy drove off, that touch made her nipple stiffen.

* * *

When they first tried to kiss, Lee pulled her lips away before they touched Stacy's. On the second try, Stacy pulled away. "Maybe," Lee said, "we should start in reverse."

As Lee smiled and Stacy chuckled, Lee undid the button to Stacy's blouse. A shiver started above Stacy's butt and darted up her spine to shake her shoulders, and that vibration shook her breasts as Lee undid the next button. When Lee eased her tongue down Stacy's chest, her nipples stiffened, and the shiver shot back down her spine from her shoulders.

"What do we do? How do we do it?" she asked as Lee's tongue stopped between her breasts, and Stacy shrugged to let her blouse fall away and hung her head back to let her hair touch her naked back.

"I don't know," Lee said.

They groped, fumbled, and grew excited because sex was clumsy once again. Then they lay in bed and held hands. Lee had led Stacy to a bedroom tucked into the interior of her crumbling old house. And Stacy looked around at the playbills framed and hung on the walls. The touring company musical productions featured a Lee Tomlinson. "You want a cigarette now?" Stacy asked, and Lee laughed.

Stacy had wanted the experiment to fail so that she could go back to Don because he was a man and just "because." But they met again, and once again. Lee curled away from her and cried. When Stacy rested her chin on Lee's shoulder and asked why she was crying, Lee said, "Because it is not good enough. Not even this." Stacy pulled away from her, surprised that she would be insulted, and started to dress. Lee wrapped a sheet around herself and whispered to Stacy, "No, no, I'm sorry." She rose, held the sheet in place with one arm, and gently wrapped a strand of Stacy's hair around her forefinger. "You misunderstand. It is not dance. Nothing can be. I thought it may be."

When Don asked Stacy who this "Lee" was who kept calling, Stacy said, "*a friend*." The arguments started. Don finally pushed her into saying that she had slept with this "Lee guy." Then he asked if it was a one-time thing, if she could quit it with this guy. Stacy said "no," but knew that she could no longer return Lee's calls or meet her at the Ginger Man.

Stacy and Lee were never able to really kiss each other. And Stacy wanted to tell Harry.

* * *

Don couldn't hear Tony Valdez over the buzz on the cell phone. "What, what?" Tony asked. Tony Valdez was the type who wouldn't get things right unless you drew him pictures.

"You pick up the stuff in the living room," Don yelled into the phone, "and you move it to Hawthorne apartments. They're off 10 just before you get to Calder. L-45, second floor." Don chuckled for Stacy's sake and added, "with a real nice view of the freeway."

"What do I do with the freeway?" Tony asked. Don should have hired a real moving company instead of a couple of guys with a dilapidated old truck and an ad in the classifieds, but Don trusted the Valdez brothers because he trusted his fellow salesman, Earl Hutson. Earl moved around all the time because women kept kicking him out. He had a tab with Tony Valdez. Except for Stacy and his ex-wife, Don had always stopped short of moving in with the ladies that he got.

It wasn't that hard; that morning, after she left for work, Don piled her cosmetics, dishes, pictures, TV, boom box in the living room. All the Valdez brothers had to do was pick up the pile of shit and move it to the apartment. Don even charged her a bed at Sears and had it delivered to her new apartment, so she'd have a soft place to put her lean, young, cheating body.

Don blamed himself. He should have known that a woman like that was too good for him to keep. Don knew about her urges. He had courted his own for years. A specialist at the Ginger Man, Don could talk to, then leave with the "older" ladies who came in. He liked the way they looked, the way they pretended not to be concerned with the way they looked. Their concern for their kids. Their willingness, nearly on the verge of desperateness. That allowed Don to provide them with some spark of excitement before they went back to their lives of habit.

Don had known about habit and had divorced his wife to court excitement. He could have gotten hurt in his journey but luckily survived. He found habit again with, surprisingly, a young Stacy. He should have known that she was not old enough to have fully exhausted that urge for excitement. Hell, he was still not old enough, or rather, he prayed that he was still suited for habit, comfort, relaxation with one woman.

Don shot around a slower car. He missed his antique Mustang with the old American V-8 that could pass anything made today, but his Lexus had comfort as well as speed.

Three days before, before the discussion and then the yelling, Stacy met Don at the door with a scotch, the way he liked it, on the rocks, a splash of water on top, and told him how much she loved him. The way she wrapped her voice around the words, the way she moved, Don, who knew about women's moves, guessed the pledge of love was a cover for some shock, for some disappointment. The cop passed him by, and then Don pulled behind a Mercedes, the worst damn cars on the road, always belching out black smoke. After Stacy told him how much she loved him, Don pushed the right button, *Lee*, and the argument started.

Goddamn Stacy could make your teeth itch. Sex was great of course, those strong angular legs resting over your shoulders or against your outer thighs. Those toes. They were slender and graceful, and he always found himself with his fingers interlaced with her toes and gently rubbing their backs. With those long legs, she had a powerful swing, and because she lifted weights and went to dance class, she had strength in her arms, so she was a great golfer. He liked to be seen with her. He liked to be with her. She was habit, but one that he enjoyed.

And as habit, she had robbed him of his old life, the exciting one with potential women, the perfect one always at the end of the bar. By necessity and by choice, he had forced a new life on himself, the type of life married people have, full of habits and little rituals you create, not a bad life, just one that took the old one away from him. He pulled out of the black smoke of the Mercedes, and then felt his eyes tickle.

Over a rise, the traffic bunched up, and Don hit his brakes too hard. He stopped within inches of a bumper, and some truck stopped inches away from his bumper. Don could see it coming. Lee was just the first. There would be others. And each time, it would hurt more, and as excitement finally outshone habit, as it had in Don's first marriage, so Stacy would finally leave her habit, which, of course, was Don. Only older women—no, only older people, Don corrected himself—who have risked excitement to find habit, only to grow weary of habit and again risk excitement, can draw a truce and be content with habit. He would cut this off now before it could cause him real harm. A quick amputation is best; no gangrene that way.

In the traffic jam, staring at a bumper and a back seat full of kids, Don was thinking clearly. He could go back to the therapist, the one he liked to see, the one with the nice legs.

Then some idiot behind him, probably some redneck who had come to Beaumont for the refinery jobs, started honking, just like all country boys, like if they showed that they were pissed off, the traffic would automatically start moving. Don gripped the wheel tighter and thought about flipping him the bird. He thought about getting out of the car and yelling, "Fuck you, you ignorant hillbilly." Instead, stuck between kids and a baboon, Don bounced his head against the steering wheel. Safe in his air-conditioned car, safe from the outside, he began slamming his fist into his leather interior and yelling at the sons of bitches to start moving, just like the ignorant hillbilly behind him. And no doubt, the kids in the car in front and the hillbilly in the pickup behind stared through his windshield and into his safe air-conditioned shelter from the outside to watch him beating up his interior.

* * *

Harry was at home with the air conditioner turned on, but the cool, dry air hadn't yet spread through his apartment. He sweat into his sofa, shook his glass of iced tea to tinkle the ice cubes against the glass and sucked a joint. He dug under the foam pad sofa seat, found his remote, and clicked on the TV to catch the evening news. After the news, he went to the refrigerator and pawed through the freezer to find a microwave dinner, then sat in front of his TV and flipped through the channels as he tried to find something worth watching during prime time.

The phone disrupted the opening of the CBS Evening News. As soon as he said hello, he heard his name, and he knew it was Stacy. "How are you doing, Stacy?" Harry reached for his second joint.

She hesitated before she blurted out the trouble: "He left me, Harry. Rather he kicked me out. He just phoned me and told me that I didn't live with him anymore. He gave me a new address. He's paid the deposit and the rent for three months."

"The shit hook," Harry said. "Why did he do it?" Harry need a deep drag from his joint, so he sucked in the smoke and held his breath while he listened.

More silence, then a hesitant voice said, "I had an affair." Harry smiled to himself because what had happened to him had now happened to Don. Then another reason for smiling occurred to him; maybe Stacy wanted him back. "With a woman, Harry." The smile in Harry's mind went away.

He inhaled again, "Jesus."

"Just an experiment really, Harry. It was like it was the next step. Something I had to do. It wasn't what I thought it would be."

"Jesus, a woman, really?"

"Yes, Harry. I thought you might understand."

"Jesus, what was it like?"

"It was just different, that's all."

Harry tried to picture this fantasy that might now have turned real. "Got any pictures?"

"Harry!" Stacy actually laughed.

Another piece of reality caught his mind. "And Don found out?"

"He never found out it was a woman."

Harry's head slumped. It felt as though his brain had rolled forward and crashed into the back of his skull. "So you call me." An ash formed on the end of his joint.

"I can tell you things, Harry." The urge to hang up shook Harry's hand, but a tiny vacuum sealed the receiver to his ear. "Harry, I miss you."

"Goddamn," Harry muttered.

"Harry, this apartment is empty. I have no furniture. All I have to my name is this new cell phone."

Harry clicked his remote and the TV flickered off. After a lot of other failed occupations, Harry had just become a social worker. It was his business to listen, to reserve judgment. "Get a hotel," he told Stacy.

She hesitated. "Could I stay with you?" Harry pressed the receiver harder against his ear. He heard the hum of the mobile phone's transmission through space; he closed his eyes, gritted his teeth, and tapped the glass of the iced tea against his forehead. "I want to sleep with someone, I mean, really just sleep, to lie next to somebody, for the night I'm exhausted."

"Anybody? You want to sleep with anybody?"

"You, Harry, you."

"Call your girlfriend."

"I can't," Stacy said as though that was the natural answer.

Then there was silence, and Harry said into the silence, "I'm sorry. I didn't mean that." He had said a lot of "I'm sorry"s to Stacy; he had meant most. He wasn't sure about this one.

"Harry, please. I don't want to be alone. I need to talk to you."

Harry wanted to wrap up what he felt and tell her about it, but the more his tongue tried to wrap around the right phrase, the more the words got harder to make, so he stammered and tried to think his way through the stammer, and so he stammered some more. "Goddamn, goddamn, goddamn," rolled off his lips.

"Forgive me, honey," Stacy said. The automatic response came to him: invite her over. But the fear forced him to reconsider, and the past, as it forced itself into his mind, made him want to grow angry. But Stacy, as always, thought faster. "You are luckier than I am, Harry. Really, you are. You know what you are. I've lost that, Harry."

The gears in his mind and his mouth clogged. "Think about the times that you told me to fuck off or the times you said 'fuck you' when I called you and cried."

"You were mean to me, Harry. Now I'm begging."

"But I never told you to fuck off; I never said, 'fuck you.'"

"No, you didn't," she said, then added very calmly, "Thank you." Harry closed his eyes so that he could get an image of her in his mind so that with some picture of her, he might be able to see what she really wanted from him. Her voice destroyed the image so that all Harry had was just her voice. "Harry, I'm not asking you to take me back. Haven't you ever just needed?"

"If you come over tonight, I will end up telling you to fuck off."

"Oh, Harry." Stacy sounded as if her will had left her. He waited. He could not hang up now. The phone seemed like it had grown into his ear. Harry could not pull it away. He heard her breaths and a sob or two. "Goodnight, Harry. This is just so damn bad," Stacy finally said.

Harry tried to blurt out, "I'm sorry; no, please come over," but he heard the phone click. The suction between his ear and the receiver almost popped as he pulled the telephone away from his head.

He had every excuse to say what he had. She deserved justice, karma, fair play. But a desire from the pit of Harry's stomach worked its way into his throat. He talked to himself. Mercy, no, not even that, a little care, would have done him good too. He reached for the phone, and as his forefinger tapped the first digit of her old telephone number, the one she had before she moved in with Don, Harry realized that he was dialing the wrong number. She had given him neither a telephone number nor an address. But he had a *redial*. The phone rang until Stacy's voice told him to leave a message. When he heard her digitalized voice, he had nothing to say. She must have heard his call and chosen not to answer. If so, Stacy knew before Harry did that all this ringing had to stop.

The Golden State

In the Chiricahua National Monument they saw a coatimundi and shared a campsite with a co-ed. The Chiricahua National Monument was the northernmost range of the coatimundi and was probably as far south as any co-ed from Kansas was likely to roam. Her old Nissan's battery had died, so they gave her a jump from Harry's brand new, fully-loaded Honda Civic, and she drove her Nissan as far as their assigned campsite, and then they all took a hike and saw the coatimundi. As they hiked, it was clear that she liked Greg best. First she held his hand, then she gently kissed him on the cheek, and Harry tried not to watch as they twisted and writhed inside Greg's sleeping bag.

It was June. They had a campfire; they were in southern Arizona. Coatis liked it so hot that they lived in South America. There were no showers. Still, Harry felt jealous that Greg had Angie's sweaty, stinky, taut body next to him. Before they had crawled into the sleeping bag, after Harry had faked that he was asleep, she had rubbed her swollen feet, which were lined with a red creases. Her hair had twisted into strings that dangled in her face. But in the firelight, her skin was golden on one side and smooth all over. Her eyes caught glints of the flames. And the dark line of cleavage began at the top of her V-neck T-shirt.

Both Harry and Greg could have benefitted from curling around a woman's body. This was why Harry left his life in the East Texas swamp and was going to California. Harry's third one-true-love had married another guy. Likewise, Greg's wife of seventeen years had packed up their two girls and left. So Greg was going to ride along with Harry to the magical Silicon Valley, where Harry would stay and grow wealthy and loved. Greg would then catch a plane and return to his family problems.

Harry watched the rolling rises in Greg's sleeping bag and sipped his beer. Greg's head poked above the sleeping bag. His copper-colored face, lit by firelight, was beaded with sweat. The firelight caught in Greg's eyes, and he shut one to wink at Harry. Harry raised his beer bottle in a salute. In a wish almost like a prayer, Harry wished that he had a joint. With no joint, he turned around for a glimpse at his new Honda Civic.

Greg needed the co-ed more than Harry did. The co-ed meant more to Greg, a black man, newly separated, with only one woman for seventeen years—as far as Harry knew—and now rolling around in a Thinsulate sleeping bag in southern Arizona with a young, hard-bodied white woman. It was only fair. Still, Harry thought, a quick roll in a Thinsulate sleeping bag with any woman would help his outlook on the world. He was on this quest, this trek, this mission to find the woman who could save him: the second one-true-love of his life. She had left for the state where a computer programmer's fist could rap on the door of a Silicon Valley employer's door and turn her vocation into wealth. When she first got to the San Jose area, she had urged Harry to come out, to take a chance, to turn his talents into riches. Now, finally, he was.

He had quit his job, wrapped up his life in Beaumont, that dark, damp, smelly town that lived in the shadows of Houston and Cajun Louisiana, packed what he couldn't sell into his new car, and hit the road to the Golden State to join his previous one-true-love. Over a beer at the End Zone, he told his best buddy, his racquetball partner, his college roomie—the man now writhing under the sleeping bag with the co-ed—about his new life, about his new car. Then Greg Giddings told him about his separation. Greg, the tough vice principal of Central High School, the man in charge of disciplining football players, drug addicts, thieves, and nice kids who screwed up, actually sniffled. So Harry invited him along. For these two Texas boys, it was the adventure of their lifetimes, and Harry would pay half of Greg's return air-fare, once he got a job paying him big bucks.

Kenya Castile Johnson also helped send Harry to California. Harry had worked with her for some time, advising her about food stamps, getting her career counseling, getting her children into day care or *Head Start*, guiding her to the Texas Employment Commission. Harry was on the bottom link of the Texas Department of Human Services, the guy who checked on any number of Kenya Castile Johnsons in order to guide them to productive lives. Ahead of him lay promotions to a point where he wouldn't have to see the people whom he was hired to help. Social work was Harry's latest career; he had had several. He also had had several addictions—the usual, but also women, boredom, and impatience —that caused him to lose careers. He was determined to make social work work.

A few days before camping in The Chiricahua National Monument, Kenya Castile Johnson had come to his desk. She picked her way around the desks of the other social workers, through the hum of voices talking into phones, interviewing, jesting, and cussing the whole process, and stood in front of his desk until Harry told her to sit down in front of him. She pushed her new miniskirt down her thighs and looked away from Harry. "Kenya?" he asked. She turned her head to face him and, at first, smiled at him. She was in her first week on the job at *Dollar General*. It was her lunch hour. "Kenya, how's it going?" Harry asked.

His fellow workers rubber-necked away from their own interviewees to see Harry. And Kenya looked hard, directly into their stares, to send their rubber necks twisting back to their own business. "How's your job? Do you like it?"

"The boss already told me I couldn't use the phone to call and check on my babies."

"Is that what you came to see me about?" Kenya stared at her red toes sticking out of her white sandals. Her feet were pretty. Dressed for work, she looked fresh and clean. "Do you have any problems at work?"

Kenya raised her head to look at Harry. The hum of voices grew louder. "Doctor says I'm pregnant."

The hum of voices stopped, or so Harry thought. "You're pregnant?" Harry dropped his head. "You're pregnant? Didn't you go to the clinics I referred you to? You should have . . . . gotten some condoms. I'd have gotten you condoms." First, Harry felt sorry for Kenya, but then he felt shamed because of his second thought, which he let come out of his mouth in a mumble: "The paperwork."

Kenya didn't hear him; if she had, she probably would have started cussing him. She was too busy looking around at all the social workers as though each one would get up and wait in line to scold her. Harry rolled his chair along the edge of his desk, rounded the corner of his desk, until he was almost knee to knee with Kenya. "Kenya, Kenya, after all the budgeting we did, with the food stamps, you barely have enough for your boy and girl."

Kenya's eyes widened. Then she gave that black girl head roll, that simultaneous front to back and sideways movement that Harry had seen so often from frustrated pregnant teenagers, from women whose husbands were simply missing, and from divorced mothers. Kenya said in a loud, intense whisper, "What right you got to look at me with that rich white man staring. You judging me right now to be some whore. Some 'black woman got herself knocked up again' staring. What right you got?"

Harry dropped his head to look at his toes. He had on his racquetball shoes. He had risen early and gotten in two games with Greg before Greg had to go threaten, cajole, and plead with the troublesome students at the mostly-black Central High School. He had forgotten his soft soled work shoes. "The attitudes these days, Kenya. It's politics. We've got pressure not to increase entitlements. You were doing so well."

Kenya's voice grew louder. "I know he a worthless two-timing son of a bitch who just gonna leave. And it ain't for him I become pregnant. I know better, sure. I know what he want. I know what you sitting there thinking, proud of your rich, white ass and your good job."

Harry's latest pay stub was in his pocket. He wanted to pull it out to show Kenya what he made. But instead, he said, "Kenya, I'm a long way from rich. I'm not trying to humiliate you or judge you. I've got rules I have to follow." He had said that *he had rules to follow*. He blanked out for a moment while his past flashed inside that space between his eyes and his brain. Too much pot, too much alcohol. Quit as a teacher at Central High. Quit as a beer distributor salesman. Fired as a car salesman. Once married—for three months—before she left. Latest girlfriend, Stacy, married to a rich guy with a BMW nearly paid for. Kenya was staring at him. "Sorry," he said to Kenya. "What the hell, huh?"

Kenya relaxed; her shoulders drooped. "Can I smoke in here?"

"No," Harry said. More rules to follow.

She started explaining herself. "Didn't get pregnant for nobody. I know what's what, but sometimes at night. I just want to forget; I just want to have that feeling. . ." Modesty must have stopped her "So what we gonna do now?" Kenya asked.

After speaking to Kenya Castille Johnson, Harry drove to see his spiritual advisor, Lee Tomlinson. Harry pushed the buzzer next to the iron gate and watched the gate roll out of his way. He heard untrimmed toenails scraping concrete and the low growl of Lee's mutt. Harry knew that the gallop and the growl were only fake. When the dog got close to Harry, he skidded to a halt, then jumped up to rest his front paws against Harry's stomach. "Down, down Balanchine," Harry said. He got the dog out from in front of him and walked up the steps of the sinking porch and then knocked on the door.

Lee wore a taffeta mumu that floated around the slim body inside and made her seem as though she dressed in pastel clouds. She held a cigarette between her fingers and pulled her hand back over her wrist. "Come in Harry," Lee said. Wafts of smoke flowed along with the folds in her mumu as she led Harry through the house. And Lee and Harry flowed through open, empty rooms flooded with sunlight and dark rooms lit in garish lights—blue, red, and orange. Her home was filled with paintings and photographs, most of dancers, many nude, some of Lee. Lee needed a lot of space to contain her and her things, but she couldn't afford both space and upkeep. So wasps, roaches, spiders, lizards and sometimes mice and squirrels crawled into her house through the widening cracks. Lee had made a zoo and an exhibit that only she appreciated in this old mansion in the bad part of old town.

She led him to her screened-in patio. Harry had earned the right to be welcomed into the inner most part of her house, into her *salon*, where the screen kept out the mosquitoes so that she could sit with the plants. They overgrew their pots, dangled their tentacles from the ceiling, bloomed and blossomed intermittently all year round. And Lee liked to sit in this hot house and listen to music she used to dance to and to the mosquitoes humming outside of her screen. She dropped her ashes where she pleased.

She sat in the wide, throne-like wicker chair, and Harry sat in the lounge chair, nearly at her feet. When he first came into her house, expecting to see the type of woman who would excite Stacy, he thought he'd see some tough-talking woman in engineer's boots and a black T-shirt cussing men, or some teenager with pierced body parts, or some exquisitely delicate but beautiful southern lady. Instead, he found a woman with lines that were now etched into her eyes, with a body that looked as hard and as tight as her face, but with eyes, gestures, and movements that suggested softness, the human need for beauty—the way she smoked, for instance.

The neighbors whispered that on some cool nights she'd raise the blinds, open the windows, turn on the lights, and dance naked through the large house. She still had a good body, they said.

"It was curiosity at first," she had told Harry at that first meeting. "We had just met. We had lunch. We both needed women friends." She waved her cigarette in front of her face. "And then I simply kissed her, to see what it felt like. Things went from there."

Harry had wanted to think of her as a seductress, a pervert who had cast some psychopathic spell over Stacy. But then Lee said, "You know, she dumped me too."

Lee had been a dancer. She had almost made it to Broadway. Had she started stripping younger, she could have made it to the finest gentlemen's clubs in Houston. She came to Beaumont to dance and teach aerobics at St. Elizabeth's Health and Fitness Center. It was where she met Stacy. Lee had said, "I lost the ability to take or to receive whatever it was a man might give me. Love, sex all went into the thing that I did, even as I was losing my talent and my ability to do that thing. And when dance went, I had no real interest in sex. I thought that a woman might be different."

"You seduced her," Harry had muttered.

"No, Harry," Lee had said as though she were disappointed in him. "It's the old cliché that a woman alone knows what a woman wants. There's some logic to. But as with any intense relation, logic left. For me, Stacy was an introduction back to other people, to romance. She wasn't dance, but she knew about dance. She could almost take the place of dance. The strangeness must have frightened her . . . so she went back to Don."

Eventually Harry kissed Lee too, but nothing else, just lunches, movies, and occasional drives to Houston. So, instead of a close female companion, Lee had Harry. And Harry had a woman who could advise him about women.

On this visit, the one after Kenya Castille Johnson had announced her third pregnancy, Harry pouted, then came to the point of his visit. "She phoned again."

"Who? Who?" Lee asked. Out of nowhere, Fosse appeared in her lap and meowed until she stroked him between his ears.

"Stacy. When she has a problem, she phones."

"She phones me too. Don't make more of it, Harry."

Harry looked at Lee's face—the crinkles on her upper lip, the long lashes that swooshed over bright eyes, the taut skin—and he wondered how she could be so serene. "But this time she phones to tell me that she's gonna marry this Don guy. She says that it's only fair that I know, that she ought to tell me."

"She's probably right." Lee dragged her hand from Fosse's head down his neck and spine, as he arched it under her palm, until her hand was wrapped around the tip of his tail.

"Well, I mean, goddamn. How do you think it makes me feel when the woman I love the most calls and tells me she's marrying this other guy?"

"Would you rather she not call?" Lee asked.

"Jesus, Lee. You've got ice water in your veins. Not everybody's like you. We can't all be so goddamn stoic."

Lee rose and pushed Fosse out of her lap. She knelt in front of Harry and grasped his hand. "I know about this great injustice you feel. I think I know frustration pretty well." She smiled at the cat. "But bitterness is even tougher. Harry, she called you, as she called me, because she still has some regard for you. Maybe she called you because she had to."

"I'm going to quit my job. It sucks."

Lee pulled Harry up out of his chair, wrapped her arms around him, and started some Samba. The music was only in her head, and Harry began to shake his hips a little. "Lighten up, Harry," she whispered, and she shifted into a country two-step, something Harry could follow.

"You can't just dance around and clear everything up. The problems are still there."

"Exactly. Have any better ideas?"

"I'm changing my life."

"You're too old to change your life," Lee said as she slid her hands down Harry's side and then shook his hips so that they were both swaying to some rhythm that only she heard. "Go make us a drink," she whispered.

Harry found his way into her kitchen and returned to her hot house with two gin and tonics. She took one drink from him, pushed him into her padded wicker throne, and sipped her drink while she danced for him.

With one hand, she pulled her mumu above her calf. She stretched on her bare toes. She swayed. She was still shapely, could still conjure up fantasies in male minds, but her dance, Harry realized, was not merely sex and thrust. It was not a stripper's dance. It was smooth, slow, but sad too. She twisted and rolled her arms into waves in front of her face, in front of her body, then made them cascade behind her. One hand went into the air, then slumped, she strutted. Then her shoulders went limp, making her look like a rag doll or an ape, and she slouched toward Harry. Lee's dancing confused Harry, but he knew he was watching art.

"Some things, we must endure," she said and reached for her pack of cigarettes.

"You ought to quit smoking," Harry said.

"I've paid for my vices. I've gone too long being too much on guard, too disciplined."

"My whole life here suddenly sucks," Harry said.

Lee sat across from Harry. "Get her out of your mind, Harry; I got her out of mine." Lee stroked Fosse from neck to tail, and he arched his back and stiffened his tail. "It's time to get old."

* * *

So three women's pronouncements caused Harry to listen to a fourth. He called Jen, his second one-true-love, and asked how she was doing. She told him about the golden apples falling off the trees, about the wild sexual escapades in the new Garden of Eden, one with no snakes, no retribution, no angry God. To Jen, Harry was still young enough to turn his life around in Silicon Valley. Way back in his head and behind his heart, Harry knew that he had decided to go to the Silicon Valley, not to make money, for money had never been a factor in any of his misguided decisions and directions in his life, but to reunite with Jen. In Beaumont, they had had a year-long affair. But she was married at the time, and when Jen and her husband divorced, she didn't run to Harry, as he had hoped, but told him about her new plans to strike out for the Golden State. Harry helped her pack and waved as she drove out from her apartment complex in the big U-Haul with her Subaru towed behind.

So Harry quit his job. His manager warned him about his shortsightedness. He felt like calling Kenya Castille Johnson and telling her what he had done, but instead he met Greg for a beer. Greg cautioned him, said that he would be missed, asked him to reconsider. Harry refused. Next he got all of his money in traveler's checks, went to a Beaumont Honda dealer and, using his savings as a down payment, bought a fully-loaded Civic. He began throwing away or storing his stuff, and stripped himself down to just enough heft to fill the Civic.

As Harry closed his life in Beaumont, the school year ended, and Dianne told Greg that she wanted to live apart from him for awhile.

* * *

Things were quiet in the morning as Harry, Greg, and the co-ed stuffed their camping equipment back into their packs and boxes. After coffee and eggs, Greg suggested that he ride with Angie to Phoenix.

Even with an automatic, the Honda shifted smoothly and built up power fifty. It felt like a sports car. Harry wanted to let it go, but he kept it in check and glanced in his rearview mirror to see Angie's rattling, shaking Nissan. And once, he saw Greg lean across the front seat to sneak a kiss from Angie. He couldn't begrudge his buddy, but he wanted to be in California land with an old girlfriend. In Phoenix they stopped at a Denny's for lunch. And as their cars baked outside, Harry, Greg, and Angie sat in the air conditioning and talked about their upcoming adventures.

Greg looked out of the Denny's window as he chewed his burger in one side of his mouth. Angie preached. "Northern New Mexico has so much. California is

85

over. There isn't there what there once was." Harry watched the shimmering heat rise up from asphalt, cement, and car hoods in transparent shaking waves that diluted your vision. His own bright-blue Honda Civic glowed in the sunshine. "Why don't you come to New Mexico with us?" Angie asked. Her dirty hair fell in long uneven bangs in front of her face. "We could have so much fun." Both Harry and Greg watched the Arizona city-scape melting in the sun.

Harry swung his gaze away from the shimmering heat to look at the young woman with her dirty hair falling in front of her eyes in her long, uneven bangs. "We could have so much fun." Harry looked back at Greg, but Greg kept his eyes on the Arizona city-scape that seemed to be melting under the sun.

"You've seen my car. It doesn't run too well. It sure would be nice to have a man with me." Her remark was not enough for Harry, and he could tell that Greg, too, saw it as a sorry-ass excuse.

"It's something I've never done," Greg said. They watched each other as their smiles straightened, turned into frowns, then stretched into smiles again.

During their senior year at Southwest Texas State, Harry and Greg's team, the Black Mollies, was in the flag football intramural play-off game. Fifty yards away from a touchdown with only seconds left, Harry was two passes away from victory. The first was a dump-off pass, and then, for the last play of the game, everyone knew what was coming. Harry dropped back and watched Greg make his cut to the sideline. Harry gave a fake pump. He turned his head to pull a safety away. Then Harry saw Greg's inside fake, then his outside move toward the flag. Never in his life had his arm, his heart, his head been so sure. The ball was on a long slow arch to a spot right at the goal line. Arm, head, heart were all in time with Greg. But Greg's foot didn't take hold of the sod. His left foot slipped. But he regained his balance and watched the ball come over his right shoulder. He pivoted his head as he watched it spiral and float in front of him. And dove.

From where he was, Harry saw both of Greg's hands grasp either side of the ball. Then Greg began a slow-motion fall as he tried to pull the ball in. But Greg's stomach hit the ground first. A puff of breath blew Greg's lips apart. The ball, still in Greg's hands, hit the ground and then bounced out. A little flat, that ball was crammed into the back of Harry's Honda.

Outside the Denny's, Harry and Greg transferred Greg's stuff to Angie's car. Harry checked the trunk one last time and saw the nearly flat football from their long ago intramural game. Harry scooped up the scarred, mushy old football in both hands and tossed it underhanded to Greg. Greg caught the soft underhanded shove, smiled, and tossed it back to Harry.

From his rearview mirror Harry watched as Greg and Angie pulled away. Fitting, he thought, that he should be going to his new destiny alone.

* * *

Down Fremont, right on Sunnyvale, up three blocks, and Harry pulled his packed Honda, his new life, up to Jen's apartment. He parked alongside the curb, stepped out, and felt what made California different. It was June, but the Pacific cooled the air, made it feel like eternal spring. Three times a year maybe Southeast Texas had a California day. The rent was high, groceries and meals expensive, but this was the price of paradise. And a lot of people, Jen included, must be able to afford this climate. He closed the door to his new car and patted the roof.

He trotted up the stairs to her apartment and rang the bell. He smiled, expecting a hug, and this guy with strings of long dark hair opened the door. "You must be Jenny's friend," he said. "Come on in." He stuck out his hand, and Harry let his hand go limp as he shook the guy's hand. "Anthony," the guy said. He was at least ten years younger than Harry.

Anthony jerked his head toward the inside of the house, and Harry followed him in. The apartment was smaller than the one he had in Beaumont. The couch took up most of the living room. Anthony plopped across the couch, and looked at the ashtray on the coffee table in front of it. Harry too looked at the still-smoking joint in the ashtray and smelled its piquant aroma. Anthony shrugged. "You mind?" he asked. Harry no sooner shook his head than Anthony was sucking in on the joint. Harry looked around, but among the sports posters, the books stacked into the corners, and the trophies, he saw nothing that reminded him of Jen. Anthony leaned across the coffee table, picked up the remote, hit the mute, and suddenly the sounds of a soccer game filled the living room. "I love soccer," Anthony said.

During a commercial, Anthony turned his attention to Harry and said, "You want to share a joint?" Harry had shared enough joints, so he shook his head. "Beer?" Anthony asked, and before Harry could answer, he disappeared around the sofa and went into the tiny kitchen and appeared with a Budweiser. "Have a seat," he said, and Harry placed himself away from the TV set where he could watch Anthony.

"Jen's running late," he said as he watched the soccer match. "She ought to be back soon."

Harry nodded, then tried to converse. "So what do you do?"

"I've got the graveyard shift, tech support," he said and stretched his arm across the coffee table toward Harry. The lit end of the joint was about to burn Anthony's fingertips. Harry's past made him reach for the offered nub.

As Harry chased the smoke with a sip from his beer, Anthony said, "So you're from Texas."

"Well, yes, but Beaumont is more like Louisiana. I've never thought of it as Texas."

Anthony nodded. "You couldn't tell by me. I've lived in California all my life. Don't think I'd ever leave. I like to have the ocean nearby."

Harry stretched to hand the ember back to its rightful owner before it burned his fingers. "We've got a coast nearby in Beaumont."

As he took the joint, Anthony asked, "Oh, yeah, which one?" Harry smiled, but Anthony didn't.

After thirty minutes, Jen showed up at the door with a six-pack of Sam Adams and sushi to go. Harry felt this warmth rise up from his chest and catch in his throat. When she smiled, her whole mouth moved into the left side of her face. She hugged, then kissed Harry, and he couldn't tell whether the lingering smell of the Calvin Klein perfume was from her or only wafting in his mind because of all the memories suddenly flooding his head. Jen told Anthony to put his pot away. "Are you here for good?" she asked Harry, and he didn't know if she meant Silicon Valley or in this apartment.

For dinner, Anthony and Jen expertly scooped sushi into their mouths with their chopsticks. Harry squished a quail egg and splattered rice across the living room carpet. He begged for a fork, but Jen wouldn't let him have one. And after small talk, exchanging some photos, ESPN's coverage of the women's national sand volleyball finals, Anthony excused himself for bed. Harry and Jen discussed the old times, her ex, her future, Harry's fate with Stacy. And after a lull, with two skinny candles lighting the living room, two beer bottles on the coffee table, Harry stretched his arm above his head and around Stacy's neck. She turned to look at him and smiled. He pressed his lips against hers and kept them there.

For awhile, Jen actually returned the kiss, but then she pulled back. "Harry, wait." Harry was intent on sliding his open hand between her shoulders and the back of the couch. "Harry," Jen said, and Harry reluctantly pulled his face and his hands away from her.

"So he's this roommate, right? Rent's expensive."

"He's my lover."

Harry caught himself in mid-lean toward her. "You didn't mention him on the phone."

"You never asked."

Harry found himself scooting farther back from her. "He's not some minor detail, you know."

"Harry, you're my friend. Anthony wasn't too excited about your coming out. But I told him that you were my friend."

Harry grabbed his beer and took a long sip. "Why do you think I came out?"

"To change your life."

"To come back to you."

"You've got a one-track mind," Jen said and stood. "You think only with your groin. You think if I'm not humping you, then I don't love you."

"Well, I was kinda hoping that since I drove two thousand miles that I might get to exercise my groin a little."

Jen doubled her fists, closed her eyes, and stomped her foot. Her body grew taut all over. Harry knew that this act also meant an argument. "You don't change. Everything is physical. You need the most blatant proof."

With the candles flickering between them, lighting her face in streaks of yellow and orange, but still showing the gentle curves of her body, Harry stood and said, "And Anthony is smooth? Not blatant?"

"He's my lover!"

"He's a computer nerd crossed with a jock."

She turned away from Harry and marched toward the bedroom she shared with Anthony. "You can sleep on the couch. It folds into a bed. I have work in the morning."

* * *

After driving around, Harry found himself at a mini-brewery in Sunnyvale staring into a dark brown beer with a golden, foamy top. Not only did he not know where he was, he didn't know where Sunnyvale was. He had followed Jen's directions and knew only that he was south of San Francisco and somewhere close to San Jose. On his drive, all that he noticed was the changing architecture lining the freeway, unlike in Texas, where eventually, on whatever highway you drove, you'd run out of stacked buildings. Further, he had looked around the bar, walked outside, walked down the street, got in his car and drove around. California was full of Asians but no black people. In the bar he listened to gossip and decided that the inhabitants of Silicon Valley were young, dyed their hair blue, wore earrings or pierced other body parts, and voted Republican. He felt out of place. He had never felt himself a Texan, but he felt a long way from home. So with a beer to go, he hit the freeways and found himself in downtown San Jose bar where older people drank domestic beer or shots of whiskey. There were Mexicans and black people in this bar. It was a bar Greg might have liked.

By midnight Harry was listening to Rene Garcia, a short little man with a bulging belly. "When I was a kid, we rode go-carts through these orchard groves. Then the defense people, then the aeronautics people, then the computer people buy up the orchards, give us a good price for our houses, then kick us out." Harry found himself mumbling, "Sons a bitches." Rene went on, probably because Harry had bought him a beer. "So I done right, got a goddamn degree in computer science. But what they don't tell you is that, soon as you get a job, the company goes broke. So now I live with my mama, drive a fifteen-year-old Camaro. Got a ol' lady who is as out of date as my Camaro, and I can't even take her out 'cause I got no gas to put in my Camaro." Harry was grateful to have Rene set him straight about the Silicon Valley.

Since he was now a resident of Silicon Valley, Harry decided that he would change things. He'd start by changing Jen's mind about him. He'd start by paying

89

his tab. With Rene patting him on the back, he pulled several bills out of his pocket and laid them on the bar. He stumbled for the door as the bartender counted the money and Rene waved.

He concentrated on keeping himself straight as he walked down the street. Harry accepted his new-found identity. He was a drunk Texan. And by God, a drunk Texan might just go off on your ass. It wasn't that he was mean, he was tired of all the hazy, undefined bullshit.

He knew that he was closing in on his new Honda Civic, but he wasn't sure about which parking lot it was in. Worse, he had to pee. Downtown looked deserted, so he stepped into an alley, unzipped his pants, and stepped behind a trash dumpster. He felt a poke in his back. An exaggerated deep voice said, "Give me your wallet. What you feel is a switchblade." Harry couldn't pee.

Harry was a social worker, a counselor of sorts, and his job was to advise people how to control themselves, not to give into violent or passionate outbursts. But on this night, he was a badass, kick-'em-in-the-balls Texan, who had been dumped by his third one-true-love, and now twice by his second one-true-love, and he was not about to take any more shit from these wimpy-assed Californians. He swung himself around and brought his elbow up to catch this thief in the face.

His elbow caught no chin or cheek. Harry whirled right over the head of his assailant. He thought that he was being held up by midget. Harry stopped his spinning, braced himself, doubled his fist, and waited to feel a knife blade in his guts. He was prepared to die. And then he saw this ragged lump of clothes holding a knife. The twelve-or-thirteen-year-old boy was about to cry.

Harry's instinct and muscle suppressed his mind and any sympathy. He kicked the kid in the shin. While the kid reached for his shin and hopped on one leg, Harry pushed the flat of his hand, not his fist, no broken knuckles for Harry, into the bridge of the kid's nose. The kid stumbled back against the opposite wall, dropped his knife, grabbed his nose, then slid down the wall. Harry saw this blackness ooze from between the kid's fingers. "Sorry," Harry said and reached for the child, who jerked away. But Harry caught the kid's stocking cap and pulled it off the kid's head. Her hair fell down, tears mixing with blood. She heaved. Harry had just kicked the shit out of a pubescent girl. He ran.

He felt he was getting closer to his car when the world behind him lit up in flashing, circling, yellow, white, and blue lights. He turned to see a cop get out of her car, and Harry said, "Thank God you're here." The cop held her hand on the top of the billy club and sized him up. She told him to walk to her patrol car; then she cuffed him and curled his head down as she helped him inside the backseat.

The officer took him to the station, and he confessed his crime to a sergeant. "Probably another runaway kid," the sergeant mumbled. Then the sergeant read him his rights and fingerprinted him, not for assaulting a homeless pubescent girl but for public intoxication. For his one call, Harry called Jen.

Jen didn't say much when the police brought Harry from the drunk tank to the lobby of the San Jose police station. Anthony smiled and put his arm around her. Harry promised to repay the bail money. And from the way she looked at him and then the way she looked at Anthony, Harry knew that she'd never let him back into her life.

While Jen preached to Harry, sitting in the passenger side seat next to her, about going to detox, Harry tried to guide her toward the parking lot where he had left his new Honda.

The sun was just coming up, and the earliest of the downtown commuters were pulling into town. Jen parked next to a curb. In the middle of the police and plastic streamers was the charred, ex-ember that used to be Harry's new Honda. Harry placed one foot in front of the other as he slowly made his way to the only real money, property, or pride he had left in the world. The police officer who brought him in held her hand in front of him and said, "I figured it was yours."

Harry looked at the police officer, pulled his keys out of his pocket and held them up for the police officer to see. Jen was suddenly beside him and patting his shoulder. "Oh, shit man. You're screwed," Anthony whispered

The police officer said, "I guess the little bitch knew what you were driving." Harry looked at the cop. "We never found her," she said.

* * *

The only good thing about losing his car and the luggage that was in it was that Harry had only a carry-on, and a nearly flat football to carry on the plane back to Houston. He had taken the carry-on up to Jen's, and the football had miraculously survived the fire. As he was about to enter the loading chute at the San Jose airport, Jen kissed him goodbye. When he stepped out of the unloading chute into the gate at Houston Hobby airport, with his football under one arm and his carry-on in the other, Greg was there to greet him. "Jesus, so you lost your car," Greg said.

Harry smiled. "So you lost your girl."

"Her car crapped out in Santa Fe. I thought I better get my black ass away from this disaster waiting to happen. I came to my senses." Greg looked at Harry and smiled.

"Who picked you up?"

"My wife. I'll show you my new apartment."

On the way back to Beaumont, Harry found out that Dianne was still not sure about whether she wanted to be married or not and that the two girls were staying with her mother in Houston. "What you gonna to do now?" Greg asked him and shook his head. Harry didn't know, but in a way he envied his friend. The mostly-black kids at Central High respected their former coach and vice-principal. He was one of them, hometown ex-high school football hero. He could understand. He was a role model. He was black. Harry, who walked through a predominantly black part of town to check on food stamp recipients and children's welfare, would always be this white guy, some foreigner.

Back in Beaumont, Harry and Greg sat on the stairs outside Greg's one-bedroom apartment and sipped beers. Harry felt suffocated by the humidity. He had come from paradise with its cool ocean breeze to this steam bath with its muggy Gulf air that killed all breezes. "You know, I've been called an Oreo by some people here in this town. They say because I work for white people, because I run around with this white guy, that I'm trying to be white."

"Nobody's ever said I was black on the inside," Harry said.

"Well, some folks say I'm supposed to act like this, get involved. Hell, it gets old." Greg sipped his beer. "My wife's out experimenting to see if she wants to stay married to me, heard she dated some white guy stock broker or something. I got students and school board members bitching at me. I'm living in a dump, but I look at you, and I think I ain't got it nearly as bad."

"You didn't fuck up nearly as bad." Harry stood up and grabbed his football. "Go on, out and up."

"What?"

"Go out for a pass. The best thing we almost ever did was to complete that pass."

"You crazy?"

Harry trotted down the steps and Greg followed. Harry slapped the football against the palm of his left hand, and Greg started a slow trot down his apartment complex's parking lot. "Go on," Harry said, and Greg picked up speed. Harry faked a pass. From somewhere shoved way back in his brain, a memory or a feeling took over Harry's mind and arm. He remembered how fast Greg *had* run, and without physics, calculated how fast Greg was now running, and he knew, when Greg swung his arms and really started to zoom past the parked cars, how far to throw the ball. His arm obeyed. It cocked farther back and came forward, and his wrist started to roll even before he let loose of the ball, and his fingers let go and followed the roll of his wrist to let the ball glide in an easy arch and start its descent ahead of Greg's arms and pumping feet.

A loose bit of gravel, old muscles, fear, doubt, caution slowed Greg. Harry could see that in his last stride. He leaned too far and was falling as the ball was falling toward his upturned palms. Greg turned his palms in, pulled them under his body, hit the asphalt on them as the ball hit in front of him and bounced away. He skidded on his palms and then slid farther on his belly and knees. Harry was running toward him even before he quit sliding.

Harry stood over Greg as he lay on his belly and moaned. Then Greg slowly pushed himself up to his feet and held his bloodied hands out for Harry to see. Harry looked first at Greg's palms and then at his bloody knees. "Maybe that was a bad idea," Harry said.

Greg turned his palms in so that he could look at them. "What's my wife gonna say?" he asked.

* * *

After mercurochrome and cotton swabs, Greg gingerly steered his car to Lee's house. Harry waved good-bye to his friend, rang the buzzer, greeted Balanchine, and stepped to the front door. Lee answered the door in tights. Sweat rolled down her forehead to her nose, then dripped off the end of it. "I hear you fucked up, Harry."

Harry could never quite figure how much older Lee was than he because, for all her smoking and unhealthy habits, she had good habits as well and kept herself young—more so than Harry or Greg. She led him through her decaying house back to the screened-in back porch, had him sit in her wicker throne, and brought him back a gin and tonic.

"You need a place to stay, right?" Lee asked. She sat on the floor, and curled one leg, then the other under her. Mosquitoes buzzed outside the screen, and sweat welled up at the small of Harry's back and under his arms.

"I got no place else."

"When are you going to forget these women, Harry?"

"Now, right now." Harry sipped his gin and knew that he was lying. "Maybe, if I go back in, they'll hire me back. Oh yeah, sure, at base. I'd have to start all over. But I haven't been gone that long."

"You're always starting over," Lee said as she bent her forehead over her left leg and touched it to her knee.

"How many times have you started over?"

Lee blew at a bead of sweat dangling from the end of her nose and sprayed it into the air. "Stacy called," Lee said, and Harry felt himself scoot forward in his seat and his gut twist half-a-turn. "All this time, after the surgeries, endometriosis," Lee hesitated to breathe. Harry urged her on by scooting to the very edge of his seat and leaning toward her. "She thought she couldn't get pregnant." Harry's shoulders slumped, and he pushed himself back fully into the chair. "But it's a medical miracle." Lee rested one hand on his knee. "She's ecstatic, Harry. Stacy's pregnant."

While Harry stared at his toes, Lee said, "I just met this beautiful black man. He has a questionable reputation, but he's smart, smooth, and seems to like me."

"That's nice," Harry said. He cocked his head to let the thought roll around in his mind, and he saw that Lee cocked her head in the same direction. "Can I use your phone?"

He thought he had forgotten the number, but his finger knew it and punched out the tone. When a woman's voice answered he said, "This is Harry. How are you doing? How's the pregnancy?"

"Why you want to know," Kenya Castille Johnson asked.

Part III
Bobby and Velda, Vic and Wendy, Bessie and Charlie

Hemingway's Lighthouse

Dean Bobby Snyder turned up the collar of his tweed sport coat to prepare for his departure from his office in the Buchner House and to step into the cold, unusually crisp Oregon evening. The Dean of Humanities at Willamette Valley College, a prestigious liberal arts school with a high ranking in *U.S. News and World Report*, felt the stiff Harris wool against his neck, rubbed the polished wood of his desk (no cheap prefab, Office Depot furniture for Willamette), opened his door into the foyer and his Asian-American secretary, dipped his chin to that woman who was beyond age, exited his office, walked down the wood-paneled halls, heard his heels tap against the wood floors, pushed with one hand to open the door to his building, stepped out into the falling snow, and thought: except for all of this, this was almost like his undergraduate days at Rice University in Houston.

In those days a ragged, working-class girl, who relied on native smarts, spunk, and bluff to get into Rice, shamed him with her writing. Velda Ortego was from Port Arthur. Her Cajun daddy had left dying Acadia to come to the refineries of Southeast Texas. He was white, he worked hard, he could learn valves, switches, and basic chemistry, so he got a job in a refinery. Daddy wanted his little girl to be happy, preferably with a man like him. Of course, Daddy only knew men like him. Mamma was content to follow Daddy. She converted from Catholic to Baptist against Daddy's will because what she did well was adapt, and in Texas Baptist had the edge in social propriety and advancement. Mamma raised her daughter to look for a man slightly better than her daddy, a man who could provide her with a tract house in one of the all-white suburb towns around Port Arthur. But something went wrong with Velda, and she gave up on her Momma and Daddy's low-level dreams, won a national merit scholarship, got accepted into Rice, which at that time was nearly free to smart Texas kids like Bobby Snyder and Velda Ortego, and began to write stories. Bobby met her in his fiction writing class.

Rice University, at that time in the Texas dark ages, had one of the highest suicide rates of all universities in the country. At Rice, smart, intense kids liked to read Sartre, get even smarter, and become fashionably depressed, and then kill themselves. But Velda had had too much of her father and mother's blue collar and too much of her own weirdness to ever kill herself. Bobby, on the other hand, feared that he wasn't quite smart enough to be one of those morose, intelligent kids who killed themselves so people will say "Oh, the waste."

Their writing workshop was taught by an instructor who had just seen her novel get a New York publisher and so was beginning to look at brighter jobs with tenure attached. Yes, tenure track jobs were hard to find even in the old dark ages. In the class taught by the newly-published writer and full of morose students, Velda picked her nose. Bobby and others saw her. She had shown up at the clinic with an itch on her scalp, and the nurse had diagnosed lice. Velda stayed drunk. She smoked pot. She dropped acid. Rumor had it that she pulled a train in the men's athletic dorm. And when she turned in her stories, the envious, suicidal or ambitious students tried desperately to find flaws. Only Bobby and the instructor, both intoxicated with visions of moves up literary and academic ladders, recognized some gift, some gigantic rift in genetics, sociology, socialization, and fate in Velda and defended what Bobby, at only twenty, and the instructor, at only thirty-five, knew were brilliant stories.

Bobby had his own aspirations for greatness. He worked, he plodded, he planned, he rewrote, yet in his fiction writing class only this mess—this whoring, drinking, druggy with a smirk toward everyone—could write like Bobby wished he could.

Truth be told, as Bobby found years later when he hired her, Velda worked hard at the writing. The drugs, the trains, the booze were simply excursions, breaks, time-outs from making words do what she wanted them to do. And Bobby knew that he could never risk booze, trains, and drugs to make words do what he wanted them to. So Velda Ortego, unbeknownst to her, in that undergraduate class some thirty years before, convinced Bobby Snyder that he was not a writer but an academic.

Between Rice and Bobby's step into the unusually cold, crisp, snowy Oregon evening, Velda had published a whole bunch of stories, four well-received but poorly-selling mystery novels, and gained a string of ex-lovers and ex-addictions. Bobby had made his way through tenure and promotion at two second-tier state universities and become the Dean of Arts and Humanities at Willamette Valley and helped it get listed in *U.S. & World News Report* as a prestigious regional liberal arts college. Bobby was a team player. Bobby was happily married for nearly thirty years and had two beautiful daughters in beautiful and prestigious liberal arts colleges in California. Velda was a mess.

And now, as he looked up at the unusual snow, not as rare as in Houston, but still tempered by a humidity a little like Houston's, still the same green stuff growing over everything, Bobby knew that he would have to fire Velda Ortego.

Bobby Snyder—dean, husband, father—turned his back to Buchner Hall and walked into the falling snow. It hit his face, melted a bit. Like a kid, he stuck out his tongue to catch some flakes. He had forgotten his overcoat and gloves, but he had remembered his Irish tweed hat., He pulled his hat lower to his head, shoved his hands into his pockets, and watched as his shoes made prints in the snow. It got dark early, and he and Thelma Li had stayed late so that they could both take off early on Friday. A wayward snowflake found its way below his collar and down his neck. One of the great attributes of this very liberal liberal arts college was that Willamette Valley tried to relate to students and give them and their well-to-do parents a nurturing environment, so Dean Bobby Snyder didn't need to wear a tie. So snowflakes fell down the back of his open collar.

Bobby made his tracks in the snow, past the few students—smiling and radiating health and confidence. They were Polynesian, Asian, bright West Coasters, many in berets, some in socks and sandals, despite the snow. If they were still on campus, they were probably lonely, but not suicidal. It was no longer fashionable for smart kids to be morose. Bobby stepped from the bounds of the college and into the small town, once its own town tucked between the Cascades and the Coastal range, with picturesque vineyards and orchards, now a suburb of Portland. He walked past the Mexican restaurant, started by the migrant orchard pickers, who stayed, supplying him with a hint of the Tex/Mex that he had consumed in Houston.

The Pig's Foot Saloon served a mix of students and locals. Sometimes it had fights in which Willamette Valley students lost to the locals. As he shoved the door open and stepped in, he saw mostly locals, probably the last remains of the farmers and craftsmen who used to make up most of the town's population. He saw several students but none of the suburbanites who commuted to Portland. Smoke wafted up to the ceiling, so Bobby stifled his cough to look like he belonged here. He couldn't see Velda Ortego. So he made his way to the bar.

Before too long a young bartender leaned across the bar on his elbows and asked Bobby what he wanted to drink. "Coors Light on tap," was Bobby's automatic response. The bartender with the mess of curly red hair set the beer down and asked for two dollars.

Bobby dug into it for three bills. "Is Velda Ortego in here?"

"She's always in here." The bartender stuffed one dollar into the tip jar and nodded his head at Bobby to thank him, then slouched over the cash register to deposit the other two dollars. "What do you want with her?"

"I'm her boss. Why do you ask?"

"Why do you want to see her?"

"College business."

"Not collection business?"

"No."

"If you're trying to strong arm, I swear I'll kick you outta here."

"You her guardian?"

"You could say that. I owe her."

"For what?"

The kid shook his head, and his curly hair fell over his forehead. He pushed his unruly hair out of his face, and Bobby saw the tattoos leading from the back of his hands up to his elbows. Bobby couldn't see much beyond the kid's elbows because of the rolled-up sleeves of his flannel shirt. "We do each other a few favors. You aren't going to be a problem are you?"

"I'm her dean. From across the street."

"I don't get on campus too often," the kid said, smiled, and Bobby relaxed a bit. "What's she done?"

"That's a private matter. Or she'd probably prefer that it remain private."

"Maybe where she is is private." The kid smiled. "Look, I don't want nobody hassling her, okay? I don't mean to be rude."

"How do you know her?"

In a quick, practiced move, the kid retrieved a lone cigarette from his flannel shirt pocket, stuck it in his mouth, and lit it. "She helps me with my writing."

"She's what?"

"Helps me, man," the kid said. "Helps. See, I may not look it now, but I been to a college or two. Not like yours, man. But I got these stories. And she helps me with them. See. In return I help her when I can." He exhaled some smoke. Bobby coughed.

"She's missed her writing seminar for weeks now, and she's in here teaching you to write?"

"And just so you know, no matter what them little, shit-assed, spoiled kids say, she's one hell of a teacher." The kid reconsidered. "No, no that ain't right. 'Editor,' she's a hell of an editor. You don't need 'class time' to be a good editor."

Bobby felt as though he had crossed the street through the snow to step into another world. This was the world he had avoided but the world Velda had sought. This was the world that Willamette Valley assured parents that their children would escape. He held out his hand. "I'm Dean Bobby Snyder. And I'm really glad that Velda has you to look out for her and protect her, for you and for us."

The kid shook his hand. "I'm Jeff. But some people in here call me 'Rosebud.'" Bobby tried not to laugh, but Jeff did. "Some drunks who come here said 'Jeff' is no name for a bartender, said a bartender needs a nickname. Velda heard them. So she tells them to call me 'Rosebud.' You seen that Kane movie?"

"You aren't a local are you, Jeff?"

Jeff sucked in on his cigarette, "I'm from Mount Vernon, Texas. And I ran away from that ass backward, Bible thumping country as soon as I could. Military turned me down, but not Tyler Junior College, Texas A&M at Commerce, or Portland State."

"I'm from Victoria, Texas. I got out of there as soon as I could too."

Jeff nodded. "Velda stays in the back game room nowadays. She mouthed off to a drunk, and things got ugly. She's watching how much she drinks. She's careful now. You be careful with her."

In a show of camaraderie or recognition, Bobby downed his beer, pulled out three more dollars, and ordered another. He told Jeff to keep the change. If nothing else, Jeff was bound to realize that Bobby was a good tipper.

Making his way through the wafting smoke, Bobby started to sweat. He took off his wool hat and then his sport coat and entered the game room.

When he hired Velda, Bobby had two insuppressible thoughts. First, he thought that together he and Velda would show these Yankees that they had academic pedigrees too. Second, Bobby had left that class at Rice University feeling that he owed her, for Velda made him become what he was. With her around, Bobby could see what he might have tried to become—had he the will and the talent.

Then there was a memory; back in their college days, Bobby had studied Velda. Beneath those old T-shirts, firm untethered breasts battled for position. Shapely legs with thong sandals on one end and the frayed edges of tight cut-off jeans on the other constantly flexed with some nervous twitter or stress that shot through her body. With some makeup, some shape to her hair, plucked brows, accented lips, she could have been a cheerleader. Instead, she worked at making herself unattractive. When she'd pulled her head up from her folded arms to answer a question—feigning disinterest or sleep in the untenured writer's class—Velda would show that she had absorbed the lessons without seemingly paying any attention. When she elaborated, she showed a faked give-a-shit attitude mixed with some eloquence. And the drafts of her stories revealed a rhetorical magic. Bobby was falling in love.

But he knew that he had more of a chance with a Rice sorority girl and cheerleader than this magical, destined, dangerous, lice-infested, nose-picking girl. So he dated, courted, and later married Lou Ann. She wore makeup and panty hose. She plucked her eyebrows and puckered her lips. She was beautiful and charming but not magical.

That magical girl had a faint resemblance to the stout middle-aged woman who rose from her table in the Pig's Foot Bar game room to greet Bobby: still no makeup, a short skirt that showed a bulging belly, bigger breasts, squared shoulders, and an opened-neck blouse. She hugged him, "I'm glad to see you, Bobby. Even if *they* sent you."

"Oh, Velda," Bobby said. As he lowered himself to a chair across from Velda, he said, "What are you doing here?"

"I'm always here."

"So I've heard. Why?"

Vela's eyes settled on Bobby. "So you're the Hemingway scholar. I don't know if it's true or not, but I've heard, when he was in Key West, Hemingway chose his house because it was beneath a lighthouse. No matter how drunk he got, he could find his way home." Bobby had heard the story. "I live in this quaint as shit cottage right behind this place. It's so quaint it gives me the heebies. The Pig's Foot is my lighthouse," Velda said. Velda dug in her purse for a cigarette. "I'm trying to quit. I have been for thirty years." Her smile forced Bobby to smile, even though he had no idea what the joke was. "I've been trying to quit a lot in the last thirty years."

Bobby took a match from a nearby matchbook and lit her cigarette. She pulled back blowing smoke in his direction. "What about teaching your classes?" Bobby asked.

She smiled, "*Class*, not plural. I've been teaching all but one."

"But that one was why you were hired."

"Oh, Bobby, they think only from their eyebrows up. They've never wanted. They've never failed. They expect some sort of entitlement for being smart, rich, pretty, or clever. And that's all they are. I can't criticize their stories. They want only praise, just for attempting to write fiction. What did Samuel Johnson say about women preaching and dogs dancing on their hind legs?"

"We applaud them not because they do it particularly well but because they do it at all."

Velda inhaled once more on the cigarette, then abruptly she crushed it in the ashtray. "Maybe that's our job," Bobby said. "To applaud them and send them on their way."

"You really believe that?"

"So why do you help Jeff in there?"

"He honestly tries. He has more than simple intelligence. He feels. In the long run, he'll turn out better than those precious children across the street."

"But you dismissed class. You haven't met in six weeks."

"I gave them what they wanted. I gave them a reading list. They e-mailed what they thought, then they e-mailed a story. I e-mail them back with faint praise."

"But several complained."

"I know which ones. Uppity little snits. Look, Bobby, help me hold on to this job. It's all I have."

Velda reached across the table to gently place her fingertips on top of Bobby's hand. He rolled his hand over and clasped her hand. "What about your own writing?"

"A University Press is interested in my latest novel. But how can I make a living there. Some young editor at my old house asked if I could write another mystery—or romance or fantasy, anything to put on a grocery store rack."

"A book on a grocery store rack is nothing to be ashamed of. It's no worse than selling insurance."

She pulled her hand away from Bobby's. A tear formed in the corner of her left eye. She wiped at the tear with the back of her hand. "Truth is. I can't seem to find the wherewithal to start running my fingers across a keyboard. No matter how bad I fucked up or how bad the publishing industry twisted out from under me, I could always write something. Now, I'm tired."

"Velda, something, something. You have to give me something to defend you with."

"How about thank you for hiring me?"

"I need something more, something tangible to defend you."

"To defend me to *them* or to yourself?"

"Velda, you had such promise, such talent."

"And what, I squandered it? Let it go? Drank it away? Fucked too much?" Her voice grew louder, so Jeff peered into the game room. She stabbed at the table with her index finger. "Maybe the talent and the promise are why I am this way."

Bobby checked the room for witnesses.

"The world had as much to do with my fate as I have." She took a drink and said loudly, "And goddamn it, I don't owe the world, fate, and myself your approval." Her face reddened as she scowled at Bobby. But then, through her nature or will, she pushed her face into a smile. It was the happy face of a grandmother. "Bobby, I'm sorry," she said. "Clearly, I've had too many adventures with booze, drugs, and men . . . .Did we ever, you know, back at Rice?"

"No," Bobby said.

"We should have." She reached out and rested her fingers on the top of his hand. "You know I have a son. He's thirteen. Yeah, I know, me with a teenage boy. He was an accident. I thought my biological clock had had its last tick. He splits time between his father and me. Now he's back in Houston, a smart kid. See, I'm kind of normal. Defend me on normalcy. Go for pity, sentimentality. Say my son'll starve if I don't have a job."

Bobby was too brain weary to go on. He grasped her hand, squeezed hard, and pushed himself up. "I'll try. I'll try."

"I could always trust you, Bobby."

When Bobby returned to the cold, the street lights turned the snowy world silver. Christmas lights added dashes of color. His shoes crunched the snow as he walked to his two-story house built in the odd fake-Victorian style that had become popular on the edge of town. The mile walk from campus to his house always invigorated him, even in the snow. In that leisurely twenty-minute walk, Bobby always congratulated himself on the world he had made for his family. He could walk, not drive, to and from work, in a protected, well-to-do, safe community. The rest of the world was ten long miles away in Portland. He had made himself and his family safe. But Velda gnawed at his liver with her negligence. Velda had declared war on safety and comfort. That was why he left writing behind.

* * *

Lou Ann had wine, a salad, and pasta waiting for Bobby. Normally they scrounged for themselves because mostly they couldn't coordinate their early evenings. Bobby had the more normal hours, but Lou Ann was busy selling the cozy cottages around town and the suburban tracts closer to Portland. But they had decided to have dinner together at least once during the week and on Saturdays and Sundays. Lou Ann had started on the wine.

They ate dinner without much talk. Lou Ann tried to start conversation by telling Bobby about her weird clients; then she went on to report the latest news about their two daughters. But all she could get out of Bobby were grunts while he sucked up the pasta along. She watched a documentary on one of the myriad of cable channels while Bobby graded the papers from his one class and tried not to think about Velda. The last thing that he wanted to do was to share what he felt about Velda with his wife. "The committee hearing on Velda Ortego is tomorrow. I've been trying to think of a way to defend her and I can't."

"You can't defend her, or you can't think? English teacher?"

Bobby chuckled. "I've been thinking too much. I can't defend her."

"So why even try?"

"I feel like I owe her."

"What on earth for?" Bobby fished for an answer, but Lou Ann rescued him. "You've let that woman bother you ever since she got here. You just think you owe her. You know how you get. Your dissertation, the move up here, her. Some things scrunch up your insides."

"Well, as you said, it's how I get."

In the middle of the night, Lou Ann rolled toward Bobby. He felt her breath on his ear, felt her spoon against him, and heard her whisper, "Why are you so restless? You want me to be sweet to you? You want me to please you?"

Bobby wanted to explain but couldn't. "No dear, that's not it. But I do appreciate your offer." He got out of bed and stumbled down the long hall, down the steps, into the kitchen, and poured himself a tall scotch. He had had his bouts with liquor, but nothing serious, nothing like an addiction.

As he wondered his way through his second glass of scotch, Lou Ann appeared in the kitchen door, and some lost, vagrant light coming in through a window outlined her body underneath her sheer nightgown. And wondrously, Bobby felt aroused. Lou Ann still had the body and exuberance of that cheerleader / sorority girl whom he chose over Velda. "You know, this funk of yours is getting irritating. And I'm getting tired of it." She crossed the kitchen, her sheer nightgown flowing behind her, her body silhouetted by the lost light. She sat next to Bobby and asked rhetorically and sarcastically, "Is there anything that I can possibly do?"

"Yes," Bobby said. "Yes, you can be sweet to me now."

* * *

President Miriam Stephenson had asked each member of the committee to vote "yea" or "nay" as to terminating Velda Ortego. In was an advisory committee, but Miriam would use the votes to defend her decision, or to make it. The two co-eds who had initiated the complaints showed up scrubbed and pretty in new suits, but Bobby saw the tattoo of the dagger laying across a rose on the ankle of the one co-ed, and he heard the other's tongue stud click against the back of her teeth as she made her case.

The two argued that they had paid a lot of money, or rather that their parents had, and they were not getting their money's worth. There was no encouragement; there was no "hands on" teaching; there were no classes. Worse, Ms. Ortego didn't seem to care about her students' progress toward becoming writers themselves. They recommended termination. Bobby wished for their termination. He preferred depressed, morose, and suicidal kids to indignant but cheery ones.

English Department Chair, Leslie Clark, made the argument that Bobby used when he hired Velda. She was a renowned writer. She brought honor and integrity to Willamette by being on campus. She was not a traditional academic, so her teaching strategies would be different. Leslie Clark, an attractive, well-dressed woman, an award-winning teacher herself, a feminist, voted for censure but not termination.

Vice President of Academic Affairs Leonard Jett shifted his eyes from President Miriam Stephenson to Bobby without moving his head. He needed a clue on how to vote. So he abstained from commenting and voting—for the moment

So all eyes turned to Bobby. He was glad that he had put on a tie for this meeting. He sat next to the president and felt the sunshine rush in through the large window at his back. The window filtered out the cold, and the warm sunshine made him drowsy. He bit his lip to keep his mind on his dilemma.

President Miriam Stephenson's comforting eyes told Bobby to make the decision for her. Leonard Jett's pleading eyes asked Bobby to relieve him from a decision. Leslie Clark's eyes cheered Bobby to agree with her. And the two tattoo and studded students' eyes demanded retribution.

Bobby began. "Velda Ortego's reputation does indeed benefit Willamette Valley. Her teaching methods, though, are unorthodox, but I find nothing in them necessarily harmful, destructive, or vindictive, as indicated. And at a school such as Willamette Valley, with our reputation and mission, with where we want to be, we should welcome Ms. Ortego's reputation and be open to her methods." He glanced at the co-eds, who pulled back in their chairs to put distance between him and them. Leslie Clark nodded in agreement. Leonard Jett swung his head between Bobby and Miriam Stephenson. Miriam Stephenson said with her eyes that she would follow him and protect him.

"But the fact remains that she did indeed miss class. Though she might have perfectly legitimate pedagogical aims, Velda Ortego broke school policy. Such teaching methods would also appear questionable to accrediting bodies." Bobby's hands were twittering. "She had been warned. She knows what she has done. She is not protected with tenure." Bobby couldn't finish, but the committee members got the idea. Leonard Jett, Miriam Stephenson, and the students smiled but all for different reasons. Leslie Clark looked down her nose at Bobby, but then smiled too, as though to forgive, as if to say that he had no other option.

* * *

"So you fucked her? I got eyes and ears over on that campus. I heard," Jeff said.

"Someone had to do something. I was that someone," Bobby said.

"Well shit, buddy, what about a little mercy and forgiveness? Christian ethics, huh? Ain't you guys a Christian school?"

"We're loosely Presbyterian." Bobby stared at the drink in his hand. "But we mostly answer to our benefactors, not God."

Even though Jeff laughed, Bobby resented defending himself to a townie bartender. "You want me to tell her what she already knows?"

"No. My job. My responsibility."

Bobby took his half-empty drink with him as he trudged to the backroom. Velda sat at her table, her arms spread, a smile on her face. She wore jeans, a sweater, and make up. She did not look middle-aged and worn out. She looked like the unkempt girl with the untethered tits, the shapely legs, the smart-ass demeanor, and knowledge of life's dirty secrets. She hugged him again. As they sat, Bobby began. "Velda, I don't know how to say this. I haven't prepared anything. But I was the one who. . . ."

Velda held up a hand to stop him. "I saw those two little muffins who attacked me. They were gloating. The whispers floated in here, even with Jeff's interference. So you can tell me if you want. But you don't need to."

"Velda, I'm sorry, but as you know, you couldn't have expected us to overlook what you did."

"And I don't know that I could have done any differently. Let's call this 'a learning experience' as the students would say." Velda patted Bobby's shoulder. He was startled by her perfume.

"Velda, I tried to think this through. I tried everything that I could to defend you."

"Spare me, Bobby. You did me the favors when you hired me. You don't owe me anything else."

"What are you going to do?"

106

"Write a romance novel. Chick Lit. A children's book. My memoirs. Find another trusting college. But first I think that I'll go to Houston and visit my son." Velda added, "Yeah, this motherly stuff sort of surprises me too."

"I can write you a recommendation."

"I'll let you know if I need one."

Bobby leaned back in his chair to study her. He felt intimidated by her and yet attracted to her, just as he had at Rice. "Look, a middle-aged woman is used to losing things. Once she gets used to her diminishing looks, the other losses are easy."

Bobby didn't know that Velda had ever cared about her looks. He was disappointed in a way. He stuttered, then made his tongue obey him. "Don't you regret anything? Don't you wonder if you had done something different? Would it have killed you to have met your classes?" Velda tried to answer, but Bobby's tongue had loosened. "Did you consider that my reputation was on the line too? Don't you think at all about your future? What will become of you? Is a normal life so bad for you?"

"I don't remember all the questions, but I think the answer is 'yes.' You want to go on?"

"No. I'd end up pissed off. Not at you. I wouldn't be so pissed off at you but at me."

"Why? You have the perfect life."

"I don't want to talk about my life."

Bobby wished that he could talk about his life. But when he stood to go to his perfect life, in front of Jeff, Velda kissed him on the lips as a thank you for the three years he had given her.

Outside, not yet fully dark, the usual clouds had returned to melt the unusual snow. There was no silver, no dancing Christmas lights reflecting in the snow. Bobby felt hot, sweaty, and flush in his wool sport coat and overcoat, as though he were in Houston in August.

He ate by himself, but he had wine and a microwaved meal ready for Lou Ann when she got home. She watched another documentary while he tried to read some of Hemingway's *Islands in the Stream*. Lou Ann asked about Velda's fate, but Bobby gave her the barest details. Bobby had read that, as a man ages, he senses his diminished physical capacities, so instead of fighting, he flees. A woman, on the other hand, because of her declining estrogen and increasing testosterone, is willing to fight for the answers. They annoyed each other, but they had learned to live with each other.

Late that night, in the predawn, Bobby woke and saw Lou Ann curled away from him in the big king-sized bed. He scooted across the space between them. He kissed her behind the ear. Lou Ann awoke and groggily asked, "You want me to be sweet to you? Now? What would you like?"

"I just want to hold you. I want to tell you something about Hemingway."

"Well, whispering sweet nothings about Hemingway into my ear is certainly a novel way of making love."

Bobby told her about Hemingway's lighthouse, the one right over his house, so no matter how drunk he got, he could find his way home. Then he said, "You're my lighthouse."

Lou Ann kissed him. They both lay awake. Bobby was glad he had made Lou Ann happy. Velda Ortego had no lighthouse; he was envious of Velda's confidence. He thought of her drifting, all alone, toward Houston and other choices.

Oasis of Love

Back when the Oasis of Love had just broken sod, just when I had killed off Jerri Johnson and my son had gotten killed, my sister gave me my dog. Later, when my dog got older, I would walk him to the park two blocks down from our new house and watch the construction of The Oasis of Love. Now, my dog can no longer trot beside me when we take our morning walks to the park, and the Oasis of Love is complete and thriving. As we walk down the block, he wags his thick tail and swings his stiff, arthritic hips in a clumsy, sideways fashion. As he sways, the hanging skin around his mouth quivers, and he slobbers. Sometimes he pushes himself too much, and we have to stop to rest.

I too have slowed down. I've developed some arthritis in my hips; my muscles ache a bit longer when I get up in the mornings; I don't know if I could still rein in my dog on his leash as I did when he was younger, when he'd pull me behind him to the park. It was almost as though he could recognize the large freeway billboard advertising the Oasis of Love to freeway drivers and know that our rich green grass was underneath that sign.

Then, as his paws left asphalt and touched that grass, he would jump straight up, like his legs had springs, nearly pulling the leash out of my hand, and I would slip off his leash to let him bound in the luxuriant park. After he ran, he'd roll on his back, and sometimes he'd yelp, I'd like to think, out of joy. Then he'd run into the rich foliage to scare up birds.

Now, he no longer seems to recognize the sign, and when I take off his leash, he lowers his hips to take a load off his back legs, then lowers his front legs to rest his chin in the grass. He raises his head once in a while to bark at birds. He still waits by the door when it is time for his walk and thumps his thick tail on my wall. So I wonder what the park is to him. Is it some integral part of his life, like love, like me? Does he remember his puppy days? Does he grow sentimental? Excited? Sad? I'd like to be able to account for my dog.

Worse, he has bladder trouble. After the rolled newspapers and the scoldings that I used to housebreak him, he now ducks his head and whimpers. Perhaps he is embarrassed, humiliated, wanting somehow to apologize or ask forgiveness for a house dog's greatest sin.

And for my dog's sake, I sometimes feel like writing the parks and recreation department to thank someone for the park because the designers of the park must have considered old ladies and their dogs when they made our park. It is gently landscaped and has lit, paved walkways that wind through the trees and trimmed undergrowth. Because the air around Houston is filled with water, the park stays almost too richly green. At the edges of the grassy meadows, the thick green of leafy shrubs, not weeds or wild plants, choke the domestic trees. In springtime, big bursts of white azaleas spot the green. Thus our park is soothing for old ladies and their dogs.

Only to my dog and me, though, is it the Oasis of Love. The real Oasis of Love is not the name of one of those sleazy massage parlors that used to line the interstates next to truck stops. It is the Christian Community of Rev. Richard Tivy, resting safely insulated from the concerns of the world that go on beneath the large billboard. Rev. Tivy's large church is nestled in its own luxuriant and mani-cured green backdrop of grass and trees, and surrounding the church are a swim-ming pool, tennis courts, a community center, and suburban streets. To the funda-mentalist suburbanites who cluster in Rev. Tivy's version of the American Dream, the iron and brick entrance to the Oasis of Love must look like a modern vision of the pearly gates.

I had every right to kill Jerri Johnson because I completely *made* her. And consequently, Jerri Johnson *made* me a living when I got fired from Willamette Valley College She accounted for the only real money I ever had. For notoriety I had my past life, my attempts at teaching college, and my commercial novels from early in my career. Because of her, I was able to move out of my small, smelly condominium and into a real house so that my dog would have a back yard and a daily walk to a park.

Jerri Johnson was a short, small-framed woman like me. Because she worked in a man's game, the private eye business, she wore jeans, khakis, and small inexpensive earrings. A necklace, of course, was out of the question. A bad guy could strangle her with her own necklace. But whenever she got the chance, she wore evening gowns and jewelry so that she could feel herself looking feminine. She taped her small pistol to her calf with adhesive tape, something a male pri-vate-eye wouldn't dare do. Usually, she got mixed up in cases where she couldn't line up legality, morality, and self-interest all on the same side. Needless to say, she was confused.

I didn't keep her the same age, forever thirty-eight, like every other private eye, but let her grow old. But something about a menopausal private detective walking Houston's mean streets and giving lip to pimps, crack addicts, and oil men began to seem absurd. I didn't want her getting as old as me without some sort of peaceful life.

So Jerri Johnson caught a slug in the back of the head in a dusty pool room in downtown Houston while she was attempting to locate a white man's long-lost, black daughter. She never knew what hit her or who did it, nor did she solve the case, so even though she was in business of finding out things, she never knew her own life. This, of course, was my theme.

As far as I was concerned she had done her job. Besides making me enough money to live on, she surrendered willingly to my plans for her life. With a slug in her head and thus out of my life, she allowed me to become a quiet, retired lady. So now, under another pseudonym, I write romance novels and ghostwrite celebrity tell-alls. They aren't nearly as fun Jerri Johnson.

My son was twenty-two, a senior at the University of Tulsa, a scholarship student, a football player, a quarterback even—how, given my mis-wired genes, I'll never know. I could never account for my son. Unlike Jerri Johnson or my dog, very little that I poured into his life seemed to stick with him. He was not a bad kid or a disappointment; he just turned out different from what I expected, probably because he grew up with his father.

He was coming back from spring break and lying in the backseat of a buddy's car. Up in the front seat, the two other passengers were swigging beers and didn't stop at a red light. A car skidded into the rear of their car. It tapped the outside of the door where my son rested his head, but it quickly, neatly, and efficiently broke his neck.

The repair bill was only $1200. No one else was hurt. Because the insurance companies made a big to-do about the fact that the driver and other passenger were drinking, some people from M.A.D.D. wanted me to join their ranks and to use my son as another example about the problems with teenage drinking and driving. I got drunk. I never liked causes, and I didn't want a cause attached to his death. I didn't want him reduced to a symbol. I wanted him to remain himself, a "self" that I helped make—even if I couldn't account for him, even if his father mostly raised him.

I sometimes think that there was less of me in him than I would have thought. I had diluted my genetic memory and strength by filling my life with things other than children. At his funereal, I looked more like his grandmother than his mother.

It took me so long to have Jake because I was one of those kids who, when she gets out of high school, wants so much to be someplace else and to be some-body else. I made it to Rice University, New York, and Amsterdam. I slept on park benches. Smoked pot when some people still thought it was a hallucinogenic. I developed a fondness for alcohol, that woozy feeling you get just before becoming slobbering drunk. I had affairs with all sorts of men, some of them wonderful, most too caught up with some purpose or cause to ever really love me. My mother despaired. And even though I had the early, literary novels and a movie option that never came true, my father told me that someday I'd have to grow up.

Jake was the next kick. I remember thinking as I came back from the doctor, "So I'm pregnant. This is new." Jake's father wanted to marry me so that my son could have a decent childhood and I could be proper woman. So I became a wife in the same way that I became a mother.

I stayed a mother much longer than I stayed a wife. Somewhere around the time that Jake was three, his father told me about his latest other woman and moved out. I didn't need Jake's father, but I needed his money. No commercial publisher wanted my novels any longer, and I liked good whiskey and a certain extravagance in my life. I tried writing but couldn't make any money on my new novels or my name. Then an old friend from college, a man I always wished I had bedded to see what made him tick, gave me a job teaching the overly precious and overly rich students Willamette Valley College. I left Jake with his father to adventure up to a quaint, cute, small town in Oregon. I drank away my job. So I moved back to Houston to be with Jake while he went through high school. Mostly, I embarrassed him.

At the funeral, Jake's teammates were the pall bearers, and I sat to the side of a pulpit while a rented preacher said things about Jake that just weren't true, things about being a respected member of the team, a promising scholar, an inspiration, what the Rev. Tivy of the Oasis of Love Christian Community might say to his suburbanite flock. Jake was a youngster, most interested in filling up time with what youngsters consider fun. Why make him into more?

As the rented preacher droned on, my sister placed her hand on my shoulder, something she thought she should do, something the Rev. Tivy would have done had he come to the funeral. My ex-husband and his latest wife rode in the limo with me, and they both patted my shoulders too. The pall-bearer teammates told me what a great "team man" Jake was and patted my shoulders. I didn't want any of this. I didn't want to honor him; I wanted to remember Jake, as he was, to account for his life.

After the funeral, I went to the retirement home where my sister and I kept our mother. She had gotten feeble, and so Sarah and I moved her from Port Arthur to Houston, we could watch her as she lost what had been her. As I sat by her on the front porch of the retirement home, I patted her hand and realized the silliness of the gesture. I fessed up. "Jake has been killed. We buried him yesterday."

My mother turned her head to me and squinted. Behind her eyes was a milky thickness. A cloud-colored vagueness was taking her away from herself. I patted her hand again. "My son, Mama. My son, Jake," I said. "He's dead."

"My God. Oh my God." She lifted the hand that I didn't pat and held it to her mouth. I grasped her frail, bony hand, and she looked down at her hand wrapped in mine, then looked back up to my eyes. She was lucid, and her eyes told me that there was flat out nothing that we could do.

"Mama," I said and then started to cry. "I wasn't a very a good mother. I didn't try hard enough."

She looked at me as though I were still a child. It was one of those moments in which—if TV shows, cheap novels, or even the residents of The Oasis of Love had their way—I should have hugged my mother, and with tears streaming down our faces, I should have shouted, "Oh, yes, yes, mama. I love you." I've even written scenes like that. Instead my mother said, "I wasn't a very good mother either. Your father always thought I was responsible for your misbegotten ways. He thought we should have pulled you out of college. Maybe we're both bad mothers."

I felt foolish but went on talking. "The words like *good* or *bad* don't apply. He was him; I am me," I raised my head to look at my mother. "You are you."

"Sometimes, you just gotta hurt," she said. "Mostly you don't know. So you got to be sure of what you do know."

A week later, my sister showed up at my condominium with her arms over some squirming blondish blob. In front of me, Sarah held a puppy, its eyes still wrinkled shut. It pushed itself with its flipper like paws to the edge of Sarah's fingers. "His mother died. He's not even weaned yet."

My sister took her time to get married. She became a veterinarian. Unlike me, her biological clock stopped ticking before she ever had a child. Instead of children, she brought her worst cases home.

"He'll die," I said.

"Maybe," my sister said. "Sometimes you have to take the chance." She handed me my dog. It was an outrageous gesture, something that I would never have let Jerri Johnson do. My mother and I had always been too old for such gestures, but my sister, as she grew older, risked making her life into such gestures. Besides, she had initiated the dare, as the younger sister often does. So I took the dog from Sarah, stretched him out in my flat palm, and held *my* dog in front of my face and smelled his puppy breath.

Of course, a dog is not enough. A sister is not enough. They are not a part of you. Unlike a mother or a son, they are not distinctly yours, beyond good or bad. We need things that cannot be confused with anybody else's, things that you make or that make you.

My publisher begged me to send Jerri Johnson into surgery to be saved so that she could solve more cases. Or better yet come back disabled in some way so that she had more to overcome in solving her cases. Maybe make her a zombie or a vampire. I said no. My publisher said to create a new character. I said I was retired. I bought an old brick house with bay windows and hardwood floors near the tony homes around The Oasis of Love construction site for my dog and me. I didn't even bother to name him. I wanted him to remain just a dog.

I have seen my dog get as old as I am and then even older. He will not out live me, and I don't think that I would out live another dog. I don't want to put in the effort to raise another dog.

So now he lies in the thick grass of *our* park and raises his head to watch a bird in flight, perhaps remembering when he could chase the bird. I sit in a bench in front of him and remember the day my sister placed him on my fingertips. And I remember my son's funeral, my mother's last days of coherency, my mother's funeral, and Jerri Johnson (whom nobody remembers anymore). And I look up at Rev. Tivy's sign for the Oasis of Love. I wonder how Rev. Tivy and his Christian suburbanites, sealed away in their sanitized community of love, can account for love, how they could possibly call love an *oasis*. Perhaps, an oasis *from* love is what we all seek.

Praying and Drinking

Bessie's office would normally be a bedroom. It has a separate entrance, a storm door, and a sign over the doorway. I sit across from Bessie's desk in a vinyl chair salvaged from April's redecoration and refurnishing. Bessie sits behind her buffed-topped, neatly-kept desk. I suspect that everything in the office has been done for effect or first impression, probably upon the advice of the owner. I am here to pay June's rent. I always fill my checks out in Bessie's office.

Behind Bessie is a bookshelf with ceramics: a cute duck, a little boy fishing, a little girl in a swing. Another bookshelf to the side of her desk has books, mostly religious, with titles like *When Bad Things Happen to Good People*, *The Power of Positive Prayer*, *Faith in the World*, *Good News for Modern Man*. I suspect these are for effect too. They are always in their proper place on the proper shelf. I hand Bessie my check.

Bessie looks it over to see if I filled it out correctly and legibly. I had some trouble for a couple of months. She tries to smile but looks exhausted. It is unfair that she should have to work today. "I am sorry, Bessie," I say. "I just read yesterday."

The muscles in her face sag. She begins: "He had come in from his walk, and he said he had trouble. His arm hurt up around his shoulder, and he couldn't breathe. I should have known then, should have taken him straight to the emergency room. I asked him, you know. But never to put a person out, he said 'no.'" I fidget in my seat because I am afraid that I will not be able to sit through this. I want a cigarette.

"Then at the dinner table, while we were eating, he put his hands up toward his throat." Bessie grabs her throat to show what Rich did. My fingertips start to tingle. I want to be back in my apartment.

Bessie takes a deep breath. "I ran to him, you know. And he fell into my arms. And I couldn't hold him, and we both fell on the floor." I had guessed at the death Saturday morning. Through my apartment's front window I saw the bachelor son from Dallas standing by the black limo parked in front of the complex. He held the door open and looked at his watch. The rich mourners wore tasteful black or gray tailored suits or dresses ordered from Nieman Marcus or Sakowitz. The blue collar friends wore their out-of-date, off-color suits. Their wives wore dresses they bought at sales off Penney's and Sears' racks. I saw Bessie return holding the arm of her son, her eyes red, close friends following behind her, talking to themselves. Some of the women followed her into her apartment, but most of the men stayed outside in the courtyard, folded their arms, and talked about business.

"The EMS people tried CPR, even broke a rib, but a doctor said that, even if they could have done something, he would have had brain damage. You just don't know."

"At least he didn't suffer," I say. The tingle in my fingertips moves into my hand; it begins to tremble.

"The doctor said that he was dead in less than a minute." I stand, plant my feet, then step toward the door.

"How are you doing?" I say as I push against her glass storm door.

"I'm praying. Rich will hear me, and the Lord does listen." Last month we had a brief conversation about Jesus. Bessie had said, "You say you're not a Christian? What about when you die?" The tremble in my hand makes its way into my wrist. I grab my wrist and try to relax.

"I know that I can't say or do much, but I have all summer off, and if you need any help with the apartments, I'll be glad to help. I like working outside."

"Sure," Bessie says.

"Bye," I say and push open the door.

"Thank you for the rent." As soon as I get outside, I reach in my pocket for cigarettes. I get a cigarette into my mouth, but even with two hands, I have trouble lighting it.

* * *

I sit by the large living room window in my apartment and look at the artificial pond and the waterfall powered by a pump behind the club room. The owner's son, home from college for the summer, picks out trash and rocks from the ferns around the pond. His best friend dips his hand into the pond and pulls out the trash. I met them both two days ago but cannot remember either's name. The owner's son wanted to make extra money to pay for his rent and fraternity dues, so his dad gave him and his best friend jobs at the complex as yard boys.

I have all summer off. And, though my hands tremble, I have yet to have an unbearable day. I take the pack of cigarettes off the arm of my chair and shake it. I pull a cigarette out with my teeth and light it.

From my window, I can also see across the pond, through the storm door, and into Bessie's office. As usual, she sits behinds her desk talking on the telephone. Her hair is no longer red; she lets it grow back to its natural salt and pepper; she had lost twenty-five pounds. She has since lost fifteen more. Did it, she says, by eating Weight Watchers and Lean Cuisine. I tried some of them, but like a lot of other things I've tried; they tasted bland. I have to be able to taste food to want to eat it.

Since it is nearing noon, I think about going out for lunch. I could shave, put on a pair of slacks and a knit shirt, go to Walter's Family Hamburgers, Kentucky

Fried Chicken, or Julio's Mexican Food. All are within walking distance. I flick my ashes at the ashtray on the arm of my chair but miss it, so I brush the ashes off the chair's arm.

Instead of lunch, I really wish for a cup of coffee. I have none. I remember that Bessie always keeps a pot of coffee in her office for herself and prospective tenants.

I put out my cigarette and walk barefoot to Bessie's office in my shorts and T-shirt. I wave to the owner's son (Bessie just manages) and say, "Hi, Joey."

"Josh," he corrects me.

I rap on Bessie's door. She looks up from a ledger book, and I walk in. "Could I bum a cup of coffee from you?"

"Sure," she says and hands me an empty cup, then stands, grabs her drip coffee pot, and pours me a cup. I start to sit, but she says, "Wait." She pours herself a cup, then says, "Let's go outside."

I step out and hold the door open for Bessie. We sit at the cement table to the side of her apartment and sip our coffee. Towards noon, the summer days start to cook, but this early heat has yet to build intensity. So, even though I sip coffee, I feel cooled by the shade from the second story porch and the still cool cement under my legs and hips.

Bessie says, "Rich and I used to have coffee here on Saturday mornings. It's nice here in the mornings."

"This is the first I noticed." I feel the cement bench. "Anything I can do at all, anything around the apartments. Clean up. Carry out trash. You know. Don't be afraid to ask." Seeming cheerful, Bessie pats my leg.

* * *

I hold the water hose over the flower bed and watch tiny streams turn the dirt to mud. I squat to get a closer look. The early afternoon sun pushes down on the top of my head, and I sweat, but sweating feels good.

Bessie decided to let me do some yard work. The owner's son and his best friend don't like my interfering. They don't think they can talk about fast cars and sexy girls while I'm around. I do cause them some problems. At first I couldn't tell the weeds from the plants. My first day, I had a pile of expensive ferns pulled from a flower bed. The owner's son tried to be polite, yet he did tell me how much I had cost his father. Another week, I got a rash on my fingers, and the owner's son told me that I had gotten into some poison ivy. Now they let me run the weed-eater and water the flowers.

I'm glad to have a job. The mornings are pleasant with plenty of shade. The afternoons are hot, but we take dips in the pool. During the nights I think about what I will do the next day.

Having something to think about at nights helps me get through them. My counselor and the members of my Wednesday night group all tell me that getting through the nights is the start of recovery. My hand trembles less often; I smoke less. I am getting fat. I can taste food again. I like to phone in orders for a large cheeseburger, onion rings, and a Pepsi to Walter's Family Hamburgers. Walter's claims to have the best onion rings in town—big and crispy with the grease they are cooked in soaking the bottom of the paper tray they are served on.

I walk to the faucet, lean against the wooden fence, and with one hand, turn off the water. I curl the hose up and lay it in the grass. Then I sit down and have a smoke. I am tired, but it feels good to be tired. Sometimes, when the nights are bad or long, I call my ex-wife. So far, she listens and doesn't complain when I wake her. On the weekends, when the rates are cheap, I call my son in Los Angeles.

He got lucky without even trying. He's my first wife's son, no relation to the ex-wife I call at night. For some reason, he got interested in Japan in college. He studied the language, went to Japan, and married the daughter of a Tokyo banker. Language and connections are why he got lucky. A large Los Angeles bank with a lot of international loans hired him as a translator and cultural advisor.

In one sense, I got lucky. My luck is with the Ector County School District. Because of a shortage of math and science teachers, ECSD is willing to hire a fired engineer with a drinking problem. With a teaching job I have all summer to dry out.

* * *

I sit in Bessie's office to pay July's rent. I cross one leg over the knee of the other and gently bob my foot. Bessie's books have been disturbed. *The Power of Positive Prayer* is gone. *Good News for Modern Man* lies on its side rather than being stacked against other books. *When Bad Things Happen to Good People* lies spine down and open on a bare space of shelf.

She refuses to gain weight or dye her hair back to red. She sits behind the desk looking through a stack of checks. "The boys in the back section are excited because I rented to two more girls."

"They ought to be. I saw the girls sunbathing while I was weedeating." Bessie tries to keep the youngsters in the back section by the pool and the sedate types needing peace in the front section with her.

"Sweet things, but they've both been married and divorced."

"Everybody has," I say and watch my foot bob.

Bessie shakes her head. "Everybody is quick to get rid of a man or can't find one, and I had such a good one and lost him." I hang my head; I want to tell her to get on with her life. "Even at the funeral, the minister said that he had never heard anyone say a single bad thing about Rich. He just wouldn't put anyone out."

"You were a lucky woman to have been married to him." I am glad that I found something encouraging yet realistic to say.

"Don't I know it." She looks away from me and off at the wall. "The doctors now say that he had all the warning signs: a sore left shoulder, some hard breathing, a numb hand. I knew that. I should have done something. He was never one to put a person out."

"A person has to want to help himself," I repeat my counselor's advice. Bessie nods.

"My son, Billy, you met Billy." I nod. "He's handling it so much better."

"He's off at Dallas, though, and hasn't lived here for several years."

Bessie shakes her head and looks at me. "Nights are the hardest."

"You get out any? Do anything?"

"I belong to a church group of older unmarrieds. We bowl, go to restaurants."

"That's good."

"Yeah, but I'm not ready for people yet. I can't handle crowds. I went to a family reunion in Louisiana. But all those people trying to help me. It was terrible."

"Yeah," I rub at my elbow.

"I'm not ready."

I reach in my shirt pocket for my pack of cigarettes. As I pull it out, Bessie stares at my pocket, and I slide the pack back into my pocket. "Well, I better go help Josh," I say and go outside for a smoke.

* * *

The cold water shocks me. Like in high school, when I was on the swim team, I start an overhead crawl toward the light. After I take two strokes, I am still chilly; after a couple more strokes, I feel refreshed. I open my eyes and keep my head underwater. The hazy lamp light changes shapes in the water. I feel the movement of the muscles in my arms. I feel my body glide. As I near the side, I duck my head and curl as I remember from high school and come up coughing on swallowed water. My nose, throat, and eyes itch and burn from chlorine. I swirl around and grab the lip of the pool, cough, and tremble.

It is a bad night. Expecting a bad night, I had let the air out of my back right tire. A good move because, when I go to my car at ten o'clock, telling myself that I will just go for a ride, I see my back tire and know that I shake too much to fix it. With nothing to see out my front window, unable to follow the plot or characters on TV, my hand trembling, I decide to go swimming.

The coughing quits. I catch a breath and push off the bank with my feet. My muscles ache. I had called my ex-wife and waked her. "Oh Jesus, Charlie, what's wrong?" she had said.

"I can't sleep."

"So take a pill."

"When I can't sleep, I drink."

"I know, believe me, I know."

"Why are you being so bitchy tonight?"

"This is getting old, Charlie. It's getting so old."

"I'm sorry then. I'm trying to help myself."

"Well, then, help yourself. I can't help you Charlie."

"Just talk."

"Okay, what about?"

"Goodbye," I said and hung up. I called my son, but he was out. I talked to my Japanese daughter-in-law; she wished me luck in broken English.

I reach the opposite end of the pool and grab the lip that hangs over the water. I cough again but not from swallowed water. It is a single cough that starts deep in my lungs, comes slowly to my throat, then convulsively bursts out of my mouth. I put my hands palm down on the edge of the pool, stiffen my arms, and try to swing my butt on the cement edge. But my arms give out, and I fall back into the water. Clawing water in dog paddle fashion, I get my head out of the water and grab the edge. With my fingertips and chin over the lip of the pool, I stare at the apartment in front of me and see its light go on.

Bessie is at the pool in minutes. I hear the gate slam and see her emerge out of the dark. She stands over me, the light from the pool lighting the gray in her hair, making her look fierce. I feel like a Boy Scout sneaking out for a skinny dip after lights out. "Is that you, Charles?" she says.

"Yes."

"They said it was kids."

"I thought I would take a swim."

"It's after hours."

I try to lift myself out again. My arms hold, and I get my butt out of the water, but when I try to swing my butt on the edge, I miss the lip and splash back into the water. Bessie bends down to look at me. "Can you swim?" she asks.

"Not too far."

"Can you make it to the steps at the other end?"

"I think so."

I push off with my feet and swim on my back. I use slow, deliberate strokes and try to glide as far as possible. I see Bessie walking along the edge of the pool keeping an eye on me. "Sure, you can make it?" she asks. She stops at the lawn chair and picks up my towel. My pack of cigarettes falls out from its folds, and she picks the pack up too. As I turn at the L, I reach shallow water, so I walk towards the steps at the far end of the pool. I breathe heavily and sneeze. As I come out of the pool, water dripping down my legs, Bessie slings my towel around my shoulders.

"My cigarettes?" I say, and she hands the pack to me.

"A grown man," she says then smiles.

"I couldn't sleep." We both walk back toward the front section of the apartments. Bessie walks with quick, even steps, her head cocked to one side, her eyes down. Her walk is businesslike, purposeful. Shivering, my bare feet punctured by small rocks on the sidewalk, I have a hard time keeping up with her.

As we go through the gate to the front section of the complex, she says, "Maybe you'd like to come by for a drink?" I give her a hard glance. "Oh, I mean a coke, or tea, or hot milk."

"It's late," I warn her.

"It's okay, I can't sleep either."

"The tea sounds good."

We walk into her living room, not her office. It is the first I've seen of her living room. It has the complex-issued furniture, and it's immaculate. On a side wall is a framed collection of portraits—color photographs of Bessie, Rich, the married daughter, and the young bachelor son. On the coffee table and lamp stands are more cute ceramics: cats and ducks, a little girl bending over pouring from an old-style watering can. Unlike my place, every piece of furniture is clean of dust. "Go ahead, sit down," Bessie says.

"I'm wet."

"That's okay."

I stretch my towel over the seat of the couch and sit down. Bessie goes into the kitchen. I shiver.

When she comes back in, my hands start to shake. I automatically fumble with my pack of cigarettes. I look at Bessie and drop my pack on the coffee table. She looks down at it. "Okay, go ahead and smoke." I pick up the pack and manage to get a cigarette out of the pack and between my lips.

"No light. No damn light," I say. Bessie frowns at me. She goes into the kitchen and comes back with a kitchen match. She looks around, then strikes it under the coffee table, and holds it toward me. With the cigarette in my mouth, I move my head toward the match, but the closer I get to the match, the farther Bessie pulls the match away. I grab her wrist. My shaking hands cause her hand to shake, causing the match to shake, but by waving my head I light my cigarette a quarter of inch from the tip. I inhale, blow smoke away from Bessie, and look for an ashtray.

"Why did you start to drink?" she asks me.

I blink, think for a moment. I could tell her that it was that I couldn't sleep, but I say, "Because it was fun."

She shakes her head; then the tea kettle in the kitchen screams. She leaves for the kitchen and comes back with two mugs. She hands me one. I look inside to see a floating tea bag. She sits a saucer on the coffee table. "You can put your tea bag in here." She looks at me with my open palm under the down-curled ashes on the tip of my cigarette.

"Put your ashes in there too."

I flick my ashes in the saucer and take my mug, but it shakes in my hands, so I set it on the coffee table. I pull the tea bag out, dribble tea across the coffee table, and drop the bag into the saucer. "Sorry."

"You poor man," she says, sitting beside me on the sofa and patting my back. I turn toward her. I see her shoulder, and maybe just because she is there, I want to put my face into the soft part of her shoulder; I want her to pat my back again.

I feel like crying. But I don't. Instead I shrug. "It's not that bad," I say.

She smiles like she has found me out, but then her smile grows broader and becomes like a real smile of happiness or hope. "I have a date tomorrow night," she says.

"Wow," I say. I pick up my mug and slowly lift it to my mouth. I tremble, spilling some hot tea on my lap, but I get a sip. I set the cup down. "Wonderful. Just what you ought to do?"

"I met him at our Wednesday night church group."

"Nice guy, huh?"

"Jack is a fine Christian man."

* * *

Because of the previous night, Bessie gives me the day off. I tell her that I don't need the day off, but she insists. I wake early, and the mere memory of liquor gives me that day-after drunk taste in my mouth.

I don't eat, but I nibble some soda crackers and drink several Cokes. I don't feel like Walter's onion rings. The soap operas on TV don't appeal to me. I tried to call my son at his Los Angeles office, but he was not in. I called my ex-wife at the beauty shop she owns and managed to apologize, a big mistake. So I look out my window and watch the owner's son and his best friend fish trash out of the pond and trim the hedges. They are probably glad to be rid of me and hope, I would bet, that I am gone for good. They shout about a girl named Louise and someone's Firebird. They laugh.

I sit by the window most of the day. Toward six, the sun lowers over the stone wall that surrounds the front section of the complex and shines in my eyes. The yardboys leave, so I shift my chair towards Bessie's apartment. Her office is closed early.

Then, with the sun behind him making an aura around his silver hair, a man comes through the front entrance of the apartment complex and crosses the wooden bridge over the artificial pond. He turns away from me and heads toward Bessie's apartment. I put the side of my face against the window to get an angle so that I can see better.

Though a slight breeze blows, the man's silver hair stays exactly as combed.

He wears blue seersucker pants and a navy blue knit shirt with a penguin on the pocket. He rings the doorbell and turns away from it, folds his arms, and rocks back and forth on his heels. When Bessie opens the door, he turns to face her, quickly runs his hand over the top of his head, squashing his pompadour, and holds the door open as Bessie steps through it.

* * *

She wears a smile and red sun dress with matching red sandals. Her hair looks like she has touched up some of the gray. As she steps on the sidewalk, the man takes her elbow and leads her away.

This night of Bessie's date is not as bad as the previous night. My hand shakes; I go through a pack of cigarettes and get a cough from them, but I know that I can make it through. I sit by the window and watch Bessie's apartment. Shortly after midnight, they return. Bessie walks ahead of the man at an even faster pace than usual, her head cocked like a charging bull, looking out of one eye. He has to trot to keep up with her. When she gets to the door, she does not turn around to say goodnight. "Kiss him," I say to myself. He leans against the door with one hand, his arm to one side of Bessie's face. She looks at the arm, then he straightens, leans away from her, and lets the arm dangle at his side. Bessie goes in and turns off the porch light.

The man stands in the dark a moment, then walks towards my apartment. He stops by one of the wooden beams that brace the second story and bangs the heel of his fist on it. He continues walking, and as he crosses the foot bridge, he bounces his fist on the rail.

I get up from my chair at the window and sit cross-legged by my coffee table. I fold my hands, lean toward them, and bounce them on my forehead, and it occurs to me that I might be praying. I try harder, am even tempted to say "Jesus" or "Lord" out loud. I want no archangel or heavenly bell, not even an answer; I want . . . I want maybe to feel better, maybe just to feel I'm praying. But I see my ashtray on the coffee table in front of me filling with butts. I smell the ashes from the ashtray and the tobacco on my breath and know I cannot pray.

* * *

I am up at six, sitting at my window, listening to the early morning farm and ranch report, the morning exercise program, then the Today show. I wait for Bessie to open the office. She opens early at 8:30. I immediately walk to her office in dirty khaki work pants and a T-shirt.

She smiles and looks at me through the storm window. "Come in, Charles," she says.

I step in and say, "May I have a cup of coffee?" Her coffee is made, her office straightened and ready for business: desk clear, ceramics and books in proper

123

places on the bookshelves. She pours me a cup of coffee. I take it and sit across from her. I smile. "How was your date?"

She looks at me with a wicked smile. "I thought you would ask."

"Well?"

"It wasn't very good."

"Why? What went wrong."

She closes her eyes and folds her hands in front of her. "He was improper and his manner inappropriate."

I sip my coffee, think a bit, cock my head. "So what is that?" She doesn't answer but sits in front of me with her hands folded and her eyes still closed. "Then again, it's none of my business."

She opens her eyes and blinks. "We went to his house after a very nice, pleasant, and expensive dinner. We watched a movie from his video machine, some old John Wayne thing he likes. And then, he tried to put his hand down the front of my dress." She blinks, doesn't smile. I lean back in my chair, amused and happy for her. I smile. I almost laugh.

Her eyes now wide open, her hands unfolded and motioning in front of her to help her talk, she says, "I was married twenty-eight years, so I've been out of this dating business. But twenty-eight years ago, with a simple acquaintance, that sort of action was wrong."

"Oh Bessie, I don't think what's his name . . ."

"His name is Jack."

"I don't think Jack meant anything. I'm sure he's a nice guy."

"Charles," Bessie says and leans on her elbows across the desk top and toward me. "Isn't it still wrong? Have things changed that much?"

I wait. I feel the tingle in my fingertips. I want a smoke. "No, things haven't changed. Men have always reached down the fronts of women's dresses."

Bessie comes up from her elbows and leans back into her chair, even scoots it a bit farther away from the desk and me. "Well, to me, it's not right." Her face sags. "I'm not ready for that."

"Give him another chance. Or give somebody else another chance."

"No, I think I better stay from people for a while."

"But you shouldn't. You don't have to."

She cocks her head to look very closely at me and smiles faintly. "I have my job. I love my tenants. I think the Lord sends me all my tenants."

"Call him up. Talk to him." My hand now trembles.

"No, I'll pray. The Lord will help me."

"God damn it; don't pray. Do what you want, but don't pray." The words come out almost on their own, without my help.

Bessie starts to say something, but her mouth opens and closes like a fish. "NO. NO. NO. Don't say that."

"Don't say what?" I grab my hand and swivel my butt to turn away from Bessie.

"That word or not to pray."

"Call Jack."

"I'll pray." Bessie crosses her arms and scoots close to the desk. She has, after all, smitten the devil.

I stand, my hand jerks once. I turn away and say over my shoulder, "It's not my business." As I reach for the door, my hand has its own way. I look back at her. Her face softens, and she gets up to open the door for me. "No, sit down, please." I open the door with my other hand. As I step through, I look back at her and shrug my shoulders.

"I have to do this my own way," Bessie says, sits back down, then shrugs her shoulders.

"Good luck," I say.

As soon as I walk out the door, I grab for my pack of cigarettes. I put one in my mouth and light it. The yard boys are at work. The owner's son waves to me. "I'll be out to help in a minute," I say to him. The best friend giggles at me. No doubt, without my working with them the previous day, they had time to come up with drunk jokes. No doubt, they tell Jesus jokes about Bessie. But they are young. I exhale the first puff. I hope—maybe I pray—that someone will answer Bessie's prayers and tell her to give herself and Jack a break. And I hope for my own break.

Like in the Movies

My truck had to choke and spit out black smoke if it was to get much over 55, so most of the long, empty way from Hobbs to Santa Fe, I stayed in the right lane and watched the wide cars that West Texans like to drive whiz by me. You count anything—fence posts, cows, cars—on the long stretch of that ugly moon-looking desert land from Hobbs to Roswell then the high plains between Roswell and Santa Fe, especially if your Tom's Snacks truck is sputtering and coughing and Texans are whizzing past you.

I furnish several bars and convenience stores with Tom's snacks, so the bosses put me in this taller-than-wide truck with sliding side and back doors. Most of my routes are between Hobbs, Portales, and Carlsbad, but the company gave me this temporary assignment, so I have to drive long hours in this stupid truck. Used to, I drove a Peterbilt, long haul, and could pass Texans and most anything else on the highway. It took some skill to drive a semi, not just patience. But I've got trouble at home.

After a night in Santa Fe, I headed up to new territory, Española and then Taos. New accounts, new cheesy crackers, Slim Jims, Nabs, or whatever the hell it is in the back of my truck. I don't make the sale. I just deliver. And I don't eat the stuff. Fifteen years in a truck gave me a paunch and a temper, which in turn made me make a lot of mistakes at home. But I have dropped two pants sizes and am talking to a counselor about the stuff that makes me blow up. I have to learn to accept my own family's differences from me. And my wife thinks it best if I stay at home more. So now I choke on the dust and gravel thrown up behind Peterbilts.

But Taos had this weird effect on me. Hobbs, New Mexico is not a place anybody but my wife would choose to live. But her mamma and daddy are there, so so am I. Taos is where tourists are. Writers and artists and movie people have been coming there for years for whatever reason they come. I was glad to be going; I wanted to look at the scenery, feel mountain air, figure out what it was the writers and artists and movie people come to see. Maybe talk to some locals. Maybe slide off the straight and narrow, open up the old diesel and barrel around some curves.

After I stocked my stores, I found the cheapest motel that I could, the Sun God Inn, checked in; and just before sunset, I bought a six-pack and walked around the Taos plaza, then I sat on this bench in the plaza to drink my beers. With the sun setting, with the altitude, I shivered while I drank my beer. Worse than being cold, there wasn't much to do but look at the tourists gathered on the balconies of Oglevie's restaurant or the La Fonda hotel and the local teenagers gathered at the plaza. We all got some excitement when the teenagers set down their boom boxes and began dancing. It was kind of like watching a dance in a western movie, only the kids weren't doing the right dances.

An Indian with gray streaks in his braids sat on the opposite end of the bench from me. He glanced at me, turned away, then looked again. "Mooch one of your beers?" Local custom, I thought, and gave him one of my beers.

He took a long sip, then pulled a bottle out of his Levi's jacket and took a sip. He pointed the bottle toward me.

"Chase your beer?"

"No."

"White people never want to drink with me, and every goddamn Indian I know does." He took a long pull of the whiskey, then put the bottle back in his pocket. I hadn't seen many Indians, and I knew the movie ones were mostly fake, but he didn't look real. "Where you from?"

"Hobbs."

"Bullshit place, almost as bad as Texas. I lived here most all my life, except for when I grew up in Oklahoma. Been coming to this square for years. I'm Billy." We shook hands.

"Vic Arriola," I said.

Billy looked me up and down, "You Mexcan?"

"Half. My mother's side. My wife's white."

"Good to have a white wife."

I looked over at him, "She's still the old lady, the yoke around your neck."

Billy chuckled: "I had two wives, neither was white. But one stabbed me in the shoulder when I was asleep. She severed some ligament or such shit, and I had to quit the construction business."

"What'd you do?"

"Stopped fucking other women. I really loved her." Billy pushed his rolled-up sleeve over his forearm and showed me the inside of his arm. "Look at this shit." A long scar trailed his vein. "Did that myself when the other wife left. Hurts like hell."

"Why?"

"Scar, man. When the scar heals, you're healed." He shrugged. "But that's mostly Indian bullshit. Now I go to this counselor."

For a second I thought that he could give me some advice. "What kind of counselor?"

"A little old white guy been here for years, long as me, had this hot-looking white woman leave him and kinda gave up on it, if you know what I mean. He talks to me for free 'cause he likes Indians. You stick around, you'll see him walking this black lab he keeps. You want to talk to Clayton Tanner?"

"No, I don't think so." For all I knew, this Tanner guy might be some snake handler, Jesus freak, or witch doctor.

Billy again pulled his bottle out of his pocket and took a sip, then leaned forward to cough, forcing over his shoulders. He chugged my beer to put out the fire from his whiskey, then pointed his bottle toward me. "Exchange a snort for another beer." He straightened and swooshed his braids back over his shoulders with the backs of his hands.

It was a mistake, but I pulled another can loose from the plastic. He grabbed the can and shoved the bottle up under my nose. There was no label on it. I held up the bottle to look at the liquor and swirled it around. "It's gin," Billy said. As I'd seen guys do in the drunk tank, I rubbed the lip with the palm of my hand and raised the neck of the bottle to my lips. Something slick was on the lip of the bottle. I threw my head back and let a big gulp of what Billy said was gin burn its way to my belly.

"Thanks," I said. "Don't taste like any gin I ever had. Gin always had this carrot juice taste to me."

"That's 'cause this is good gin," Billy said. "No carrot juice in this shit."

We both hugged ourselves. "Guess you're cold 'cause your Mexcan. Me, I guess I'm cold cause I'm Kiowa, that's a southern tribe. Kiowas are always in the movies attacking something and killing white people."

"Where's a Mexican go to party?"

"Hey, I know what you're after. Nothing but this local trash hangs out at La Fonda, and somebody ends up cutting somebody. You need a classy joint where white tourists go."

"I'm feeling lucky."

"The Sagebrush Inn, high class, white babes."

* * *

I walked back up the road out of Taos toward the Sun God Inn. I checked on my truck, no broken windows, no flat tires. Kids practicing to be real criminals sometimes broke into my truck and stole the snacks. With my truck okay, I took a hot shower, thinking about how amazing it was that I could be so cold in July. Showered and shaved, I put on two T-shirts and a clean long sleeve western shirt and wished I would have brought a sweater or a jacket. I squashed a golf cap over my head, hoping it would keep me warmer.

Hands in my jeans pockets, my shoulders up around my neck, I hit the road again, walking down the dusty gravel sides of the road, stepping over trash from the new Sonic, the beer bottles, and condoms until I got to the Sagebrush Inn. I wasn't about to drive my Tom's Snacks truck to a place where "classy white people" hung out. So I walked where I drove, next to the gutter.

My wife's favorite movie was the one where this guy is killed and then comes back from the dead and meets Whoopi Goldberg who gets him back together with his wife, and then they do it one last time. My wife even bought the video, and the last time she watched it, she looked over at me like, if I was to get killed, she'd rather me to just stay dead.

People with money stayed at the Sagebrush. It wasn't adobe, but lumber, like an old Western town in the movies. Inside was the bar Billy told me about. It had a long cowboy-saloon-style bar with cow hides in back of it, and hats, lariats, and chaps nailed up along the walls. It had over-stuffed lounge chairs and hard-backed wooden chairs around tables crowded together to give room for a small stage. A trio played on the stage, and some of the customers tried to two step in between the tables and chairs. I decided to avoid the crowd and sat at the bar, my back resting against it, a glass of beer resting on my knee, and looked for a woman.

A pretty woman with a girlish grin and a nice figure, with long brown hair that hung below her shoulders and untrimmed bangs that hung in her face, sat down beside me. As I looked at her, she swiveled in her chair to face the bar, then I swiveled to the bar, and our eyes met in the mirror at the back of the bar. She pulled her head away to look at the people dancing. She kind of jerked her head around, acting like she was looking for somebody, which of course she wasn't. She was alone and scared of being a woman alone in a bar. I've made a few notes while I been on the road. I kept looking at the brown hair, remembering a time in an Oklahoma City motel pool skinny-dipping with a woman who turned out to be a teenager, remembering my wife's own short brown hair.

Finally, when she put a cigarette in her mouth and fished around in her purse for a lighter, I picked up one of the Sagebrush's matchbooks, leaned in front of her, and lit a match smooth as hell, like somebody in one of those old late night movies. She smiled, then put the cigarette in her mouth, and sucked in on it. Now she had to talk to me.

"Could I buy you a beer?" she asked.

This was a surprise. "Sure," I said, glad because of my finances. She dangled her cigarette from one hand. The bartender brought my beer, and I thanked her.

"You're a tourist, I bet," she said.

"How can you tell?"

"You just don't look like a local. Maybe it's your hat."

I took off my golf cap, then put it on her head, leaned away from her, and looked at her. "You're right. It don't look right here. I need one of those mock Western hats you see people wearing."

She reached up and took off the hat, holding it in one hand, her cigarette sticking between her fingers. "You ought to get a new one."

"I'm growing to like it."

"I work in a photography store over off the square. If you have any pictures

130

you want developed, bring them by."

"I don't even own a camera. I like to remember stuff." She looked at the band, then turned around to look at me, trying to get a good look at me without my hat, to see if she was passing the time with a real bow wow of a guy. "Would you like to dance?"

While we danced, she pressed herself close to me and rested her face on the soft spot of my shoulder, and I tried to steer us around tables while keeping step. I thought about my wife teaching me to dance years ago, so I wouldn't look foolish at a wedding reception. I couldn't remember the last time I had danced with her, and here was this poor girl suffering from my lack of practice. "My name is Vic," I whispered.

"My name is Wendy, Vic. Do you have any pot?" she asked.

"All the pot I have is three hundred miles away." Every once in a while, with the kids in bed, the Mrs. and I liked to roll one and smoke it in bed. I've heard doctors say it hurts your sexual drive, but friends tell me it's supposed to make you uninhibited and help you get laid.

"I don't smoke too much," she added quickly.

"Neither do I," I said.

After our dance we got our drinks off the bar and found a quiet, dark table in a corner to sit at. As the night wore on, as we bought each other more drinks (she liked tequila sunrises), we reached across the table and held hands. "What do you do for a living?" she said.

I hesitated, then said, "I work for Tom's Snacks."

Her eyes opened widely for a moment, "Are you going to move to Taos?"

"I'd like to."

She dropped her head, and her eyes looked up at me, making her look like a teenager. "It's a nice place, huh?"

"Yeah."

"The Sagebrush is a nice place too," she said. Again she dropped her head, so she had to raise her eyes to see me, looking like this sixties French actress, all sexy and innocent at the same time or like those photos of the girls of the Big Ten or such in *Playboy*. She had probably used that look to attract high school football players. "I stayed here the first night I was in town." Then she lit up a cigarette. The words of my wife and my counselor about delaying my impulses, being content with what my life was and such, kept sneaking into my brain, kind of like the good angel Goofy in those Disney cartoons that beans the bad devil Goofy with his harp. Then I wondered what kind of advice Billy's voodoo, witch doctor, white-guy counselor, whatever he was, might give me.

"Maybe I better go," I said. Wendy again dropped her head, and I looked into her round, innocent eyes. "Tonight, now?"

"I've got a few phone calls to make."

"Maybe, I better be going too," she said, "I've got work tomorrow." I held her hand, and she said, "If you want a cup of coffee, I live right up the road. Take a left at the Ranchos de Taos cut off. First road to your right, a mobile home park, lot twenty-three." She got up and slung her jean jacket over her shoulder, and I watched her butt and the way it moved around on the underside of her jeans. Bad Goofy kicked Good Goofy's ass.

I had a dilemma. I couldn't drive up to her mobile home park in my Tom's Snack's truck. What if she lived with her parents? What would they think? Since I had already walked so far, I thought I could hoof it to her trailer. I had trouble at home, and walking to her mobile home sure wasn't going to help with what I had been working on.

I walked to the bar, pushed between two guys, and asked the bartender for directions. I felt this one guy watching me. I turned and saw this Indian with graying hair tied in braids hanging down over his shoulders. He swooshed the braids back over his shoulders with the back of his hands. It was dark, but I could see that his eyes were shiny red.

He tilted his head and said, "I know Tae Kwan Do." He held up his hands and wiggled his fingers. "I could rip your throat out with my fingers, or I could pray to my ancestors to grant you a safe trip back home."

"I'd ruther you pray for me, Billy," I said.

He shook his head like he was clearing it and leaned his head closer to mine, "You're that Mexcan guy."

I made a stupid offer. "If I buy you a drink will you give me a ride?"

Billy turned back around to face the bar and banged on it with the flat of his palm. When the bartender came, he ordered two bourbons, straight, neat, one for him, one for me. "How'd you get here, Mexcan?"

"Walked. All I got is this stupid truck. And this woman says to come by for coffee. She lives in the mobile homes toward Ranchos de Taos."

"Know right where it is," he said, slammed his flat hand on the bar, brushed his braids back over his shoulders, and ordered another bourbon as the bartender sat our two shots in front of us.

"You ain't drunk that one, yet," I said. He downed it.

We each sipped our bourbons, and I got a little of the fuzzy head, too fuzzy to figure right. What kept working its way through the fuzz was that some good-looking young woman, who dipped her eyes like this French movie star did, was waiting for me. "Come on, let's go," I said.

"Drink your whiskey," Billy said.

I took a sip and then paid my tab. I had seven dollars left in my wallet, and Billy still looked thirsty. "So what do you do around here?" I asked, hoping to take his mind off the whiskey he wanted me to buy him.

"I could make a living around here if I'd dress the part for the tourists and talk shit. You know like in the movies. Some old fart around here wears a goddamn loin cloth wrapped up under his ass. What the hell for? I ain't gonna do that. I'm a fucking artist."

"You mean a real artist at fucking or you mean you're sensitive or something?"

"Shit no, I'm real. Come on out to the Pueblo. I got paintings out there. I'll make you a good deal." He sipped his bourbon, then added, "But don't tell no white people or Indians look like they are in charge I'm a Kiowa."

I got interested. "You're really an artist? You can make a living at that?"

"Hell, I made $5,000 six years ago." He banged his hand on the bar. "Bought a truck, wrecked it right after that."

"What you driving now?"

"Motor scooter."

Sure enough, the drunk Indian had this little moped. With me on the back, holding him around his chest, we drove on the very edge of the highway, on the gravel, in amongst the beer bottles, Sonic wrappers, and condoms. My shoulders hunched up around my neck, and my teeth chattered. I'm not a little man, and Billy was bigger than me, so that moped grunted worse than my truck and shook sideways. But Billy knew right where he was going, and from the right hand edge of the highway, he cut across one lane, the center stripe, and then the other lane to turn left on the Ranchos de Taos Road.

Wendy lived in Talpa in a trailer park full of broken tricycles and rusting beer cans. I prided myself on being a financial step or two out of this kind of place. I begged Billy to stop at the gate. He leaned his moped against the gate and reached into his pocket. He brought out two joints. "I ain't no cheap mooch Indian." He handed me two joints. "White chicks get horny when you even show them this shit. Give 'em peyote, they're your slaves. But I ain't got no peyote." He walked with me toward number twenty-three, and I told him to wait away from the front door but to make sure I got in.

Before I could walk away, he grabbed my arm and jerked me back to him. "When somebody pulls a knife on you, you gonna get cut, man. None of this Rambo, jujitsu shit, like in the movies. Your ass is gonna bleed. When that bitch stabbed me a second time, she punctured my liver and gave me some kind of poisoning. Had to quit my job again."

"What'd you do to her?"

"Hell, I was bleeding. Couldn't do nothing. I loved her, but I had to leave her after that."

I pulled away and walked to the door. I heard one of those theme songs from an old TV show, the kind that is so awful you don't want it humming in your head, but it's always there, even if you've seen the show only twice.

I jumped back when a sliver of light spread the length of the door. I heard

Wendy, "Vic?"

I looked back at Billy, who clasped his hands together and raised them over his head like he was a winning prize fighter; then I looked back at Wendy. "I don't really have a car. I got this stupid Tom's Snacks truck. And I don't do this too often. And all I want, really, is maybe a cup of coffee and a little talk." I looked to see Billy walking down the gravel road of the trailer park. He got his feet tangled in some tricycle or other such kid toy. I heard him say, "Fuck," and saw him fall down. Before I could see if he got up, Wendy grabbed my hand and pulled me into her trailer.

We started kissing in the living room; then she steered me down her dark hall and into the bedroom. We plopped on the bed fully dressed but started tugging at each other's pants, shirts, underwear, neither one really sure there in the dark if the other was all the way undressed.

I wanted to see her, to know what kind of body she had, and to memorize this whole thing for times when I would need the memory. Memory of this notch on my pistol might keep me off other women. Then, while we rolled around, she gasped like the air was sucked out of her. I heard her whimper, and I stiffened my shoulders in case she had a knife.

"What's wrong?" I asked.

"I don't do this very often."

"Neither do I," I said.

She pushed me off her, then rolled up in a little ball under my arm. She rested there, and after awhile, she breathed in deep, then rolled toward me and started kissing me a lot slower and stroking the back of my head, and I felt her hand gliding down my thighs until it came to my underwear, which was halfway down my thighs because she hadn't gotten me all the way undressed before.

I started shaking because I was excited and because I was cold, but I stopped being cold when she called me "honey" and rolled over on top of me.

* * *

I woke up too early the next morning and rolled over to look at Wendy in the dawn light. Her smeared purple mascara made war paint marks down her cheeks. The makeup on some parts of her face cracked; at other places it sparkled in tiny little crystals in the sunlight. Her tits had been touched up with silicone. They pointed straight up whichever way Wendy rolled. My wife had a pair just like them; we bought them instead of the newer used car I wanted.

I pushed myself up and slipped into my jeans. I walked through her narrow hall toward the trailer's kitchen. When I got to the kitchen, "Hi," someone said.

A curly-headed boy, about eleven or twelve, sat at the table drinking from a large glass of milk. "Hi," I said back.

"I'm Kevin. Wendy's kid," he said.

I reached my hand across the table and said, "I'm Vic." He shook my hand, then took another drink of milk.

"You Indian?" he asked.

"Mexican," I said.

"We got some Captain Crunch if you like that," he said.

"No. No," I said.

"How about some coffee?" said a voice from the hall door. Wendy was slumping against the doorframe.

"Hi, Mom," Kevin said.

"I'd like some coffee," I said.

"Instant is all I have."

"Fine," I said.

Wendy dug into a drawer next to her stove and came out with a black pan. She filled it with water and put it on the stove. As she stretched up on her toes to reach into a cabinet for the jar of coffee, the short robe rose up over her full butt and showed her panties. She quickly tugged at the hem of the robe and dropped to the soles of her feet. I got the jar of coffee.

"Bye, Mom," Kevin said, grabbed some books from off the drainboard, and walked to the door.

"You too big for a kiss?" Wendy said, and Kevin walked to her and kissed her on the cheek. In another year or so, he would be. He would start to bitch about his dumb mother and worry her stupid. But now he kissed her.

"Bye, Vic," Kevin said as he went out the trailer door.

We sat across from each other and dipped our heads to keep from staring at each other, but we both wanted to see what we had gone to bed with the night before. The water started to boil, and I went back to her bedroom to dress. When I got back to the kitchen, Wendy had two cups of instant coffee sitting on the table. "Do you need a spoon, milk, sugar?"

"No," I said. I took a quick sip of coffee and burned my lip and tongue.

"Be careful. It's hot," Wendy said. I was just another pick-up, another mistake, another try. She looked me straight in the eye but was polite. "I'm thinking about moving to Seattle," Wendy said. "I hear the schools are better there."

We finished drinking our coffee, saying nothing. After a while, when it was time to leave, I leaned across the table to kiss her. Not expecting a kiss, she raised her coffee cup to her lips. I waited, poised above her. She laughed, lowered the coffee cup, and kissed me. Her breath was sour, as I was sure mine was. She put both hands behind my neck and hugged me. "See ya," she said.

"I really wish I could."

"I do too. Could you stay another day?"

I shook my head. She dropped her head, looked up at me like she did the night before, and said, "It was nice. See ya."

I walked out of her trailer and hunched myself against the morning chill. I realized that I had no ride home. On top of that I didn't know where I was. I knocked on the door, and she answered it, laughing at me. As I hugged myself, I said, "I got no ride."

"Give me time to make myself presentable," she said and let me back in. I watched her walked down her narrow hall. Her butt was indeed big, her legs had some veins lining them, the back of her neck had gotten way too much sun and was kind of leathery-looking. She looked like my wife.

After Wendy showered and dressed, we walked to her Chevy parked beside the trailer. At the entrance a moped leaned against a barbed wire fence post that made one end of the gate. "Shit," I said and ran for the moped. I saw Billy curled up in the homemade drainage ditch that ran alongside the drive. I bent over him and heard him snoring. I felt his shoulder. There was this lump on it, not muscle but some twisted, damaged flesh.

Wendy was beside me. "Who is that? Should we call the police?"

"No. . ." I said, then thought, "No, honey." She closed her eyes while she kissed me on the forehead.

"You know him? Is he a friend?"

"He was my ride last night."

"You want to wake him up?"

"No, I don't want to listen to him."

Still shivering, I reached into my shirt pocket and felt the two crushed joints. I put them back in Billy's shirt pocket, then pulled the braids out of his face. "Shit," I said to myself, and for no good damn reason, opened my wallet, pulled out my last seven dollars, and stuck those three bills in Billy's shirt pocket. "You're giving your money to that bum?" Wendy asked.

"I guess so," I said. "You think I could borrow a couple of bucks? I'm good for it. I'll mail it." Wendy gave me a twenty.

When she dropped me off, several parking tickets lined the windshield. I turned back around and saw her still looking at me. If it was like in the movies, I would have run up to her and kissed her, and we would have driven off together and left my truck to rot. Or we would have slowly pulled ourselves out of each other's arms and driven away to always remember a special night. But Wendy didn't look like she'd be that interested if I was killed and come back from the dead. All I could do was wave bye, leaving her to her trouble, and drive back to my trouble at home.

Part IV
Walter and Sarah

The Truly Talented Writer

TTWs [Truly Talented Writers] will surely slow down the dread development process. . . TTWs can't be seduced. They want to be, but don't know how it works. . . .Not that they don't like company—they crave company—it's just that they seek it at more unconventional settings than you do.

Lynda Rosen Obst, *American Film* April 1987

1

To Walter Boone, writing was mainly bullshitting, and he figured that the Lord himself loved a good bullshitter. Walter was a great bullshitter. It was the other parts of writing that he had trouble with.

You couldn't really say Walter was a failure. He didn't so much fail as refuse to succeed. Walter would do any wrong thing to avoid doing the right thing if somebody, even his wife, wanted him to do that right thing. When wives, lovers, friends, or colleagues urged Walter to succeed, they seemed to lose their appreciation for bullshitting, so they lost their appreciation for what Walter did best and what he most valued. This is why he wrote one good screenplay and then no more. But Vance Orton, not knowing he was an easy tool for Walter, gave Walter yet another chance to re-write his one good screenplay, *The Circles of Hell*, one more time. And Walter once again had a chance to be a really great bullshitter.

Walter Boone first saw Vance Orton between the V that his feet made as he rested them on the edge of his bathtub. Sally Curtsinger had just whispered to him, "Who is that man?" And Walter spread his 10 ½ s apart to see Vance framed by the empty rectangle that had been his bathroom door.

Walter didn't know that Vance meant him no physical harm. In fact, as Vance was then saying, he meant to catapult Walter over the mundane, work-a-day walls that confound most of us and into the privileged world of Hollywood glory and money. As Walter was to realize, Vance was nearly harmless. If Walter had listened to his answering machine or paid attention to more of his mail, he might have learned that Vance was eagerly looking for him. In fact, Vance was so desperate to find Walter that he trailed him through a series of cheap Mexican restaurants and sleazy bars.

But, since Walter knew none of this, he reached across his tub, crooked his finger through the handle of the linen cabinet under the sink, opened its door, and grabbed the .38 that he kept under his towels. Walter leaned back into the warm bath water and aimed the pistol at Vance Orton.

Walter saw Sally lower herself into the water until her tits floated. They were like giant apples, worth bobbing for, even in dirty bath water. "My God, my God," Sally muttered as she watched. Walter and Sally had heard Vance's knock at the front door. He should have answered this knock. But Walter did not want to get out of his bathtub, leave Sally, drip soapy water through his house, and answer the door to listen to a Jehovah's Witness witness to him, the neighbor complain about the high grass in his front yard, or a bill collector try to repossess something. A sane man, Walter figured, would have turned his ass to the door and left. But Walter did not then know that Vance worked for the movies.

Vance saw Walter before Walter could pull the trigger and shot both his hands into the air. Walter aimed and watched Vance shake. He decided not to shoot Vance. Burglars rarely worked in daylight and rarely wore shiny, loose-fitting suits, pink tuxedo shirts with no tie, Italian loafers that looked more like house slippers, gold rings, and sunglasses. "You got him. You got him," Sally said and squiggled in the water, making a wake that splashed over the sides of the tub and nearly got Walter's gun wet.

Walter cocked his head to see Vance out of his good eye and rested his elbow on the side of his tub and pointed the gun up at the ceiling. He probably couldn't have hit anything without his glasses. "You want something?" Walter asked.

Vance kept his hands up and took a careful step toward Walter. "Are you Walter Boone?" Vance asked.

Walter slowly lowered the gun. Vance stepped back. "The car and the microwave are paid for."

"I'm not here to take anything," Vance said. "I'm here to give you something." He smiled like the investment counselor who had talked Walter into buying stocks that still were losing money.

"I don't want anything," Walter said and stretched to set the gun on the toilet lid.

"Talk to him, Walter," Sally said and poked Walter in the side.

Vance stepped gracefully into the bathroom. "I'm here to save your reputation as a screenwriter." Walter then knew that this man was not a burglar but another movie man with a deal.

"I don't want to be a screenwriter," Walter said.

"I can offer you an advance and an option."

Walter leaned across the tub, took his pistol off the toilet lid, and put it back in the linen cabinet. "Why don't you grab a seat," Walter said, and Vance sat on the toilet. "I want to be the man responsible for finally making *The Circles of Hell* into the film that it deserves to be." Walter looked at Vance's sheer socks that looked almost like a woman's dark tinted hose.

"Why don't you sit in the bedroom?" Walter said.

Vance stood up. "No problem. You got it. No problem."

140

"A movie deal," Sally said and looked at Walter. "You didn't tell me you were in the movies."

Walter shrugged and stood up. Water ran down the outward curve of his belly and dripped into the bath. Sally wiped at the water that dripped off him and onto her face. "Excuse me, Sally," Walter said. Vance kept talking. Walter grabbed a towel. Then, he bent into the linen cabinet and got a towel for Sally.

Vance kept talking: "I'm a producer, and I mean to make my mark. And your screenplay is just what I," Vance hesitated, "*We*, what *we* need." Walter figured the kid to call himself a producer. Most of Hollywood's overpaid "concept" men called themselves producers. The kid continued, "One of my secretaries who reads our optioned scripts during her lunch hour found your script. She brought it to me and said it was one of the most interesting she had ever read. I agreed. Then I did some research on you and *The Circles of Hell*."

Walter held the towel while Sally stood. She took the towel, wrapped it around herself, pushed it against her chest, making her tits bulge into a fold above the towel, and clasped it behind her with her other hand. Walter admired her tight can that barely drooped at all. Then Sally cleared her throat so that he would take his eyes off her private parts. She jerked her chin toward Vance Orton, who was now talking about distributions and profit percentages.

"Excuse me" Walter said. "But the lady, as inviting to look at as she is," Walter turned to smile at Sally, and she smiled back, "would like a little privacy in order to dry those good-looking parts." Vance's mouth hung slack.

"Oh, oh, my, okay, okay," Vance said. "Excuse me. Please, ma'am. Please forgive me."

Vance turned his back. Walter would have closed his bathroom door, but he no longer had one. Three months before, a little drunk, Walter thought he had heard a real burglar. Walter's had turned into a bad neighborhood, and so Walter closed himself in the bathroom and waited; then he fired one round into the door. He chuckled and fired two more rounds into the door for the hell of it. He couldn't afford a new door, so Walter took the old one down.

Walter dried himself as he walked into the bedroom. He found his jockey shorts on the floor and pulled them and a pair of shorts on. He found his glasses with the one thick lens for his aiming eye in the folds of the still warm sheets on his King-size bed. Just before their bath, Walter and Sally had chased each other around his bed, one of his few remaining pieces of furniture, and had eventually caught each other. Walter walked to Vance, who obediently kept his back to the bathroom door, and tapped him on the shoulder, "Maybe we ought to talk in my living room."

"Oh, yes, yes," Vance said and followed him.

Walter shoved a month's stack of *Times* off his couch and motioned for Vance to sit down. Vance sat down and started talking. To make a house payment four months ago, Walter sold all of his living room furniture except his sofa, so he went to the dining room and brought back a chair, stepping over the pizza carton with the two left over pieces of pizza, the open can of bean dip, the half empty package of Fritos, and the empty beer cans. He sat the chair across from Vance. "Sally and I had a party last night." It was more like an orgy. Walter looked back toward his bedroom and interrupted Vance, "That woman is forty-seven years old. Can you believe it? Have you ever seen a chassis like that on a woman over forty?"

Vance blinked and said, "She's a regular Madonna."

"It's all done with mirrors in the movies," Walter said. "Sally is real."

"She's quite a lady," Vance said.

Sally came in as Vance finished his sentence, and Walter was glad that she got to hear Vance. She had her hair pushed up and pinned, a couple of strands hanging down. She had on her jeans, her aerobic dance shoes, and one of Walter's T-shirts. She bent to kiss Walter goodbye and to whisper into his ear, "Thank you." Walter got up to walk her out to her car, but she said, "Oh please, stay and entertain your guest." She blew a kiss at Walter as she left.

"You're a hard man to find," Vance said. "I tried to call. I left messages on your answering machine."

"I forget to play them." Walter wished that Sally had stayed. After the bath together, they might have had another roll in the sheets. He had met her two weeks before eating a meal alone at one of those late-night pie shops. In the mornings, she had to get back to her house because her husband would call from a truck stop.

"A neighbor told me that you like to go to the poker games in Gardena."

"I like to watch the people there. Little old ladies staining the cards with their greasy fingers."

"I went there, and the man who lets you in gave me your address," Vance said.

Walter wished that Charlie, the deskman at the Gardena poker club, had kept his mouth shut so that he would have had more time with Sally and her body.

Vance then told Walter his life story and about how he happened upon a copy of *The Circles of Hell*. All Walter wanted from the movie people was his $8,000 a year for the option on his script. He had two more years on the option. Sometimes, Walter wished that he had never written the script and come to Hollywood. He'd still be married and teaching at that Texas cowboy college, Sul Ross State University. But the screenplay bought him a good life during the five years that it twice went into production. It got him some bonuses and up-front money for other screenplays, which he never quite finished, and the options on it allowed him an escape from complete destitution.

Vance was the latest young hot shot out to make a name for himself. In the last six years, three Vances had found Walter. But none of them mentioned the name *Robert Redford*.

"Redford has expressed an interest," Vance said. "And Redford plays 'good'. We need a rewrite. The hero needs less trouble. The divorce is okay. The neurosis, the booze, the depression are out. And we need fewer literary types in hell. Some more show business people. Some more contemporary people, some people impersonators could do."

Walter rubbed his chin. "Contemporary, meaning that you want people not yet dead in hell?"

Vance smiled. "Some deserve it."

Walter shoved the nose bridge of his glasses back up his nose with his thumb. "This means money, right?"

"You'll get points, and not just of the profits but of the gross."

"What can I have now?" Walter asked.

And, due to synchronicity or serendipity, Vance pulled $5,000 out of his pocket and said, "That is just a start. I'll give you another $25,000 against the $100,000 for completion. That's $100,000 and points." Walter knew that he'd get screwed out of most of the $100,000 and the points too, if the picture ever got made. One time, he got an advance on $200,000 for a script. He never finished it. Then his price dropped to $75,000, then to union rates. He couldn't even pay his union dues this past year.

Vance Orton stood over Walter, patted him on the back, and said, "I mean to resurrect your career." Then Vance added, "And start mine. Partners?" Vance asked and stuck out his hand for Walter to shake.

"You bet," Walter said and counted his money.

* * *

Vance Orton was not insecure. Rather, Vance, knowing himself well, knew his limits. All through his college then Wall Street careers, he kept bumping against his limits. So he needed some reassurance after he committed a sizeable chunk of his studio's money to Walter Boone. He knew how to pitch the project, but he wasn't too sure how good the project was. He was operating on rumor and reputation. That is why he called his personal secretary, Traci Miller, into his office after he finally found Walter Boone.

Traci Miller had been the secretary of a chain-smoking story editor, but ambitious and trying to teach herself how to write, Traci had used her lunch breaks to read the old, unproduced screenplays gathering dust in a backroom of the studio's. She had found *The Circles of Hell* and asked her boss why it had never been made. The chain smoking story editor told her the legend. Then she saw Vance in the elevator and told him about the wonderful script that she had found. Vance asked her to his office to tell him about the script.

Traci Miller could pass for a co-ed. She had small but scoop-like breasts that matched the naturalness of her hair. She had worn her hair and breasts that way when she walked into Vance's office, stood across from his desk, and told Vance why she thought *The Circles of Hell* deserved the reputation it had. And when she talked about movies, she sounded like a college professor.

And, to Vance, with the sunlight from his large picture window making her hair a golden halo, she could have been a prophet. Vance knew his limits, but he also knew about that grand kind of luck that slaps you in the face if you can position yourself into the right place at the right time. Vance was not about to blow the chance that the prophet Traci Miller had given him. Despite a year in an assistant directors training program and another two years being groomed by the studio, Vance then realized that it was Traci, the story editor's secretary, who was showing him the glamour and sizzle of Hollywood. Vance began the deliberate and careful manipulating that was his strong point. The story editor's mind was as smoky as his office, so Vance wasn't about to trust him. What he did was to promote Traci to his own personal secretary. And then he began his search for Walter Boone.

Now Vance squinted to see Traci better and thought how he could really go for this girl. But Vance knew better than to mix romance and work. And, since he knew his limits, he knew that Traci really was smarter than he was.

"Have a seat," Vance said to Traci and watched her as she sat in the padded, swiveling chair in front of his desk and cocked one knee over her other. She wore no hose under her short denim skirt, and Vance, in what time he had before he gave himself away, stared at her bare knees.

"Mr. Orton?" she said, and her smile lit up Vance's office.

Vance tapped his Cross pen on the table then stood. He caught himself staring at the first button of Traci's blouse and the cleavage formed by her white sculpted breasts. "Is *The Circles Of Hell* really that good?"

Traci's chair squeaked as she swiveled toward him. "It is the best script I've read since I've been here."

Vance wanted to kiss her, but instead, he dropped to his knees in front of her chair and said to her, "You really think so? I've committed a lot of money to this. I have to feel good about this."

"It's self indulgent."

Vance looked in her blue eyes. "That's bad. Right?" Vance said.

Traci grew cute as she slid her mouth to one side of her face and stared up. She looked this way when she thought, and when she thought, she looked like a youngster asking to be seduced. Vance touched her upper arm. "Walter Boone wants more to please his own fantasies and humor than to tell a good story. But that self indulgence gives it a certain extravagance."

Traci bit her bottom lip and looked up. Vance looked at her eyes. She really was delightfully young. Vance grabbed the arms of her swiveling chair, slightly shook it, and said, "Yes, yes. So?"

"That extravagance gives it a 'certain magnitude.'"

"Like Aristotle says." Vance remembered the term that wriggled itself loose from a sticky place in the back part of his brain. "I studied that."

"It has 'spectacle,'" Traci said.

"And that's good for the movie business." Vance waited for Traci to confirm him.

"Aristotle would like movies," Traci said. She couldn't be as young as she looked, but she couldn't be as old as she sounded.

Vance sprang up and rubbed his hands together. "It's gonna be a great movie," Vance said and turned to look at Traci. She wasn't smiling. In fact, she hung her head and stared down at her bare knees. "Traci, Traci?" Vance uttered.

"I said that it was a good script, but I can't quite see it becoming a Hollywood movie."

Vance clamped his jaw shut, and somewhere way down in his guts, below his stomach, some hot liquid began to gurgle. It was a feeling that he had had on his best day and worst day on Wall Street. It was the feeling he had had when he took his oral exams for his M.B.A. "You didn't say that before." Vance lowered his hand down his chest and over his stomach. "Why didn't you tell me that?" Vance began to think that maybe Traci was manipulating him.

Vance concentrated on keeping the boiling liquid in his guts out of his throat. "Mr. Orton, with the right director . . ."

"But it wouldn't be an embarrassing movie. It would be a noble attempt because it would be a difficult movie to make." Vance's vision let him see the easy, highway-like path up the studio's corporate ladder. He needed the bosses' enthusiasm and a respectable movie. He didn't need good reviews or box office. What mattered was vision. With this project, Vance could prove to his bosses that he could recognize talent, develop it, and put together the deal and the production. If he could prove to the execs that he had movie savvy, he could be into the really big chips.

"It is more literary in its vision than cinematic," Traci said. She stood and faced Vance. As he mulled over her words, Vance thought she looked like an ingénue. He wanted to kiss her.

"Even if we fail, we win," Vance said to her.

Traci did not have the movie savvy that Vance knew he had, "What?"

"Who could criticize us for trying? Just think what we could do with a less ambitious project. Think of the public relations. Our integrity. This studio's dedication to giving art a chance." Vance's mind was racing and subduing the burning in his gut. Vance grabbed Traci's shoulders and looked at her face. Her mouth slid to one side of her face and her eyes raised. She may know about plots and celluloid images, but her mind could not keep up with Vance's inspirational 20/20 foresight of reality. That was why he was the executive producer, and she was the unknowing messenger of God.

"Thank you, Traci," Vance said and patted her shoulder. "I needed a little support."

Vance pulled his hands behind him, smiled, and rocked back and forth on his heels. Traci got out of the chair. "Thank you, Traci," he said again, and Traci took two steps backwards, nodded, and backed out of Vance's office.

When Traci Miller closed Vance's door behind her, Vance leaped into his padded leather chair and spun it around. Walter Boone was putty in his hands. Traci could be an easy tool. Vance Orton was now certain that he would become the next hot shot wunderkind in the studio. Vance propped his feet up on his desk, dreamed about the future, and entertained the vagrant thought that maybe he should have kissed Traci.

* * *

When Vance's check and an American Express Card arrived in the mail, Walter Boone almost forgot all the philosophy he had studied and prayed to an old-fashioned Christian God. He spent nearly $500 getting his aging Porsche cleaned, waxed, and tuned and taking Sally out for an expensive meal, a play at the Mark Taper forum, and a late night walk along Santa Monica beach. First class all the way. That night, while Sally lay beside him and snored sweetly, almost inaudibly, the way you'd think your grandmother might, Walter fingered his newly vitalized checkbook and the American Express Card. In the two days that Walter had again been writing, he had written nothing, but he was financially solvent.

Walter knew about his guardian angel. Vance Orton had gone to some eastern school, not Harvard or Yale, but one that would look prestigious enough to West Coast Hollywood people. He put in time on Wall Street, where he probably got bored because he craved something more serious than making money. So he took his chances, went to the assistant directors school, and landed a peachy job with one of the movie studios. He put away his Brooks Brothers suit and dressed himself in the looser Hollywood fashions. Walter knew that they weren't really studios anymore, just packagers and distributors, but they had money and a gambler's mentality, kind of like the old ladies at the Gardena poker houses. And, every once in a while, an Orange County widow or divorcee would take home a bundle. Vance intended to use Walter's screenplay to chisel his star into the Hollywood boulevard running through the minds of the studio execs.

Walter's screenplay was about a professor of popular culture. This professor studied his own culture in order to excavate the minds of his contemporaries. As a result, the professor got confused. Everything he saw was a metaphor or a footnote to his next article or book. Context was reality for Walter's professor. So his wife left him. His students dropped his classes. And he became lost in a dark woods and wound up in hell. Charlie Chaplin was his guide through the circles of hell. The script had some cultural allusions to warm the calloused hearts of critics, great special effects, and the artistic merit that made movie makers feel good about themselves.

Unlike his protagonist, who made Walter a living for the past twelve years, Walter Boone was not about to confuse what he did for a living with living. So he enjoyed Sally Curtsinger's body. Her husband would soon return from his trucking, so the next morning, Walter dropped her off at her San Fernando Valley home, kissed her goodbye and, with a functional American Express and a fat wallet, drove to Alpine, Texas to find his ex-wife.

* * *

2

Traci Miller lay on her back on her sofa, her head propped up by two pillows, held open *The Circles of Hell*, the spine of the bound script resting on her belly, and read about the cultural scientist, who was to become Robert Redford, and Charlie Chaplin in hell. She was reading about hell's surgery room.

Hitler, without any anesthesia, howls and cusses in German as Jews, dressed in concentration camp pajamas, cut on him, stick their dirty hands inside of him, and pull out his organs. Also in the operating room are Karl Marx and Sigmund Freud. They are under anesthesia and babble unconsciously about the proletariat's surrender to consumerism and about feminism as another form of domineering mothering. Meanwhile, two teams of surgeons cut open the crowns of their heads. The surgeons take off their surgical masks and introduce themselves to Robert Redford. Then Anna Freud, Carl Jung, and several professorial looking types begin to eat Freud's brain, and Mao Tse Tung, Uncle Joe Stalin, and Nikolai Lenin begin eating Marx's brain.

Traci slammed the covers of the script shut and sat up on her sofa. She sniffed the air around her. Her sweat was making the acrid smell in her apartment. She had hurriedly gone out for her jog to get her four miles in before the sun set and the muggers came out.

Even as she had broken a sweat and even as the shock of jogging shoes on concrete had worked its way into her hips, she could not keep from thinking about Walter Boone's script. Walter's script had such a spell over Traci that she didn't shower after her jog but lay down on her sofa and began reading. And, like all the producers and directors before her, this mere secretary was confirming that *The Circles of Hell* would probably be a terrible movie.

Traci got up off her sofa and walked to her bathroom. She left a trail of sweaty, smelly jogging clothes—sweat top, T-shirt, socks, shorts—across the floor of her efficiency apartment as she stripped on her way to her bathroom.

Tonight she was lucky. The water was lukewarm. At this time of night, the mostly Asian tenants of her apartment building, which was just west of downtown Los Angeles, had used all of the hot water. Traci quickly shampooed her hair and soaped herself, then held her head under the nozzle of the shower until the water started to grow cold. She stepped out of the shower and dripped water on her bathroom floor as she dried. She wrapped a dry towel around herself, walked to her kitchen, pulled out a chunk of cheese and a diet coke from her refrigerator, got crackers from her cabinet, went back to her sofa, and with her food and drink on her coffee table, curled around Walter's script.

Despite the fact that she had quit U.S.C. and had flunked out of two community colleges because she had been bored to distraction (and thus failure) by the students and the instructors, Traci knew that she knew enough to figure out what was so intriguing about this script. So she read the script over and over.

Now, no longer a five-dollar-an-hour story editor's secretary but a salaried personal executive secretary, she could move into a one-bedroom apartment farther west in L.A.—if she could keep her new position. Her new position was tied to Vance Orton's sense of his Hollywood destiny, and Traci didn't know what telling Vance about her misgivings about *The Circles of Hell* might do to his destiny.

* * *

Walter Boone had figured out his Hollywood destiny, so his old Porsche was kicking up dust while he wondered if he was on the right gravel road. Fourteen years earlier, he had bought property and built a house off the highway between Marfa and Alpine. Walter remembered a cattle guard and a slow climb until you reached the flat grazing land in Texas's Davis Mountains meadows. He had gone over a cattle guard and had passed several grazing Herefords, but he was still not sure where he was. Then he drove through an open gate. A rancher wouldn't leave it open. Then he recognized the two-story log house that used to be his.

Fifteen years before, the rancher who owned this property got tired of hopelessly trying to make a living raising cattle, so he got together with a real estate man from Fort Worth and a builder from Alpine, divided up some of his property, and tried to sell rustic cabins on ten-acre lots. Rustic retreats were "in" all over Texas, but the Davis Mountains area was just too far away from anything. Only Walter and two others bought the rancher's rustic lots.

Walter heard a chainsaw bite into wood, and he knew that Sarah was home. He got out of his eleven-year-old Porsche and walked toward the direction of the whir. He had left the perfect 72-degree weather of Los Angeles and stayed in 80-degree weather in Tucson. But now, in Texas, which he remembered as hot and dusty, he shivered. He passed the side of the log cabin and saw logs in different widths and lengths stacked against its wall. He heard the chainsaw sputter, and he

148

rounded the corner of his house and saw Sarah bent over and dusting the rough-textured wooden Indian face that she had just cut out of a log. Her breath sent a cloud of vapor into the Indian's face.

It was cold with a few clouds, but the sun was out. Walter hugged himself then put his flat hand over his eyes to keep the sun's glare out of his face and to see Sarah better. She had a pair of bug-eyed goggles pushed back on her forehead. She wore an insulated vest and a long-sleeve flannel shirt with the sleeves rolled up. She still had the forearms and biceps of a man. Even before she starting freeing the faces and figures trapped inside pine logs, Sarah had a man's muscles from slinging clay. Around her were discarded sculptures with split or splintered faces or weird contorted features.

She had married Walter when they both finished graduate school; then he brought her with him when he started teaching at Sul Ross State University, a school whose most distinguished alumnus was Hoss Cartwright. While he taught Plato and comma rules to ranchers' and illegal aliens' kid, she taught a pottery class part time. When she filed against Walter and left him in Los Angeles, she needed a better living than what Sul Ross State University was willing to pay her for teaching a couple of art classes. So she became one of this country's most prominent chainsaw sculptors. You could see her work in nearly every souvenir and curio shop off every major highway in the southwest.

Sarah straightened, lowered the goggles, and yanked the rope of the chainsaw. Just as it started to whine, she saw Walter. She turned off the chainsaw and stared at him through the bug-eyed goggles. Walter could have used this image to describe the alien in the one science fiction script he had tried to doctor. "Walter?" she said and cocked her head to look at Walter and slowly approached him as if he might be a rattler. "What do you want?" She held the large chainsaw idly in one arm as though it were a purse or a light sack of groceries.

Walter approached her, knowing that his smile was beaming. "I have money and a studio's credit card."

"My God, did you rob somebody, Walter?"

"No, it's legit."

"What's it for?"

"I'm writing again."

"What?"

"*The Circles of Hell.*"

"Again?" Sarah smiled, and the smile made her relax so that she felt the weight of the chainsaw, looked down at it, and then laid it down. "You could have been a good professor, a good writer, a good husband. But you've turned out to be a really good bullshitter."

"Thank you," Walter said and spread out his arms, and his ex-wife walked to him and wrapped her arms around him. Walter and the bug-eyed creature, whom he was hoping would let him stay a while, squeezed each other in a tight hug. When they broke the hug, Walter said, "Why don't you take the goggles off."

Sarah pulled them down below her chin so that they became a lumpy necklace. "I've squinted through them so much that I don't even notice when I have them on anymore."

"It's cold here."

"It's almost fifty."

"I've been in Los Angeles."

"Well, let's go to the house and drink some beer."

On the way to the house, Sarah asked casually, without even looking at Walter, "When you going to stop fucking around, Walter?"

"Never, I hope." They stepped into the house.

What used to be *his* log house was now *her* log studio, where Walter could see the finished products: standing Indians with mournful faces and upraised hands, Indian faces with drunken smiles, sad cowboy faces, drunk cowboy faces, birds, bears, and copies of Remington and Russell. The wood was varnished and shiny but not smooth. Sarah had sand papered the rough edges, but the wood was still chunky from the bites that the chainsaw had taken out of it. And somewhere near the base, where Sarah had stopped whittling with her chainsaw, was her signature: Sarah Boone.

Walter stooped, adjusted his glasses, and cocked his head to read that signature. He raised up and said, "I thought your mother wanted you to keep the family name."

"Thanks for the name. *Sarah Boone* sounds authentic. It's real American, Daniel Boone, you know. It sells. I'm kind of the Whistler or the Wyeth of chain-saw sculpting." Walter was glad to know that he had some small hand in Sarah's success.

His cabin had walls when he lived in it. Now, he saw just space. "Where's the walls?" he asked.

Sarah walked across the open space, past the wooden statues, past the kitchen table, and into the kitchen area. She opened the refrigerator and came out with a six-pack. "I knocked the walls out. It was cheaper than building a studio. I still have a room for Greg when he comes home." She hesitated. "But he rarely comes home." She pulled a sweater off the hat rack next to the backdoor. "Here, this'll keep you warm." She walked out the backdoor. Walter followed her and stuck his arms into the sweater. It didn't quite reach his waist and, even though Sarah had big arms, the sweater squeezed his shoulders and biceps. Sarah laughed at him. "Let's watch the sun set."

"Damn, you have gotten to be rustic," Walter said. They squinted into the sun that was setting beneath two orange and purple winter clouds and started drinking the six-pack of Coors.

150

When the sun set and Walter begin to shiver again and begged to go inside, Sarah said, "Are you going to finish this script?"

"I'm going to try. That's why I came here." Walter cocked his head to see Sarah through the thick lens for his bad eye. She turned to face him, but Walter could not see her face in the dark. "You can stay the night."

"I thought I might stay a little longer."

"How long?"

"Jesus, it's cold," Walter said. "Couldn't we go in and discuss this?"

Sarah turned and tipped her half-empty can of Coors at Walter, "We go in, and you'd hug me, then kiss me. And I haven't had none for a long time, so you'd probably end up convincing me to get in bed with you for old times' sake."

"Not a bad idea," Walter interrupted.

Sarah took a sip from her beer, shook the can to see if it was empty, then chugged what beer was left. She let the beer can drop and hit the back porch. "Goddamn it. I'm trying to be serious, and you're bullshitting."

"I take bullshit serious," Walter said and held out his arms, the tight sweater biting him up under his arms.

Sarah backed away from him. "You're wasting your life."

"It's mine to waste," Walter said.

"How many times have I heard that? That's horseshit."

"I was hoping you would have said it was bullshit," Walter said not smiling. "Jesus, let's go inside," Walter said, hugged himself, stomped the wooden slats of the back porch, and smiled with his whole body. Walter had a certain smile that almost made a hissing sound, like the snake in the Garden of Eden.

"I'm not cold. And I like having the advantage."

"Jesus, Sarah, I need a place to stay. Let me finish the script here."

Sarah walked to the six-pack and pulled a beer loose from the plastic. She opened the beer and coolly took a sip. "You kind of shit in your nest, Walter."

"I have money. I wanted to see you."

Sarah jumped off the porch, some of her beer spilling, and looked up at Walter while he hugged himself and stretched the sweater and smiled, in his hiss-like way, like the snake in the garden. "Couldn't you have left the women alone?" Sarah asked.

"I like women, the smell of them, the feel of them."

"You had me."

"I'm back."

"Not for long you're not."

"For a while?"

"Are you as desperate as you sound, or is this your same old horseshit or bullshit? I forget the distinction."

"I gave you ten good years."

151

"Try eight. The two in Los Angeles were hell on me." Sarah put her foot on the edge of the porch and with her other foot pushed herself up on the porch. She walked to Walter and said, "Walter, you're like this old, inoperable tumor. It hurts. But I've had this lump hanging from me for so long, I wouldn't know what to do without it."

"That's sweet. You really mean that?" Walter asked.

"Did you have to fuck around so much?"

Walter put his arm around his wife: "The world is composed of two types of tragedy: unbearable and bearable tragedy. The unbearable kind is truth. Truth is that undeniable fact that that son of a bitch time erases all words, memories, nations, etc. Bearable tragedy is the lies we tell ourselves to keep away unbearable tragedy. We call the best lies art, music, philosophy, or literature."

"I've heard that before too," Sarah said.

"It's bullshit, not horseshit," Walter said. Sarah put her arm around her ex-husband and led him into the studio that had once been his house. And, after they finished the six-pack, for old times' sake, she let him sleep with her for three nights. Then she kicked him out. But Sarah never could get rid of Walter; he was like a tumor.

* * *

Traci's feet pounded the pavement. The sun was about to set and thus the muggers and dopers were about come out of the alleys and into the streets. Traci was not paranoid. She was trying to make it on her own.

Traci's dad, a liberal midwestern bigot, had sent her to Temple Bethel, sort of a West Coast imitation prep school for Jews. Traci's family was not Jewish, but Traci's father wanted Traci to be as smart as any of the Jews that he worked with at the investment agency. His plan worked. Traci became smart and got a partial scholarship to USC. She made the honor roll for her first term but suddenly turned radical and socially conscious. She rejected her father's money. She dropped out of USC.

Unfortunately, because she had been in an honors program at U.S.C., because U.S.C. was a private school, many of her credits wouldn't transfer, so she was stuck in community college freshman classes with the mostly socially disadvantaged, who were also mostly stupid. She grew tired of her classmates, her teachers, and her study of punctuation and practical math. So she joined the work force. But her job as a secretary forced her to live in a part of town that her father and the rest of her family had avoided.

As Vance's secretary, she sorted his mail, helped him schedule his day, and advised him about pending projects. This job was own step toward a career in the movie business, toward the production of her own script. But as her feet slapped the concrete, she worried that Vance would derail his career trying to produce

Walter Boone's unflimable script. Then where would she be? Still Jogging close to downtown rather than farther West

Traci Miller ran into the entrance of her apartment building, charged up the steps to her room, unlocked the front door to her efficiency apartment, and then, still sweating from her jog, curled around Walter Boone's script and began reading.

On successive readings, so much in the script seemed perfunctory to Traci. She thought that Walter's imagination was far more agile than Walter's fat, sweating, exhausted, hoarse Elvis, who stuffed himself into a sequined suit and performed for an audience of blue-haired old ladies. After the performance, he threw handkerchiefs to the ladies who rushed the stage to kiss him and fondle him. Walter's mind was faster than his Margaret Mead who ran away from a tribe of horny pigmy cannibals. Walter had the good sense to place Elvis' performance and Margaret's flight as background action to Charlie Chaplin's and the pop culture professor's descent into hell. But, to Traci, even foreground action began to seem false.

Like all good works, *The Circles of Hell* had layers. Traci had peeled layer after layer from this script but still couldn't see its heart. Traci got scared. The script was not an artichoke; it was an onion, all translucent, intricately-wrapped layers, but no heart. If ever filmed, the resulting movie would be like watching a kaleidoscope; richly textured scenes would flash in front of the viewers' eyes, but they would forget one scene as soon as the next appeared. Traci couldn't underestimate the American viewing public enough to believe that they would pay the price of movie ticket to watch a kaleidoscope. This script could turn into the next *Heaven's Gate*. Maybe the French would like it, Traci thought.

Then as Traci sniffed and smelled her own sweat, the thought occurred to her that perhaps Walter Boone had never really written the script to be filmed. And if it were filmed, maybe, Walter Boone, courting failure and infamy, would create an elaborate joke on the culture that he was stuck in. Was Walter Boone that daring, that devious, that talented a fuck off?

Traci started pulling off her sweats. As she walked to her shower, West L.A. seemed to be moving farther and farther west, away from her nearly down town apartment. She would have to tell Vance Orton that Walter Boone truly was a talented writer but that he was just fucking around with *The Circles of Hell*.

* * *

After Sarah kicked him out, Walter drove into Alpine, stopped at a Western clothing store, bought a Levi's jacket to keep his back warm and a cowboy hat to keep his bald head warm, and then drove to Houston to see his son. On the way, Walter had time to think about *The Circles of Hell*. Robert Redford, who wouldn't be neurotic or drunk, would find himself in a dark woods where he would be met by Charlie Chaplin who would take him on a tour of hell. Charlie talks with a squeaky voice like Peter Lorre's, walks in his flat-footed waddle, and uses his cane-like a pointer to make his points to Robert Redford. The first circle of hell is a bar. Dashiell Hammett, Ernest Hemingway, Scott Fitzgerald, Humphrey Bogart, John Barrymore, and Clark Gable are trading shots of scotch. Once in a while, they walk to a door down a hall and stare into a keyhole. They don't pay much attention to Redford when Charlie introduces him, but they lead him down the hall and let him peek in the keyhole. Through the keyhole Redford sees Marilyn Monroe slowly stepping out of her nylons. Then she slowly takes off her bra. She does this over and over again. They can look, and they can drink, but they can't touch Marilyn.

That was what Walter remembered and wrote as he drove from Alpine to Houston, which was 65 degrees with a spirit-dimming drizzle. Feeling and cussing his way through Houston on the freeways, Walter eventually found Rice University and drove around campus, looking at co-eds, stopping long enough to talk to a student or two, and visiting the student union and the library. Eventually, Walter found the dorm that Greg lived in.

Walter walked up several flights of stairs to Greg's floor. As he looked for Greg's room, he smelled urine, dirty laundry, stale beer, and Lysol. Greg's room door was open, so Walter peered. Somebody else's kid was lying on one bed and shaking his feet and head to the rhythm he heard through the headphones over his ears. He had *Being and Nothingness* open in front of him. Walter knocked, but the kid couldn't hear. Walter stepped into the room and tapped the kid on the shoulder. The kid pulled off his headphones, looked at Walter, kept shaking his head, and said, "Yeah?"

"Where's Greg Boone?"

"At the library,"

"I'm Walter Boone, Greg's father."

"Wow," the kid said. "I'm Greg's roomie, Ricky Van Buren." They shook hands, and Walter looked at Ricky's high top, red tennis shoes, his jeans that had indiscriminate holes cut in them, his hair with the unraveling pig tail in back, and the earring dangling from his left earlobe. Walter remembered Sul Ross State University. The drinking fountains at Sul Ross on campus had signs over them that said, "Please don't expectorate chewing residue in fountains." The cattlemen's and farmers' sons went ahead and spat in the fountains. Rice didn't need to tell its students not to spit in the drinking fountains.

Ricky followed Walter's gaze to the open book, "You read this, Mr. Boone?"

"Yeah, Ricky. Call me Walter. You like it?"

"Bitchin' book," Ricky said and gained enough self consciousness to stop his bebopping. "I don't understand all of it, but a friend of mine said I might like it."

Walter cocked his head to look out of his strong lens at Ricky, "You mean you aren't reading it for a class?"

"Naw," Ricky said. "I'm a finance major." And Walter thought that maybe there was some hope for the world.

Just as Walter was about to ask Ricky about the book, Greg came to the door. Some stray gene in either strong but small Sarah or stocky Walter must have accounted for their lanky, slender son. He had long arms, a tiny waist, and a pigeon chest, but he had a chiseled face, a face Sarah might have chainsawed out of a log. It was a face that the young co-eds would like. Walter hoped that his son was getting some.

Greg Boone wore round, plastic glasses, jeans, a crisply-pressed pale blue shirt, a tweed sport coat, and tennis shoes that looked more expensive than his roomie's. Greg walked into his dorm room with a stack of books in his arms. Walter and Ricky stood up. "Greg, this is your father." Ricky pointed to Walter then smiled, "I guess you know that, huh?"

"Yeah, Ricky," Greg said and stuck out his hand while he balanced the books with his other hand. "Dad," he said.

Walter gently shook his son's hand so that he didn't disrupt the books. Walter said, "I'm glad to see that you're studying."

"Oh, man," Ricky said. "He studies all the time."

"Well that's good," Walter said.

Greg stepped toward his bed and let his books fall onto it. "Hey," Ricky said, "this is going to be like tender. I'll go down to the lobby, read my book, and maybe get a beer."

Walter was about to ask Ricky to stay and to go have a beer with them, but Greg said, "Please do."

Greg sat down on his bed, started to say something, then shifted his head toward Ricky walking out the door. "He's really kind of a jerk."

"Seems okay to me," Walter said.

Walter cocked his head to read the titles on the spines of Greg's books. One book spine said *Inhuman Relations: Quality Circles and Anti-Unionism in America*. "These are books for my research paper," Greg said. Walter nodded like he approved. "I'm majoring in business. I want something solid when I get out of school."

"Well, you know you've got plenty of time," Walter said. "You ought to enjoy yourself a little. So look, Greg, I have a pocket full of money. Let's go out on the town."

"I have a research paper that I absolutely have to work on."

"We could have a dinner. You name it. Get some drinks. Find some girls. Huh?" Walter smiled at his son. "Son and Dad team, that'd impress them, huh?"

"Dad, I have to study."

"Live a little."

"Like you?"

"How often am I in town?"

"Now, you've figured out the problem."

"One beer," Walter said. When he was little, Greg liked to put on a cowboy hat and boots and go to the bars around Alpine with his father. He would sit on the bar, and while his dad drank beer, Greg would sing crying-in-your-beer country songs, talk to the bar patrons, and drink Big Red soda waters. Both Walter and his son would flirt with the waitresses.

Greg stood up and rubbed his hair. He looked exasperated. "I haven't seen you but maybe three times since I've started college," Greg said.

"So this is the fourth."

"Don't you have any responsibility? Where were you when I was growing up?" Greg held his hands out in front of him to show that he had little tolerance for his father. "Don't you have any sense of right and wrong? Of what you ought to do?"

Walter caught himself wishing that Ricky were his son. "You've seen too many TV movies."

"Dad, I just don't have the time, now."

"Loosen up, Greg. Not just for me, but for yourself. You have a girlfriend? Ever go out on the town?"

"I'm here for an education."

Walter pulled out his wallet. "Here, here's some cash. Save it for some free time and take out some girl, get a little drunk."

Before Walter could hand the money to his son, Greg wrapped his hands around his father's hands and said, "No."

Walter stuck his wallet in his back pocket and sat on Ricky's bed. "So what are we going to do?"

"Maybe if you could come back at the end of the semester. Maybe we could meet at Mom's or something. This is just real bad timing. Why didn't you call?"

Walter slowly got up. "Yeah, okay."

"Tomorrow, maybe we could have lunch?"

"Maybe, maybe," Walter said.

"Dad, I really don't mean to be this way."

As Walter left the dorm room, Greg sheepishly stuck out his hand, and Walter, for the second time, shook his son's hand. "Greg," Walter said. "You think of me what you will. But I don't care about what I 'ought' to do. I would rather live a beautiful life than a moral one. And beauty ain't always pretty; and unfortunately, sometimes colleges totally ignore it."

When he got to the lobby of Greg's dorm, Walter saw Ricky reading *Being and Nothingness* in front of a giant screen TV. Walter interrupted Sartre again and asked Ricky out for a drink. Ricky was glad to go. Ricky first took Walter to a couple of the bars around Rice. Then they drove around Houston in Walter's Porsche and stopped at a variety of bars and strip joints. It was nearly one o'clock before Walter got Ricky back to the dorm. And Ricky gave Walter two pellets of speed in case he wanted to drive back to West Texas that night.

Actually, Walter didn't know where to go. Back in far West Texas, he could find plenty of isolation so that he could write—and maybe talk Sarah into letting him move back in. He had vowed when he left Sarah and his son not to interfere with Greg's life, but now he wished that he had. Walter knew that he wouldn't be able to go to sleep tonight, so he took the speed and concentrated on driving and distance. He got as far down I-10 as Junction before the speed wore off. At a roadside park west of Junction, Walter spent a cold night in his Porsche with his jacket, an extra pair of pants, and a blanket that Sarah had lent him to keep him warm. Just before he went to sleep, Walter tried to think of a place in hell for Sartre.

* * *

From the way the three men moved—stiffly, formally, each extending a hand—an observer could tell that someone beyond mortal status had entered the room. When Vance Orton saw the evenly tanned face, the crinkle in corners of the man's eyes, and the casual smile that barely lifted one side of his mouth; he felt the tickle of the warming liquid in his stomach.

"Please Mr. Redford," the promotions chief said and motioned for Mr. Redford to sit between him and the studio chief.

Mr. Redford nodded and said, "Bob. Call me Bob."

Vance stood while Mr. Redford walked to a padded chair and rested his hands on top of it. Vance gently tapped his pen on the desk. When Mr. Redford looked at the tapping pen, Vance immediately stopped. "Please, Bob. Sit," the studio chief said with British formality. Redford lowered himself into the plush leather upholstered chair then smoothed the lapels of his suit. Were not the luke-warm liquid in his gut keeping him firmly rooted in reality, Vance would have thought that he was stuck in one his daydreams about Hollywood glory. Now, Vance could sense that his daydreams were in fact forecasts. God was good.

Redford shifted his squinty gaze, which had started chills in women's loins, from one man to the next. And Vance felt a chill of jealousy (why should this one man have so much?) mix with the chill of his anticipation. Vance could see Redford's cheek bulge a bit as Redford pressed his tongue against the inside of his cheek. "I won't keep you. I've decided not to make this film." Vance felt his gut grow hot. "I want to direct my own picture. But . . ." Redford hesitated and again squinted at the men, "I don't want to direct this one."

"Well, then," the promotions chief said and looked at Vance, "That is that."

"But Bob," Vance forced out of his throat while he tried to subdue the burning liquid and think of something to say.

"Yes?" Redford asked

"I have the writer doing a revision just for you. He's a talented writer. A great writer."

Redford chuckled, "You better watch Walter Boone. He's full of shit." The lava rose up out of Vance's stomach and became a scorching lump in his throat. Both the studio chief and the promotions chief chuckled along with Redford, but Vance felt like jabbing his pen into his abdomen to then rip it open and let his hot guts spill on Redford's shoes.

"Gentlemen," Redford said, stood, and smoothed the wrinkles out of his suit. The promotions chief was up and to the door before Redford could get to it. He held the door open for Redford to walk through. Before Redford exited, he turned and let his crinkling eyes and crooked smile fill the room with his charm.

Vance thought about excusing himself and running to a restroom to heave up his guts, but he wanted to appear calm in front of the studio's head and the chief of the promotions department. So Vance tapped his Cross pen on the table in front of him and tried to look pensive.

"We will have to scrap this whole notion," the studio chief said in his precise British accent. The chief of promotions hung his head, then nodded. Because he was out of ideas and knew no way to promote *The Circles of Hell*, the promotions chief would look foolish when the picture was released. So, as Vance well knew, the promotions chief was against the picture.

Vance swallowed to push the bile back into his stomach. "Look, we are not here because we found a Redford vehicle. We are here because of the promotability of this concept."

The promotions chief looked at Vance. Then he looked at the studio chief and put a smirk on his face that scoffed at Vance's naiveté, "I can promote Redford. I can't promote Dante."

Despite the burning in his throat, Vance's mind revved like a high-powered motor, but he could not downshift fast enough or build enough R.P.M.s to win an argument with the promotions chief. The studio chief said, "And isn't that a shame. It is quite a world we live in." The studio chief had made several movies with continental money and had gotten good reviews and good box office in this country. So the chairman and several board members of the corporation that owned the studio thought it a gesture of goodwill and great public relations to make him studio chief. For several years, the studio chief had dedicated himself to making quality pictures that could make money. Now that his job was in danger, he was mostly interested in pleasing as many people as possible. Vance had been hired after the chief's conversion to American methods.

"I'm just saying that this is a sleeper. This is what movie making is about. If you look at what films have been popular in the last five years . . . " Vance stood, opened his brief case, and sorted through his flow charts. Vance had prepared for this possibility.

The promotions chief twisted his face into a scoff. The studio chief smiled. Vance was undaunted. "Let me show you," Vance said as he pulled out his red and green chart.

"Oh, my. Another one of these computer things," the studio chief said. "I believe I will never understand them."

"They lie," the promotions chief said. "You can make statistics say anything."

"Maybe our reliance in such devices got us in this trouble," the studio chief said.

Vance swallowed, scooted his flow chart back into the brief case, and slammed the leather lid shut. "All right, then. We won't go with facts. Let's just go with our gut feelings." At that moment Vance's guts were churning.

"And what should we infer from our guts?" the studio chief asked. The promotions chief laughed.

"We should infer that this is a good picture. Ask anybody who's read it." When the studio chief cocked his head as though he was wondering about what Vance had said, Vance hesitated and thought too. But hesitation, Vance had learned, was always a mistake. He regained his momentum. "Since the day it was written, every screenwriter and producer who has ever seen this script has praised this script. My secretary, who has no more than a high school education but is bright in her own way, loves it. She, gentlemen, is the American movie audience."

The promotions chief laughed. "We're going to spend more than the GNP for most small countries because a secretary likes it?"

"Go on Mr. Orton," the studio chief said. The promotions chief swiveled away from the studio chief to look at Vance. Vance could see the scowl on his face. Vance's next swallow cooled the lava in his stomach. His self-charted course was clear again. "After fourteen years, someone should have the guts to make *The Circles of Hell*, and whoever does make it, despite receipts, will win the admiration and praise of this community." The promotions chief looked at the studio chief as though asking him if he were really going to believe Vance. "And we know that this community's favor is as important as box office grosses. I am talking Academy Awards, here."

"Come on Dave," the promotions chief said. "You going to buy that?"

The studio chief raised his head, "Not without a star. We need insurance. We lost Redford. We need to find someone of nearly equal stature." Vance could think of no one with equal stature, but he was not yet out of hope.

* * *

Walter took a room at the Limpia Hotel in Fort Davis. It was an old hotel that was newly restored, served good food, but competed with the cheaper Indian Lodge, the state-run hotel at the Fort Davis State Park. Walter got a corner room so that he had two windows. He liked to sit in the sunlight and try to write. But mostly he read what he had already written. The problem was that the sunlight that filled his room was distracting. The world was full of distractions for Walter. He needed a dungeon to write in.

Walter found other distractions. He liked to have lunch at the Cadillac Grill. The owner, Sam McCord, had bought a wrecked '62 Cadillac and put its front end in front of his hamburger joint. He painted the Cadillac pink and decorated the interior of his restaurant with the hub caps and nameplates from Cadillacs. The locals (teenagers cutting school and the coffee and gossip crowd) came in to have Fleetwood milkshakes, greasy Coup de Ville burgers, El Dorado chili, pre-made Seville chicken fried Steaks, or Biarritz stew. This was high-concept marketing in Fort Davis, Texas. Walter Boone liked to eat some of the cholesterol and listen to the locals.

After a week in Fort Davis trying to write, Walter Boone walked into the Cadillac Grill on a windy, chilly noon and sensed that the locals whispered and wondered about the fancy man in the strange clothes. Vance Orton wore some properly-faded jeans (the kind with an even fade throughout the material, no shiny fade on the thighs and butt), Italian shoes, a white silk shirt, and a leather jacket. Walter didn't know about any of the important developments back in Hollywood. Vance had been desperately trying to tell him.

For three days Vance had tried to call Walter and tell him that the whole project was near death, but he talked only to Walter's machine. Then he called American Express and picked up a trail of bills across Texas. The bills settled on a place called Fort Davis, Texas. Traci Miller found Fort Davis on a map, then looked for the closest city. She found none. She did spot El Paso, so she reserved a flight for Vance to El Paso.

Vance was about to cancel the American Express card when God smiled down at him: Robert DeNiro expressed an interest in playing the popular culture professor to his hair stylist. So, instead of pulling the money out from under Walter, Vance decided to fetch Walter back from Fort Davis, Texas and bring him to Los Angeles where someone could keep an eye on him. Vance had gone to the Limpia, but the desk clerk told him to go to the Cadillac Grill.

"Walter, I have got to talk to you." Walter shook Vance's hand and told him to sit down and bought him a hamburger. "What the hell are you doing here?" Vance whispered to Walter as he sat down. "This place is barely on a map."

But Walter didn't seem to hear, he turned away from Vance and looked at a middle-aged man who was dressed in insulated overalls and whose head was a fuzzy cue ball. Walter turned to look back at Vance, "This guy is great. His name is Alton."

160

"Walter, I have important news," Vance said to the back of Walter's head.

"Look," Walter said.

"My God, Walter," Vance said, pressing in on his stomach. "What have you written?" Vance asked Walter.

"Watch," Walter said to Vance.

"You've got to cooperate with me," Vance told Walter. The hot liquid began to warm in his stomach.

"Watch, watch, watch," Walter quietly spit out at Vance, and Vance shifted his gaze to Alton.

Alton took several symmetrical bites out of the rounded top of his hamburger to make its top flat. He then grabbed the ketchup in the squeeze bottle sitting in the middle of the table behind the napkin container. He squirted a stream of ketchup across the flat top of the hamburger. He took a bite. Then he looked at the mustard. He squeezed a stream of mustard across the top of the hamburger. As Vance watched, the burning inside his stomach cooled.

"Why doesn't he put it inside the hamburger?" Vance asked Walter.

"Watch," Walter said to Vance.

Alton looked at the honey. He couldn't resist. He reached behind the napkin holder, grabbed the squeeze bottle of honey, and let the honey ooze on to the top of the hamburger and mix with the ketchup and the mustard. He took a bite, chewed in one cheek, and smiled. "Yuk," Vance said and pressed his stomach. "That's disgusting."

Walter turned to Vance and said, "Alton likes honey. He's what these folks call 'simple.'"

The wind, which shook the front end of Vance's rented car all 250 miles from El Paso, rattled the window panes and crept in through the cracks in Sam's wall and foundation. A plain-faced waitress brought two hamburgers, a beer for Walter, and a cup of coffee for Vance. The waitress sat all of the food in front of Walter then leaned over to hug him. He kissed her on the cheek. "See you later, huh baby," she said to Walter.

"Who is she?" Vance asked.

"That's Katie, a good West Texas country girl," Walter turned to wink at her. Vance looked closer at her. Her teeth were crooked and brown from ignoring them most of her life; she had a horse face, and she had a flat chest. "She's not much, but she's the best to be found on such short notice in Fort Davis, Texas," Walter said.

Vance clenched his teeth and said between them, "What have you written?"

Walter's expression grew serious, and he looked Vance in the eye, then he said, "Back when I taught at Sul Ross, the 'bull rider' students told the outsiders that if you plan to come to Alpine or Ft. Davis or Balmorhea, you better bring your own pussy and money 'cause these Trans-Pecos towns didn't have much of neither."

Vance sipped his hot coffee, and surprisingly, it cooled the liquid in his stomach. "So what have you got?" Vance asked. He didn't have time to listen to Walter's stories about West Texas Don Juans.

"Not much," Walter said, then picked his hamburger up out of the plastic basket that it came in and slowly unwrapped it from the grease-stained paper. Pickles and onions fell out of the burger and into the paper lined plastic basket. Walter then took a bite of his burger and more pickles, onions, and grease dropped into the basket.

Vance took another sip of his coffee and squeezed the handle on the mug until his knuckles turned white, "You're supposed to be writing, not making eyes at a hillbilly waitress and watching morons eat hamburgers."

"Taking delight in Katie's good company and watching Alton is writing."

"It's not writing *The Circles of Hell*."

"So maybe you better fire me." Vance stared into his coffee. The bile in his belly turned warm. "Course who else do you have?" Walter took another bite from his burger, chewed, then washed down the bite with a slug of beer.

"Okay, Okay, Okay," Vance said. "It's just as well. Let's not get upset over this. Redford's out. But we got DeNiro interested. And DeNiro doesn't play good. So the divorce and the neurosis is back in. You need to give him some scenes where he can act."

Walter smiled at Vance, opened his burger, squirted on some mustard, and said, "If I keep waiting, I won't have to change anything."

"You've got to meet me halfway."

"Okay," Walter said. "Better eat your lunch."

"And you've got to come back to Los Angeles. You get no more money unless you come to my office to pick it up. And your credit card is now revoked."

"Why don't you come right out and tell me what you want instead of dropping the subtle hints." Walter said to Vance and bit into his burger.

Vance opened his burger, sniffed at it, then closed the bun back on top. He took a bite. He swallowed, and the liquid in his belly turned molten. A geyser of hot goo seemed to shoot up into his throat. Vance coughed and grabbed his stomach.

"Sam's hamburgers aren't really worth a shit," Walter said and munched his burger. Vance coughed some more and rubbed his stomach. He pushed the plastic basket with the hamburger in it away from him. He sipped the coffee. "Jesus, Vance," Walter said and stared at Vance, "Sam's hamburgers aren't bad enough to make you turn white like that. Are you okay?"

"I'll be all right as soon as I get this project cleared. As soon as you get the script done."

"You better not count on me. You better see a doctor."

Vance pushed himself up. "I have get back to El Paso."

"Why don't you stay over in the Limpia. They have vacancies."

"I have to get back. I have to be at a meeting in the morning."

As he moved toward the door, Vance heard Walter ask, "Do you ever get confused about where you're at?"

Vance never made his flight. Once he got to El Paso, the fire in his guts made him double over. He thought that Walter Boone had poisoned him with one of The Cadillac Grill's hamburgers. So Vance stopped by a minor emergency clinic to get a quick prescription, but the Korean doctor immediately called an ambulance, and Vance spent three days in El Paso Eastwood Hospital fighting an ulcer.

* * *

3

During his stay at Fort Davis, Walter had made three trips to Alpine to see Sarah. That was mostly what he did at night instead of write. Sarah had let him stay over a couple of times but had told him to stay away on his last trip. That's when he and Katie had dinner and a few beers in the lobby of the Limpia Hotel. Then Vance showed up to tell him to go back to Los Angeles.

On the way back to Los Angeles, Walter stopped at a curio shop in Arizona and bought one of Sarah's chainsaw sculptures. It was the one of a stern looking Indian with a trace of a smile in his eyes.

Back in Los Angeles, in his bungalow near Venice beach, 65 degrees outside, a balmy Pacific breeze in the air but nothing like the West Texas wind, Walter Boone decided that he *had* to rewrite *The Circles of Hell*. He called Sally and told her that it would be a couple days before he could see her but to please not forget him. It was just as well since her husband was in town. He locked his door, pulled down his shades, filled his refrigerator with beer and microwave dinners, and started to write.

In one scene Albert Einstein tries to lecture a college class about the theory of relativity. But the class, which was made up of the Little Rascals, the Marx Brothers, and the Three Stooges, will not listen and cannot be made to understand. Robert DeNiro, swarthy and dark instead of blonde and lean like Robert Redford, playing the pop culture professor who loses his way, tries to take over the class but has no better luck than Einstein. Finally, Groucho and Moe take the class over and explain relativity by respectively sitting on a pretty girl's lap and slapping Curly and Larry. The class understands.

Vance Orton didn't like the scene, but he didn't know why. He wished that he had brought Traci with him so that she could read the scene. He sucked on the powdery antacid tablet and read the scene once more. "This is all?"

"Yeah. You can't rush genius," Walter said.

"Okay, Okay," Vance said, "I'm not going to get mad."

"You're right. It's useless to get mad. I'm impossible," Walter said. Vance

163

had just gotten back to L.A. from El Paso Eastwood Hospital. This was his first morning back on the job with his medicated ulcer.

"You're gifted. Why don't you like writing?"

"I like fucking and drinking better," Walter said and cocked his head to see out of his one thick lens.

Vance caught himself cocking his head to look at his reflection in Walter's lens. "It's funny. It kind of fits in with the other scenes. But what does it mean?"

Walter plopped down on his couch and crossed his arms. "Isn't it enough that it's funny? You want significance too? You're so demanding." Vance reached into his coat pocket and pulled out his package of antacids.

"Ulcer, Huh?" Walter Boone asked. "Nasty bastards aren't they?"

"Yeah, yeah, I need to tell you some more."

Vance sat beside Walter and used his hands to explain the rewrites that the execs wanted. "These show biz characters stay. But you have to get rid of these philosophers and such. The ordinary guy isn't gonna understand them."

"The hero would," Walter said.

"Yes, yes, yes, but we're writing for the masses, 24 year-olds who maybe flunked out after their sophomore year in college. Keep that in mind. There's your market."

"I'm going to get a beer," Walter said.

Vance rose, stepped over the dirty microwave dishes and beer bottles on the floor, and followed Walter into his kitchen. "And DeNiro's gone. We've got Rob Lowe, and he plays young."

Walter stopped, "What about the character? What about what he's like?"

"We're stuck with Rob Lowe. But we'll appeal to a younger audience."

"All right," Walter said, opened his refrigerator, and pulled out a beer. "Who's Rob Lowe?"

Vance put another tablet into his mouth and sucked on it. "Don't you go to the movies?"

"I watch a little TV," Walter said.

"He's a young guy. Make the hero a graduate student."

"A middle aged, burned-out graduate student?"

"No, he has to be young." Walter opened his beer, chugged it, crushed the can, and threw the crushed can against his kitchen wall. "Walter, I'm on your side," Vance said, but Walter turned his back to Vance followed him.

"And Charlie Chaplin has to go."

Walter whirled around. "What?"

"He's a trademark for a corporation. That may make him illegal. We might have to go to court to use him."

"You write it, then. You write it and sue me for the money you paid me. Hell, I'd be a whole lot happier in some minimum security prison."

"Walt, Walt, Walt. Take it easy."

"Look, I practically boarded myself up in here. What do you want? I'm missing out on Sally's sweet ass because of your goofy goddamn scheme."

"We're going to make movie history," Vance said.

"Horseshit," Walter said. "We're fucking around."

"Don't give up faith in yourself. I'm backing you on this all the way."

"You really are a pisscutter."

"I'll take that as a compliment," Vance said.

"What you better take is a vacation," Walter said.

On the way back to the studio, Vance's ulcer stopped throbbing, but he was able to think. He needed someone to watch Walter for him. A woman might be able to watch Walter and to keep him amused. And then Vance thought of the casual way that Traci fixed her hair and the casual upward scoop of her breasts and the way he thought about her when she met with him in his office.

* * *

After Vance left, Walter went out for a couple of tacos and a margarita. As he drove his Porsche back toward his house, he decided that Marilyn Monroe could take time out from stripping in front of Humphrey Bogart, Ernest Hemingway, and Clark Gable to find graduate student Rob Lowe in a dark woods, even though the graduate student was too young to be lost in a dark woods, and lead him into hell.

Lowe could watch while Vivien Leigh (who mixed up Blanche DuBois's and Scarlet O'Hara's costumes) and Errol Flynn took a couple of drinks together, then copulated with as much enthusiasm as they might have had in brushing their teeth. Doomed to fuck for eternity would, Walter supposed, make fucking dull, but Errol and Vivien endured with stiff upper British lips.

Next, Lowe helped defend John Wayne. Marilyn gave one of her proper shrieks as Walter Brennan, Andy Devine, Gabby Hayes, a bunch of Indians, and some forgotten cowboy actors who never got as far as second billing beat up the star. After the ass whipping, while Walter Brennan cackled at the Duke; Wayne, Lowe, and Marilyn argued about what it took to be a man before the next beating started.

With Walter Brennan's laugh and the Duke's voice in his head, Walter missed his exit. He eventually got on the Pac Coast Highway and drove north, no doubt endangering the lives of other motorists as he squinted into the mist and tried to see Rob Lowe and Marilyn Monroe in hell. When he got to Malibu, Walter's visions left him, so he turned around and drove back.

The next day, Walter had a cup of coffee, planted his butt in the chair in front of his computer, and tried to remember and write down what he had seen while driving around the night before. Just before nightfall, Walter again had someone pounding on his door. On his way to the door, Walter realized that he had on only his underwear, so he went back into his bedroom, picked his jeans up off the floor, slipped them on, and pulled a dirty T-Shirt over his head. This time he found a blonde lady with a nice body, a low-cut blouse, and a full skirt at his door.

"Mr. Orton sent me to help with your script," Traci Miller said and stuck out her hand. Walter Boone limply shook her hand. "My name is Traci Miller." She stepped through the door that Walter held open for her.

Traci could not bring herself to tell Vance that Walter Boone was just fucking around. Afterall, if so many people had at one time or another believed that *The Circles of Hell* was really among the best scripts ever written, maybe Walter could eventually pull off his joke. What Traci found herself thinking about was the nature of the man who would try to attempt such a joke. He stood in front of her now with the bulge of his stomach pressing against a dirty T-shirt, his head cocked and his jaw slack.

"Want a beer?" he asked Traci.

"Yes," Traci said. Walter, she figured, was the type of man whom you'd want to sit and drink a beer with.

Walter hissed a smile and rubbed his palm over his bald head. He turned and stepped over the Jack in the Box cartons, the beer cans, and the microwave plates to go into the kitchen. Traci turned to look at his sofa, the only piece of furniture in the bare house except for a huge, shiny but rough wood carving of an Indian's face. She sat down on the sofa. It groaned and dust rose up out of it. Traci crossed her knees, folded her hands, rested them in her lap, and smiled at Walter as he walked back from the kitchen with two bottles of beer. He handed her one and said "It's time for a break." He stood in front of her looked down at his belly and said, "I've been getting fatter since I started writing again." Traci wondered what women saw in this near-sighted, chubby, bald man.

Walter sat beside her on the sofa and leaned toward her to ask, "Just what are you supposed to do for my script?" Walter asked.

Traci took a sip from her beer. "Word Process. Research. Whatever you need," she said. "I can run Microsoft and Word Perfect processing programs. I also have a new laptop computer with screenwriting software installed."

Walter took a sip of his beer and rubbed the stubble on his cheek. "Darling, don't you know why you are really here?"

Vance Orton had not fooled her when he looked her up and down, swallowed an antacid tablet, shook his head up and down, and asked her to step into his office. At first, Traci had thought that he had finally gotten around to his own attempt at a seduction, but instead, he asked her to offer her "services" to Walter Boone. "To word process," Traci said to Walter and smiled at him, "Why else would I be here?" She sipped her beer and thought about poor, stressed Vance Orton, who could not now drink a beer with her or anybody else.

"Do you really want to be a secretary when you grow up?" Walter asked.

Traci smiled. He had figured her out almost immediately. "I want to be a writer. And not just any writer, but one like you," she said.

Walter laughed at her, then rose and walked in his bare feet, stepping over the Jack in the Box sacks and the beer cans, and went into the room where he did his writing. After a few moments, he came back and handed Traci a $100 bill. Traci clenched her teeth, asked, "What is this for?"and hoped that Walter would not say what she expected.

"Go down on Hollywood Boulevard. There's a screen-something-something academy, the Sherwood Motion Picture School, or any number of other places. Or, enroll in one of the community colleges. UCLA has some continuing educa-tion screenwriting classes. I've taught at all these places. Give them $100, and they'll try to teach you to write. They're shysters. They'll take your money. But you'll have more of a chance of writing something with them than with Vance." Traci smiled and relaxed. She leaned into the couch and held the bill in front of her face.

"I've tried that. Right now, I have a better plan. I'm Vance Orton's personal secretary. And pretty soon, though he won't know until after he's read them, he'll start seeing summaries of my scripts on his desk. I don't need the school." Traci handed the money back to Walter. "In the meantime, I thought you might teach me some things." Walter took the bill and curled it around in his fingers, making it a hollow tube. He raised the tube to his glasses like it was a tiny telescope and pretended to peer through it at Traci.

"You already know quite a bit. What could I teach you?" Walter asked.

"I have a few ideas."

Walter stuffed the bill in his pocket. "Vance has this strange idea that I'm a hopeless womanizer. He suspects that I write with a part of my anatomy that's a little lower than my head."

"Wonder where he got that idea?"

"And you still came over?"

"Mr. Boone, I was the one who found your script. At first I really liked it. Those people are doomed to hell because they made the modern world the way it is. So the hero has to go to hell to see what made him," Traci told Walter.

"I was just hoping that it was funny."

"Oh, it is," Traci said. "But, with all the macho chauvinist drinking and screwing, I asked myself whether the script mocks feminism or masculinity. Then I had other questions."

Walter cocked his head to see through his thick lens. "I suspect that you are a very good secretary for Vance," he told Traci.

"I'm not as innocent or as dumb as most people want to think." Traci stood and then brushed the dust from Walter's old, groaning sofa off her butt. She didn't want to be close to Walter when she told him what she really thought. "Then I began to wonder just what the script was about. It seemed, as you said, it was just funny. Then I realized that it was just as good as it had to be to get moneyed people interested. In short," Traci hesitated. "In short, I began to think that you were just fucking around. . . . And I thought about how much you must know to fuck around and still write so well."

Walter's smile spread, and it became something seductive, charming, and then the smile that was almost like a hiss turned to laughter. The bellows came from deep inside him, and his face grew red. He laughed until he choked, and Traci sat beside him and patted his back until he quit choking. "So tell, tell me," Traci said, "What are you trying to do with this script? What does it mean? How can I do what you did?"

Walter coughed once more into his hand. He turned to face her. "At last somebody who understands me." He wrapped his arms around her and laughed again.

Traci drank four beers and talked about scriptwriting, Hollywood, colleges, the mimetic qualities of art, harmartia, Christian existentialism, and the best Mexican food in Los Angeles. They disagreed about the Mexican food. Walter preferred it much hotter than Traci did. He liked more cheese and no sour cream. As Walter said to Traci, sour cream was a bourgeois American bastardization of chiles and *cilantro* and was fast destroying true Mexican food in this country.

Well after nightfall Traci decided to leave. Walter went into his writing room and came out with a stack of pages. "I do have a job for you." He handed her the stack of pages, "Proof this and change what you want. I'll give you credit."

Traci took the bundle and looked down at it.

"It's most of the rewrite," Walter said. "You'll have the rest tomorrow."

* * *

Way down, in the very depths of hell, Rob Lowe and Marilyn Monroe encounter the Devil. He is a little cur, a cross between a muppet, a cocker spaniel, and an ape. His face looks like a caricature of Walter's lost popular culturalist. And, while he was writing, giving into ego, Walter liked to imagine the Devil as a caricature of himself. And as Walter's devil scampers around in his green, dank dungeon and whimpers, a smiling, rosy-cheeked Nietzsche tries to console him. "Cheer up. Cheer up. God is dead," Nietzsche says. (It was still his hell, and by God, Walter Boone was going to have a few philosophers in his hell.)

"Shut up," the Devil says to Nietzsche. Then, to Rob Lowe and Marilyn, he says, "I hate that sentimental shit." He plops his baboon ass on a decrepit throne, puts his elbow on the arm of the throne, and holds his chin in his open palm.

"What am I supposed to learn from you?" Rob Lowe asks.

"What? You think I got answers, schmuck? I just want a little excitement, something new. It's so damn boring here," the Devil tells Lowe.

"How do I get out of here?"

The Devil giggles, "That's amusing. Good start."

"Will yourself out," Nietzsche says. "If it doesn't kill you, it makes you stronger."

The Devil frowns at Nietzsche and says, "Asshole." Then he turns to look at Rob Lowe, "I'm confined for eternity with this jerk, and you think you got problems."

"Where is this?" Lowe asks.

"Heaven, Hell, Nirvana, Valhalla, Limbo, Purgatory, Olympus, West Texas; take your pick." The Devil frowns and lays his chin in his open palm. "What this ain't is fun. A party or something. Just something a little different."

Marilyn takes the cue and slowly starts to strip. The Devil pulls his chin off his palm and stares at Marilyn. She blows a kiss at him. "No, you don't have to do this," Rob Lowe says to Marilyn. But she and the Devil embrace and fall to the floor.

"I could take a couple of centuries of this," the Devil says and points toward a door.

Nietzsche opens the door and says to Lowe, "It ain't ruby slippers, but it'll do." And Rob Lowe takes a look at the Devil's molestation of Marilyn before he walks through the door and back into the dark woods where he started out so confused.

This was the ending of the rewritten *The Circles of Hell* that Walter Boone had handed Traci Miller. She spent the night reading it and spent the next day proofing and formatting it. Vance Orton sucked on an antacid tablet and read the computer's screen from over Traci's shoulder as she entered her corrections. "This is great. This is truly great," Vance said as he read the new ending. Then he looked at Traci, "Isn't it?"

Traci stopped pressing the keys of her word processor long enough to answer Vance. Since she didn't know whether Vance was talking about entering the script into the computer, the script itself, the fact that Walter Boone had completed the script, or the forthcoming movie to star Rob Lowe; Traci said, "Yes, *it* truly is great," and smiled for herself and Walter Boone.

* * *

After a night of real sleep, Walter woke at noon and tried to call his ex-wife and his son, but neither answered the phone. So he settled on calling Sally, but her husband was still in town, and she couldn't get away. He thought about trying to call cute Traci Miller, whose mouth slid around on her face when she concentrated, but he decided to wait before having beer or dinner with her. So Walter Boone set about cleaning up the clutter of Styrofoam coffee cups, food encrusted microwave plates, plastic wrapping, bowls with hardening cereal in them, the empty beer cans, paper cartons, aluminum foil, and bottles on his floor. He even polished the wood of the chainsaw Indian sculpture of Sarah's.

Then Walter had another visitor. Walter answered the door in his underwear. And, as soon as he opened the door, Vance almost jumped into the living room. He raised the script above him and said, "This is great Walter."

"You like it then?" Walter Boone asked.

"It's art," Vance said. "We've started the deal. Rob Lowe has signed."

Walter sat on his couch, put on his glasses, and cocked his head to look out of his one thick lens at Vance. Vance had on sockless shoes, khaki pants, a navy blazer, and a white tuxedo shirt. Walter was not afraid of success. He was not feeling guilty or indignant; he was not regretting anything. But, since talking to Traci Miller, he wanted a little honesty. "Maybe the deal was made," Walter said. "But the script is horseshit."

Vance rubbed his hands together, then sat beside Walter and patted his knee, "I think that this is the beginning of a beautiful friendship."

"Maybe so, but the script isn't even good bullshit; it's dog shit. And they'll never make a picture out of it."

"But we got a deal," Vance said.

"*You* got a deal," Walter said.

"No," Vance said and dropped the script on the floor. "You really do have talent. And I can use that talent to get us both into some high places."

Walter picked up the script and slung it toward a wall. It cracked the plaster of the wall. "Cut the shit Vance. You can't con me. Don't you see? Don't you understand? I used you as much as you used me. I'm not a fucking artist. I'm a con, like you."

Vance stood up, walked to the wall, knelt, and picked up the script. He pointed it at Walter, "You've been a royal pain in the ass," Vance said and shook the script. "I would have had the cops bust your nuts, and I could have, if I didn't think you were good. College wasn't completely wasted on me, you know. I know a little bit about art and philosophy, too. You're a two-bit philosopher, but you are a good writer."

"I'm a good bullshitter," Walter said. "Not too good of a writer."

Vance grew red, sucked some air, then gave a speech: "Don't you do anything? I've talked to some people about you. What have you done the last ten years? What are you doing with your life? You've got all this talent. People willing to give you money to nurture your gift. The chance to do something really good, and what do you do? You keep fucking up. What about your future?"

"I figure I have a good ten or fifteen years before my future gets here." Vance was standing over Walter, so Walter got up slowly. "Have you gotten in Traci Miller's pants?" Vance stepped back from Walter and turned his head to cough.

"You haven't have you? That beautiful woman, and you haven't. Don't you like her?"

"What I think of Traci Miller is not important," Vance said.

Walter looked at the red-faced young man. "And you say I'm wasting my time."

Vance reached into his jacket and pulled out a jar of antacid tablets. "All this before I've even had a cup of coffee."

"No, you couldn't. You'd never get in Traci Miller's pants. I could never get in Traci Miller's pants. She's too classy."

"Don't you care?" Vance said.

"Don't you care about Traci?" Walter asked.

"You're impossible. You're perverse."

"Look," Walter said. He tried to think about what he meant to say, "I think maybe I fucked up a kid, ruined whatever chances I had of getting back together with my ex-wife. But I've met some interesting people. I've had a pretty good time with my wasted life. What I didn't do was write. That's all."

"Such a pitiful waste," Vance said.

"Want a cup of coffee," Walter asked. He could feel Vance's stare on his back, but he did not want to turn around and have to defend himself to someone who would not understand. As he started to spoon the coffee into the paper filter, he heard the front door slam. Walter knew why his inner organs were devouring themselves.

Walter knew that Vance, Sarah, and Greg, like most people, tended to confuse life with what they thought was important in life. They were like Walter's pop culture professor cum graduate student. And they, to Walter's amusement and disgust, tried so hard to feel sorry for him.

So Walter didn't waste any of his time trying to figure out any moral to the story of his writing a script for Vance Orton. Instead he went to the poker games in Gardena and waited for Sally Curtsinger's husband to leave town. In other words, he went after beauty. The steady grind and the boredom got to Sally, just as it did to Walter's Devil. And here was Walter, like his Marilyn, beautiful and distracting. And after they grew bored of each other, after she started to feel hollow and insubstantial, Walter would again try to see Sarah and Greg. At times his wife and son might have bored him, but they weren't boring. In the meantime Walter got a job as an insect exterminator so that he might have a career and a future.

Vance Orton, as Walter later learned, put together a fantastic production team. Meryl Streep got interested in the lead. So the studio dropped poor Rob Lowe, and since Walter made his ulcer hurt, Vance hired a script doctor to change Rob Lowe back into a middle-aged professor who would now be Meryl Streep. Francis Ford Coppola wanted to direct, but David Lynch signed the contract because he had an open schedule. Unfortunately, Vance's bosses got cold feet. They were scared that the completed film would be a flop if the critics didn't like it and an artsy flop if the critics did like it.

Still, because he had found an old talent, nurtured it, and developed a project, Vance got promoted and thus got several projects with good concepts behind them and with better-than-average chances of actually being produced. And as Vance moved down the path toward his destiny and as the bile built up inside him, he took Traci with him. So Traci Miller got to move farther West in Los Angeles and started slipping summaries of her scripts in front of Vance.

Walter got screwed out of most of his $100,000. But, as a favor and as a show of faith in Walter's talent, Vance got Walter a couple of writing projects, both of which Walter accepted. Neither of which did he finish.

Jim Sanderson

In the thirty years that I have been writing seriously, I have been given many labels, emphasis on the passive voice. I went from being an "aspiring writer" to a "working class, Texas" writer when I won the Kenneth Patchen Prize (92) and had my short story collection, *Semi-Private Rooms*, published (Pig Iron Press, 1995). With the publication of my essay collection, *A West Texas Soapbox* (1998, Texas A & M Press), I became a Texas humorist and essayist. When I won the 1997 Frank Waters Prize—given for the best novel about the southwest, I was a new "rural Southwestern literary writer" When the novel that won that prize, *El Camino del Rio* (University of New Mexico Press, 1998) came out and my editor labeled it a "mystery," I became a mystery writer. With the University of New Mexico Press's publication of two more novels, *Safe Delivery* (2000, Violet Crown Award finalist) and *La Mordida* (2002), I became a "literary mystery writer." With the publication of *Nevin's History* (Texas Tech University Press, 2004), I became a "historical writer" or a "western writer." In addition, I have about sixty published short stories, essays, and scholarly articles, so to the few people who read these journals, I am an academic or literary writer. So, I'm not sure what kind of writer I am, and sometimes I'm not sure that I am a writer at all because I don't depend on writing to eat. For a living, I serve as a professor of English and as Writing Director at Lamar University. As a professor, I teach, but I'm not sure what I do as Writing Director—though I do work with other writers who cannot be labeled precisely with formulated phrases.